POWERS OF ATTORNEY

Avon Books by Louis Auchincloss

VENUS IN SPARTA
SYBIL
THE HOUSE OF FIVE TALENTS
PURSUIT OF THE PRODIGAL
A LAW FOR THE LION

Louis Auchincloss

POWERS OF ATTORNEY

AVON
PUBLISHERS OF
DISCUS • CAMELOT • BARD

Some of the stories in this volume appeared originally in various magazines, as follows:

Cosmopolitan: "From Bed and Board," "The 'True Story' of Lavinia Todd," "The Ambassador from Wall Street" (under the title "A Lady for All That")
Good Housekeeping: "The Revenges of Mrs. Abercrombie" (under the title "Office Party")
Harper's Magazine: "The Deductible Yacht"
The New Yorker: "Power of Bequest" (under the title "The Colonel's Foundation")
The Saturday Evening Post: "Power in Trust," "The Power of Appointment"

AVON BOOKS
A division of
The Hearst Corporation
959 Eighth Avenue
New York, New York 10019

First Avon Printing, July, 1971

AVON TRADEMARK REG. U.S. PAT. OFF. AND
FOREIGN COUNTRIES, REGISTERED TRADEMARK—
MARCA REGISTRADA, HECHO EN CHICAGO, U.S.A.

Printed in the U.S.A.

FOR LAWRENCE MORRIS
MY FRIEND AND PARTNER

CONTENTS

POWER IN TRUST

WHEN Clitus Tilney heard Tower, Tilney & Webb criticized as a "law factory" and its opinions described as "assembly line products," it did not bother him in the least. He knew the fashion among lawyers to affect an aversion to administrative detail, to boast that their own firms were totally disorganized, that they practiced law in a bookish, informal atmosphere, suggestive of Victorian lithographs of county solicitors seated at roll-top desks and listening with wise smiles to the problems of youth and beauty. But he also knew, from his own early days, the price paid for that kind of atmosphere: clerks unpromoted and underpaid, or kept dangling in the hope of partnership until they were too old to get other jobs, aged partners grabbing too much of the profits, an office staff bullied by those spoiled old tartars whom the hoodwinked regarded sentimentally as "treasures." And he knew what disorganization did to overhead. It might be feasible in a firm of twenty lawyers, but when Tilney had joined Tower & Strong it already numbered thirty-four, and now, under his leadership, it had risen to seventy. These, with a staff of a hundred, occupied two great gleaming floors in a new glass cube at 65 Wall Street, with modern paintings and a marble spiral staircase and a reception hall paneled in white and gold. It had not been enough for Tilney to make himself the finest securities lawyer in New York. For every sixty minutes dedicated to the law he had to devote twenty to administration. He had to be a housekeeper, a headmaster, a führer.

His only concession to the other school was that he looked like one of them. He had a large, shaggy grey head and a strong, furrowed, pensive face, and his bulging shoulders and thick frame, usually covered in unpressed tweed, were supported on long thin legs and matchstick ankles. But whether he was being charming as an after-dinner speaker, or stern with trouble-makers at a stockholders' meeting, or whimsically philosophical with the chosen group of his favorite clerks, his "disciples," as they were known in the office, he liked to think that his associates recognized that, however speculative and adventurous they found his mind, it was still an instrument capable of recalling the difference in price between roller towels and evaporating units for the washrooms.

Every leader must be prepared to tolerate expressions of individuality where they are harmless or even useful, and Tilney had had the wisdom to interfere as little as possible with such prima donnas as the litigators. But there was one member of the firm in whose continued independence of action he saw something more dangerous than the theatrical gesticulations dear to the hearts of trial lawyers. Francis Hyde, a thin, bald, bony, long-jawed old bachelor, as morose as he was dusty, represented that almost extinct species, the nonspecialist lawyer. He would take on anything, without consulting his partners, from a corporate reorganization to a scandalous murder trial, and he blandly regarded Tilney's reorganized firm, in which he found himself a rare survivor from the old Tower days, as a mere depot to supply him with stationery and law clerks. Worse still, he made no secret of his contempt for the senior partner's high concept of the role of the bar in modern society. Lawyers to Francis Hyde were simple opportunists, and he considered as hypocrites those who argued otherwise. A client's case was no more than the hand that he had been dealt. Whether or not he could win it was an elementary question of skill, as in the bridge rubbers that he played night after night over too many whiskeys in the Hone Club where he had lived for thirty-five years.

"When he came to Tower & Strong we were a law firm," Hyde used sneeringly to say of Clitus Tilney. "Now we're a boys' church school."

Matters between the two were brought to a crisis on the spring outing at the Glenville Beach Club. As Tilney was passing through the bar, after playing his eighteen holes of golf, he noticed a little group of associates, still in their city clothes, who must have been passing the beautiful morning drinking in their

dark cool corner, and his lips tightened with the disgust of one whose faith was in hard play when it was
not in hard work. It did not surprise him to spot Francis Hyde's gleaming pate at the end of the table, the
only partner in the nonathletic little group. As Tilney
paused now, perspiring freely, his sweater and flannels
a reproach to their urban darkness, all the eyes at the
table turned on him. But if there was in Tilney's gaze,
unconcealed by his perfunctory grin, some of the stern-
ness of Abraham contemplating Sodom, there was no
corresponding guilt in those answering eyes. To his
surprise and indignation he found himself surveyed as
if he were something quaint and ridiculous, a sort of
vaudeville character, vaguely suggestive of Edwardian
sports and fatuity, of blazers and straw hats and boat-
ing on rivers. They might have expected him to tip his
hat forward over one eyebrow, tuck a cane under his
arm, wink and burst into a song about playing the
game. It came over him that they must have been actually talking about him, for the sudden silence of their
concerted stare conveyed an awkward sense of interruption.

"I don't know what I'm going to do about these fel-
lows, Clitus," Hyde called over in his harsh nasal tone.
"All they want to do is booze. How are they ever going
to make the varsity team in Tower, Tilney?"

The laugh that followed had the boldness of a rebel
group that has found at last a leader. Tilney turned
aside without a word and pursued his way to the locker
room. But in that brief moment he had made, and made
finally, his grim decision. He could no longer afford to
wait for Hyde's retirement.

There was considerable discussion in Wall Street at
just this time over the contested will of Harry P. Granger, the president of a great drug firm, who had left
an estate of forty million, half to his widow and half
to the Granger Foundation. He had had no children,
but a sister, Mrs. Crimmins, a whining, petulant creature whose six sons had been educated by the decedent
and who had herself been provided for in his lifetime,
had chosen to attack the will as the product of undue

influence. Tilney had followed the proceedings with a lively interest because Mrs. Granger, the widow, had been a childhood friend of his in Ulrica, a small, up-state town.

"We have an interesting situation here," he announced at the weekly partners' lunch in a private dining room at the Down Town Association. "This Crimmins woman is making a tour of the big firms looking for someone shady enough to take her case. It really puts it up to them, because no matter how little she has to go on, she can always settle for something."

"What makes you so sure she has nothing to go on?" Waldron Webb, the senior litigator, demanded. "If you were a court lawyer, Clitus, you'd learn not to be so positive."

"But I knew Harry Granger well," Tilney explained. "A violent man, but an utterly sane one. And one who knew exactly what he wanted to do with every penny he'd earned."

"Well, if she has no case, why should the executors settle? Or do you just assume they can't be bothered to work for their commissions?"

"No, it's not that. I know the executors. They're all right. But nobody likes to take chances with forty million bucks. Haven't you always told me, Waldron, that juries are unpredictable? Besides, it may be cheaper to pay Mrs. Crimmins off than to win the case. While it's going on, the executors can't qualify. That means there has to be a temporary administration, and the Granger Drug Company, which Harry controlled, would be run in the Surrogate's Court. Any businessman knows that a few months of that would cost more than even a whacking settlement. It's simply another example of the way our law favors the grabbers and shysters."

At this point the nasal drawl of Francis Hyde came down the table to Tilney's astonished ears: "It may interest you to know, Clitus, that you have just described a client of this office as a grabber and one of your own partners as a shyster. I agreed only last night to represent Mrs. Crimmins in her honest efforts to rectify the injustice done her by her brother's will."

In the profound silence that followed, Tilney knew

that every eye at the table was on him. But he stared back only at Hyde, fascinated by the bleak cynicism in the latter's long, arrogant leathery face. "Do you think you should have made that decision without consulting the firm?" he asked now in a mild tone. "Do you think you should have taken on a client so controversial without asking your partners?"

"She's only controversial to you, Clitus," Hyde retorted, "because you've made up your mind about her case without knowing the facts. I wonder if she appears so bad to the rest of us." He turned now to address the table. "Here's a man with one of the great fortunes of the city, who cut out his closest blood relative to leave more to his widow than she could ever spend. Who are we to say that his only sister isn't entitled to her day in court?" He paused for effect and then actually dared to wink. "Particularly when I've taken her on a contingent fee basis under which we are to receive fifty percent of any recovery." There was a gasp around the table. "Some of you gentlemen who thought that Clitus was a bit grandiose in moving into our sumptuous new quarters may be less inclined to slam our expensive front door in the face of a poor supplicant like Mrs. Crimmins."

Tilney glanced around the table and saw at once that his partners were not prepared to condemn Hyde. It was not only that the new rent was high; they were not inclined to take moral issues seriously where women were the litigants. In his sudden violent anger he knew he would go too far. "Look," he said curtly, "it's a question of what you are, what you stand for. It depends on what your philosophy of being a lawyer is. Do you want to be the kind of person who helps society to make a better thing of itself, or do you want to make your money out of simple blackmail?"

This was followed by an outburst from the whole table.

"Really, Clitus," Morris Madison, the senior tax partner objected, "isn't that a bit rough on Frank? Is it so unreasonable for the closest blood relative to expect *some* remembrance in an estate of that size?"

"I think these foundations get entirely too much anyhow," Waldron Webb broke in. "It's become a racket."

"Wouldn't the sister have taken half the estate if there'd been no will?" somebody asked.

"But there *was* a will," Tilney exclaimed impatiently. "It's only a question of what Harry Granger wanted to do with his money. And it's clear as daylight that he didn't want to leave Mrs. Crimmins a red cent!"

"But you're begging the question," Madison pointed out reasonably. "How do you know that Granger was in the full possession of his faculties when he signed the will?"

"Because I knew Granger!" Tilney almost shouted. "Anyone who knew Granger knew that he was sane!"

The constrained silence that followed this second explosion was of a painful duration. It was almost a relief to everybody to have it broken, even by Francis Hyde's mocking tone. "However well our friend Clitus knew the late Mr. Granger, he obviously did not know him well enough to be his lawyer. And that would be the only thing that would keep me from accepting Mrs. Crimmins' retainer. Does anyone but Mr. Tilney disagree with me?"

Tilney, correctly reading his defeat in the renewal of silence around him, was unable to resist a last fling at his opponent. "If I know Margaret Granger, you may have bitten off more than you can chew. I doubt if *she*'ll settle, even if it costs her double to lick you!"

"With admirable foresight the late Mr. Granger did not make his widow an executor," Hyde retorted, smiling down the table. "I have two very realistic officers of the Granger Drug Company to deal with. You said yourself, Clitus, that they were all right. But I tell you what. If I settle this case for a penny under four hundred grand—which is a mere one percent of the gross estate—I'll be glad to tender you my resignation from the firm."

"You'd better be careful," Tilney muttered grimly. "I just may accept it."

For several minutes thereafter there was no sound at the table but the chink of silver and the lapping of soup, and the dirty joke with which Waldron Webb at length broke the silence was greeted with a burst of relieved laughter.

The next months were terrible ones for Clitus Tilney. Hyde initiated in the Surrogate's Court a lengthy series of pre-trial examinations, or what was known in the legal world as a "fishing expedition." He examined and re-examined, with exhaustive and exhausting care, the three witnesses to Mr. Granger's will, but he uncovered nothing but the fact that the decedent had drunk two cocktails—*after* the execution of the document. He interrogated the servants in the house, the nurses and doctors who had attended Granger's last illness, and the employees of the drug company whom the president had known personally. He showed particular interest in any evidence of the frequent manifestations of the decedent's lively temper. But above all he procrastinated. He complained to the court about his difficulties in rounding up witnesses; he pleaded illnesses and accidents; he insisted mysteriously that he was on the trail of new leads. He made motion after motion and appealed from decisions denying them. As Tilney put it disgustedly to his wife, the whole procedure, written up, would have made a perfect textbook for incipient shysters in the art of delaying tactics. The surrogate was impatient, the press caustic and the executors and their counsel livid, but time passed, and time, of course, was Hyde's trump card.

Reaching deeper and deeper into waters that he himself had muddied, Hyde at last plucked out one small, faintly wriggling eel, in the form of a modest trust fund that Granger had set up years before for a retired actress who had presumably been at one point his mistress. By showing that his client, Mrs. Crimmins, had been a friend of the actress, Hyde sought to establish a basis of Mrs. Granger's "psychopathic hatred" of her sister-in-law and her reason for "hounding the decedent until he had removed his sister from the will." At this point Mrs. Granger, driven to exasperation by her own long interrogations, snapped in answer to one of Hyde's sneering questions that Mrs. Crimmins was "a cheat and a liar." The words hit the headlines of the evening papers, and people began to shrug and say that the case was simply a mud-slinging competition between two angry women. When Hyde

announced confidentially at a firm lunch that he had
received a settlement offer of half a million, Tilney,
sick at heart, assumed that all was over.

That evening he and his wife went to a private
harpischord concert in an old brownstone on lower
Park Avenue. He had hoped that the music would
settle his nerves, but he found that the twanging exasperated him, and he slipped out to the dining room
where the butler, an old friend, gave him a whiskey
and soda. He had settled down to drink it when he
saw approaching him across the empty chamber the
small, neat, grey, compact figure of Margaret Granger.
So might Queen Victoria have crossed a room, with
dignity, with intent, with relentlessness. As he rose to
greet her, he noticed how everything about her, her
pale round unpowdered cheeks, her thin, pale, set lips,
her straight grey hair held in a knot in back, her simple
satin grey dress and slippers, her single strand of tiny
pearls, proclaimed, and proclaimed sincerely, that her
money was but a burden and a duty.

"Sit down, Clitus," she said severely, "I want to
have a word with you." They sat facing each other, on
two high-backed Italian chairs, while she eyed him for
a cool moment. "I'd like to know what you think you're
up to."

"I'm up to very little. My partner, Mr. Hyde, seems
to be up to more."

"He's a disgrace to the bar!"

Tilney glanced stealthily to his left and right and
then leaned forward to whisper hoarsely: "I agree with
you!"

"No, Clitus, I won't let you joke your way out of
this. I really won't. He's your partner, and you should
have stopped him. You owed me that much, as an old
friend."

"I tried, Margaret, believe me. My partners wouldn't
go along."

"I thought you were the senior."

"There's a limit to what we seniors can do."

"Well, I don't understand it," she said, shaking her
head. "But I should think there was some way a man

in your position could have stopped it. And now I suppose you'll get a large fee?"

"Hyde gets no fee at all if he loses the case, and he can't possibly win if you fight. What's all this settlement talk? Have your lawyers lost their guts?"

Mrs. Granger was taken aback by his sudden offensive. "They tell me it costs less to settle. No matter how sure we are of winning."

"And is costing less the only criterion?" Tilney protested. "Is there no moral issue involved?"

"You talk to me of moral issues, Clitus!" she exclaimed indignantly. "You, the partner of a man who's dragged my poor Harry's name through the mire!"

"Yes, *I* talk to you of moral issues, Margaret!" he retorted. "I have the unmitigated gall, if you will, to remind you of your moral obligation, as Harry's widow, not to give away a penny of his hard-earned money to his swindling sister."

Mrs. Granger really gaped at this. "Your *client*," she murmured in astonishment. "Is that the way you talk about your clients?"

"When I tell you that it could get me into the hottest kind of water with the Bar Association, will you believe I'm sincere?"

Mrs. Granger leaned over now to rest her small hand for just a moment on top of his large one. "Oh, Clitus, my good old friend, forgive me. Tell me what I should do." Her voice trembled. "Everyone keeps telling me it's best to settle the wretched thing. They talk about the publicity and the cost, and they tell me that Harry's foundation will pay Mrs. Crimmins out of its half of the estate, so it won't make any difference to me, anyway. But I don't *care* about the publicity and the cost. And I don't care about who pays what. All I care is that Harry's horrible sister and her horrible lawyer should not be rewarded for what they've done to his memory. And I know that Harry would gladly have paid out his last dollar to lick them!"

"You believe that?"

"Passionately!" she exclaimed and clasped her hands together. "Oh, Clitus, tell me what to do."

He hesitated a moment. "Do you still walk your poodles in the park in the early morning?"

She stared. "Yes. Every morning at seven."

"I'll meet you tomorrow at seven. At the Ninetieth Street gate."

They both rose in startled guilt at the sudden burst of applause from the next room. It was the intermission.

Tilney, of course, had made a careful study of the Granger will. It was a simple document, perfectly designed by competent counsel to effectuate the testator's twofold design: to provide sumptuously for his widow and to deprive the United States of its last penny of tax. The primary function of the Granger Foundation, at least in the mind of its benefactor, was less the study of incurable diseases than keeping the money away from the federal bureaucrats. And so the forty millions had been divided neatly in half, without a single outside bequest: twenty outright to the Granger Foundation, and twenty in trust to the widow for her life and then to the Foundation. But to qualify the widow's trust for the widow's tax exemption it had been necessary for Granger's lawyers to give her a power to dispose of her trust by will. Of course, it was understood between her and her husband that she would not exercise this power and that on her death the foundation would come into possession of the reunited halves of the estate, still virgin to the tax collector. Nonetheless, she had it. She had it, and on this Tilney had based his little plan.

The morning of his meeting with Mrs. Granger was a bright mild day of early spring, and seated on a park bench watching the pigeons and squirrels, Tilney felt as exhilarated as a young man at a romantic assignation. He jumped up when he saw her approaching, with her three absurd miniature poodles, and, taking the dogs' leashes, led her to a bench.

"Give me the little darlings, Margaret, and take this pencil and paper. I want to dictate a letter of just three lines. To the Director of the Granger Foundation. Of course, you will wish to add your own embellishments. But so long as the final version contains the

gist of my message, we'll be all right, and Frank Hyde
will be all wrong."

"Dear Clitus," she murmured affectionately as she sat
down, "what a true friend you are. I wonder if having
my faith restored in you isn't worth as much to me as
frustrating Mrs. Crimmins."

"You can have both," he assured her as she took
the pad and pencil and waited. "Now then. 'Dear Bill
or Jim, or whatever you call him: This is to inform
you of my irrevocable decision.' " He paused and
smiled while she hastily scribbled. " 'If a single penny
of my husband's estate, or any money previously contributed by him to the Granger Foundation, is, under
any circumstances whatever, given to Mrs. Crimmins
. . .' " He paused again, this time even longer than was
needed.

"Go on, Clitus!"

"I will immediately execute a new will, by the terms
of which the entire principle of my trust will be given
to charities *other* than the Granger Foundation.' "

Mrs. Granger scribbled busily until she had finished,
but when she looked up, she was frowning. "I couldn't
do it. I gave Harry my word."

"And, of course, I wouldn't ask you to break it. But
you never promised Harry you wouldn't do a little
bluffing, did you? You never gave him your word that
you wouldn't try to trick his foundation into showing
a little backbone?"

"No," she said doubtfully. "I didn't. The matter
never came up. Do you think he'd have approved
of that kind of stratagem?"

"I think he'd have been tickled pink. I think he'd
have clapped his hands and shouted!"

"And you really think this . . ." She glanced down
at the pad on which she had scribbled his message.
"You really think it will work?"

"It will work like a charm. Can you imagine a foundation tossing away twenty sure millions to save a possible few hundred grand? They're not madmen, you
know. Even if they suspected you were bluffing, how
would they dare take the chance that you weren't?"

As the beauty of the scheme sank into her mind,

she smiled at last at this vision of the perfect weapon. "But then it will cost your firm a great fee," she protested. "Is there any way I can make it up to you? Can *I* give you a fee?"

Tilney threw back his head with a roar of laughter. "My dear Margaret, what sort of crook do you take me for? Haven't I been unethical enough for one day?" He rose and reached out a hand. "Come now. Go home and write that letter. Make me proud of you. That's all the fee I could ever ask."

The next days were delectable ones for Tilney. He never missed the chance, passing Hyde in a corridor, to boom a hearty question at him as to how the great case was going, and he would chuckle loudly at the other's evasive and discomfited answers. After a fortnight had passed, he felt that it was time, at a firm lunch, to call down the table to Hyde for a report on the Granger case.

"When you last spoke of it," he added, "you told us it was as good as settled. Has the agreement been signed?"

Hyde stared at him with unconcealed malevolence. "I suppose the word's out by now that the settlement has fallen through." He snorted in disgust as he directed a less baleful stare around the table at the other partners. "I was going to tell you all today, anyway. Frankly, gentlemen, it's the damndest thing that's ever happened to me. The agreement was all hashed out, typed and ready to sign. We'd even told the surrogate about it in chambers. And then, whambo, somebody gets cold feet, the widow or the foundation, and refuses to go through with it. Oh, I can tell you, their counsel's face was *really* red. Old John Gales, of Gales & Martin, admitted to me he was thunderstruck. He actually apologized!"

"What are they trying to do?" Waldron Webb demanded hotly. "Shake you down a hundred grand at the last moment? It's the most unscrupulous thing I ever heard!"

"That may be it, I don't know. But Gales says they

won't settle for a penny. Somebody seems to have got religion on the Granger Foundation."

"In that case, what do we do now?" Tilney demanded, frowning. "Fold our tents and steal away?"

"No such luck, Clitus," Hyde retorted angrily. "If it's a fight they want, they'll get a fight. And if it's dirt they want, they'll get their fill!"

"That's a pleasant prospect," said Tilney with an acid smile. "But first of all, there's one little matter that I feel obliged to bring to the attention of the firm. I note on the monthly statement that more than thirteen thousand dollars of cash disbursements have been charged to Mrs. Crimmins' account. Of course, I understand that the fee basis is contingent, and that we get nothing if we lose, but you must surely know, Frank, that lawyers can't pay clients' disbursements. Isn't that champerty?"

"What am I expected to do? Mrs. Crimmins hasn't got that kind of money."

"Well, Mrs. Crimmins had better find it, I'm afraid," Tilney continued in a sharper tone. "She'd better beg, borrow or steal it. The firm has suffered enough from the bad publicity of this case without having the Grievance Committee of the City Bar breathing down our neck. In the meanwhile I have given the cashier instructions that no further sums are to be charged to that account."

"Does that mean," Hyde demanded irately, "that I can no longer sign a chit for a taxi to go to court?"

"It means precisely that. If you go to court on the Granger case."

Hyde pushed his chair roughly back and strode from the room while the partners exchanged uneasy glances.

"Does anyone think I'm wrong?" Tilney demanded in his highest, most challenging tone. "Does anyone want to see us continue in champertous practices?"

"I'm sure nobody thinks you're wrong, Clitus," Morris Madison put in in his reasonable tone. "But I do think it was a bit rough on Frank, springing it that way. He'll have to make up those disbursements out of his own pocket."

"Well, I don't want to know about it if he does,"

Tilney exclaimed. "It's just as bad for him to do it as the firm."

"You won't know it," Madison said quietly. "He'll simply deposit the money in Mrs. Crimmins' checking account, and she'd pay us. Frank may love his booze, and he may be crusty, but he'll give a client the shirt off his back. And he's not a rich man, either."

"You're breaking my heart," Tilney sneered, and he was defiantly glad to note, taking in the table with a rapid glance as he lowered his head over his soup bowl, that he had shocked them all.

Hyde was good to his word about giving the Granger estate a fight full of dirt, and the trial attracted even more publicity than the pre-trial hearings. Tilney was sure that his partner had privately hired a press agent and fervently prayed that the latter's bill would be a large one. But for all the dirt and the headlines, for all the weeks of idle testimony, for all the tricks and chicaneries, the defense remained adamant. The legal world found such intransigency hard to understand. It was widely rumored that Hyde had offered to settle for less than half the sum originally tendered him, and the executors made no secret of their dissatisfaction at having their hands tied by legatees. The other stockholders of the Granger Drug Company, worried by the effect of the delayed probate on the affairs of the corporation, had appealed in vain to the widow, and an editorial appeared in a morning paper questioning the right of a charitable foundation to spend more of its money in litigation than a settlement would cost. It was no use. The board of trustees of the Granger Foundation, with a disregard of public opinion unique in the gentle field of charities, issued a statement to the press that because of "the aspersions cast on the name of their distinguished founder," not even a nominal settlement would be considered.

After that Hyde's case, if case it could be really called, collapsed. When he had called the last of his witnesses, the estate moved for a directed verdict which the surrogate granted. Six weeks later the Appellate Division unanimously rejected Hyde's appeal and de-

nied him leave to appeal higher. Two months after that
the Court of Appeals in Albany refused to hear his
appeal, and Harry P. Granger's fortune was safe at last
from the attacks of his sister and her embittered counsel. Clitus Tilney felt a greater exultation in his heart
than he had known at the most splendid of his firm's
past triumphs.

Only a week after the end of the Granger case Tilney
was dressing at home to attend a dinner at the Bar
Association in honor of the visiting Lord Chancellor
of England. Ada Tilney, whose high pale brow under
her faded straight brown hair, parted in the middle in
mid-Victorian fashion, was like a rock washed clean
by the years of his absences, absences at conventions,
testimonial dinners, committee meetings, or simply at
the office, sat beside his dresser, fitting the pearl studs
in his shirt.

"I left something on the bureau for you," she said
in her placid tone. "Have you seen it yet?"

Tilney noticed a magazine, folded open under his
silver-handled hairbrush, and picked it up. It was the
Gotham Gazette, a periodical sent out free to addresses
east of Central Park for the sake of the fashionable
advertising. Tilney saw the title of an article, "Early-
morning Dog-walking" and beneath it a small photograph of Mrs. Granger and her poodles. Behind her, of
course, loomed himself, although he was not identified
in the caption which read: "Mrs. Harry P. Granger,
widow of the drug magnate, is up and out with her 'toy'
poodles as early as seven o'clock."

"Most women seem to have trouble with their husbands going out at night," Ada continued. "It's so
like you to make time for infidelity only in the early
morning."

"Ada, you're wonderful!" he exclaimed with a
chuckle as he tossed the magazine in the scrap basket.
"Let me tell you something funny about that picture.
There *is* someone who might make trouble about it. But
that someone doesn't happen to be you."

"Still another woman, no doubt."

"No, a man."

The sudden hint of grimness in his tone aroused her apprehension. "Oh, Clitus, does it have something to do with that horrible case? Is it Frank Hyde?"

"It's Frank, all right." He took his shirt from her. "But do you know something, Ada? I'm a man who's missed two wars. Too young for the first and too old for the second. I've always wondered how I would have behaved under fire. Well, tonight perhaps, I shall find out."

"But surely Frank would never see a silly magazine like that?"

"There are those in the office who would be only too glad to send it to him. Besides, it's elementary in military intelligence to assume that the enemy knows anything he *could* have known."

As Tilney entered the long somber portrait-lined reception hall of the Bar Association, filled with black ties and grey heads, Chambers Todd, straight nosed, square jawed, black haired, the "business getting" partner of the office, came up to complain about Hyde.

"He's over there, talking to Judge Caulkins," he said with a brief nod of his head towards a corner. "He's half plastered already. Something's got to be done about him, Clitus. He's giving the firm a terrible black eye. Suppose he passes out at an affair like this?"

But nothing could dull the curious sense of elation that his little talk with Ada had given Tilney. "It wouldn't be what Madison Avenue calls a good 'image,' would it?" he asked with a rumbling laugh. "Think of it. Whenever the words 'Tower, Tilney & Webb' are uttered, the picture flashed on the mental screen is one of an elderly man, inebriated, sinking slowly to his knees."

"I'm glad you find it so funny," Todd retorted.

"Leave him to me, Chambers. I'll go and speak to him now."

As Tilney approached, Judge Caulkins greeted him with the fulsomeness of one anxious to escape an embarrassing colloquy. Hyde, swaying slightly, stared after the retreating jurist with narrowed eyes. He did not look at Tilney.

"What do *you* want?" he muttered.

"I'd like to persuade you to shift to soda water. Just until dinner, old man."

"Don't 'old man' me. You had the gall to talk to me about champerty. What about betraying one's own client? Which is worse?" Hyde turned suddenly on Tilney and almost shouted as he repeated the question. "Which?"

"Do you imply that I betrayed a client?" Tilney asked calmly. "Whom?"

"You tricked Mrs. Crimmins out of half a million bucks! By some kind of rinky-dink with Mrs. Granger. What do you think the Grievance Committee will think of *that?*"

"Ask them."

Hyde steadied himself against the back of the sofa. "Do you know how many copies of that picture I found on my desk this morning? *Three!*"

"My wife had one for me," Tilney announced with a laugh. "She had a couple of questions herself." His spirits rose to a peak as he felt the dizzy joy of danger, and he regretted the wars he had missed. "But if you think you can make something out of my old friendship with Margaret Granger, by all means go ahead. Drag the poor woman to the Grievance Committee. Drag me. And don't blame anyone but Francis Hyde when you've made the biggest fool of yourself in all New York!"

Hyde's watery eyes began to twitch. He glanced around at the bar. "I think I'll get myself one more little drink before we go in."

Tilney laughed again, an elated laugh, as he saw that he had won. And won, too, not in the sneaky way of his conference in the park, but with all his cards on the table. There was bluffing indeed! But the foe had not only to be routed; he had to be destroyed. "Tarry, Frank," he called softly after him, and the other turned back in surprise. "You and I can't go on this way. You have threatened me, and we can no longer be partners. You promised to resign from the firm if you lost the Granger case. I should like to invoke that promise now."

Hyde's eyes peered at Tilney as if he had not fully grasped his meaning. "Have you discussed this with the firm?"

"They can choose between you and me."

"I see." Hyde nodded vaguely. "Between you and me."

"I would assume that an adequate pension would be arranged for whichever has to go."

"An adequate pension," Hyde mumbled with a thickening tone. "Yes, no doubt."

Tilney watched him as he ambled off to the bar, and for the first time it occurred to him that Hyde might be an object of pity. He seemed old now and frail, and the prospect of lonely days as well as nights at the Hone Club seemed dismal enough. Still, there might be work that the firm could send him, or legal aid, or committee work for the Bar Association, or even writing law review articles. And the pension would be adequate; he would see to that.

He saw that Hyde was arguing with the bartender, who was reluctant to give him another drink. The dining room doors were open, and the guests were beginning to move forward.

"Look at him, Clitus! Shall I take him home?"

It was Todd again at his elbow, and Tilney in a single grim second saw all the fatuity of his own reasoning. Frank Hyde was doomed to a lonely, miserable, alcoholic old age, and nothing on earth was going to alter that doom. But was it any sadder than the withering of a leaf or the eating of flesh by carnivores? The senior partner of Tower, Tilney & Webb had not created the universe.

"Oh, God, there he goes!" moaned Todd as Hyde fell suddenly forward on the bar table. The noise was slight and attracted only the notice of those in the immediate vicinity, but when Hyde tried to get up his right arm suddenly swept a whole tray of glasses to the floor, and the hideous crash brought silence to the entire vast chamber.

"There's your image, Todd!" Tilney called after the younger man who was hurrying to help their fallen partner. He resisted the impulse to go himself. He would spare Hyde the final mortification of having the victor help him to his feet. It was probably the last mortification that it would be in his power to spare him.

POWER OF SUGGESTION

LIKE many of the associates of Tower, Tilney & Webb, Jake Platt came from the Middle West—Winnetka, Illinois—and lived during the first bachelor years of his legal apprenticeship in Greenwich Village. He spent many of his free evenings in discussion groups and of his weekend afternoons in soft-ball games with the boys at St. Martin's Settlement House, but after he had resolved upon the serious courtship of Leila Frisby, a dark-haired, wide-eyed Bennington graduate who was determined to make her way off-Broadway, he haunted the fringes of Bohemia. Her friends accepted him because he was handsome and silent and because his easy, pipe-smoking, blond, American masculinity made a pleasant background for discussions of Rothko and Sartres. And then, too, he was helpful about leases and contracts, and for those of them who cared, the income tax. What they did not know was that behind the tireless twinkle of those ceaselessly surveying grey eyes lay the serene conviction that they were dilettantes without any real existence and that once Leila had married him and moved to the red-brick truth of Stuyvesant Town and given birth to the first of a planned family of three, she would have no more time, as he put it to himself, to "wait for Godot."

Nor was his prediction unfulfilled. After Leila had become Mrs. Platt and the mother of little Jock, she began to be more critical of her old friends. They failed to recognize the pull of her new responsibilities, and if she and Jake wouldn't stay at a party till dawn, they didn't seem to care if she came at all. Thus the connection with Bohemia was gradually dissolved without Jake's having once to suggest it. But what he had not anticipated was that her abandonment of old affiliations did not bring with it any immediate enthusiasm for new ones. Leila viewed the Saturday night supper parties which they now attended, made up entirely of young lawyers and their wives, mostly from Tower,

Tilney & Webb, with a more jaundiced eye than he quite liked.

"It's bad enough with the men," she complained on their way home from one of these, "though at least one expects them to talk shop. But Margy Schlide! She keeps it up even with the girls. She told me tonight that Barry had to make partner this year or never and that his chances were exactly two out of five."

"How does she figure that out? I would have said they weren't one in a hundred."

"Because he didn't go to Harvard, I suppose." Leila had preserved intact from her Village days the prejudice that firms like Tower, Tilney & Webb selected their partners exclusively from Harvard.

"No, of course not. Relatively few of the associates went to Harvard. I didn't go to Harvard myself."

"No, but you might as well have. You have that cool, snooty look that poor Barry will never develop."

Jake paused to control his irritation and to recapture the look which his wife had described. "It's not the way Barry looks or talks that's against him," he explained in a judicial tone. "The powers that be aren't so superficial. It's the way he *acts.*"

"How?"

"Well, he calls even the young partners 'sir,' for example. And he doubles up with laughter every time one of them makes a joke. He's always polishing the apple. That sort of thing doesn't go downtown."

"You mean, if it's too obvious?"

"No, Leila, I don't mean that at all. Naturally, none of us wants to be an associate all his life. But most of the boys expect to make the grade by hard work and not politics. If Barry Schilde became a partner, he'd turn Tower, Tilney into a kind of Oriental court, with bowing and salaaming and stabbing in the back."

"Poor Barry and Marg," said Leila wistfully. "I see them wandering about in their turbans amid all the grey flannel suits. But is that what's wrong with them? Are they the only ones in costume, or are they the only ones who *aren't?* And why do you all care so?"

Jake did not answer; in his opinion the discussion had gone quite far enough. It was inevitable that Leila,

with her quick, inquiring mind, should eventually find
out the truth about the legal and business worlds, about
all worlds, for that matter, but he wanted it to come
little by little. It was not in the least that he was
ashamed of the truth or of his own ambition. Every
man who was worth his salt cared, pretty much to the
exclusion of anything else, about his own promotion.
What else mattered, in the anthill which the world was
becoming, but to acquire a bit of space for oneself and
one's family? But it was difficult for most people, particularly people who had spent so much of their lives
"waiting for Godot," to understand this. They clung to
other values which, perfectly obviously, failed to make
them happy. One had only to look about at Leila's old
friends. And it was because the Barry Schlides, by talking and carrying on the way Leila had been erroneously
led to believe that downtown people talked and carried
on, confirmed her in her prejudice that Jake found
them so objectionable.

Originally, he had regarded Barry as a mere clown.
That round, red, rubbery beaming face, topped by the
balding dome over which the sparse long hairs were
so carefully pasted back, looming up in the center of
groups at cocktails to proclaim in a high shrill voice
the Schlide victories over Uncle Sam in the Court of
Claims or the Tax Court, had seemed to Jake simply
ridiculous. Yet he had learned that there was something about Barry, despite his outrageous conceit and
his blatant toadying, despite his never-ending loquacity
and his abominable jokes, that made the other clerks
put up with him, at times even like him. There was an
infectious quality in the intimacy that he thrust upon
one, in his unfailing good humor, even in his bland
assumption that one was in the identical craft with himself. And then, too, he was certainly a good tax lawyer.

But a partner? Did Margy Schlide who, after all,
was nobody's fool, seriously believe that Barry was
going to be a partner? Jake thought of himself as an
expert in such matters, keeping a secret file in his
desk that listed all the members of the firm since 1925,
with statistics of their states of origin, law schools, legal
specialties, religions, social backgrounds and whether

or not they were possessed of independent means. He could think of no precedent in his file to encourage the Schlides.

"Horace," he asked his office mate the following Monday morning, "have you ever stopped to consider Barry Schlide's future in the firm?"

Their desks faced opposite walls, but the slap of Horace's tilted chair against the floor was ample statement of his interest. Horace Mason was a stout, bald, didactic young man, the office politician, but the general assumption that he was apprenticed to Tower, Tilney only until he had reached an age to take up a partnership in his father's firm, Mason, Winthrop & Sears, gave to his opinions a detachment that made him the associates' oracle.

"Funny you should say that. I was just thinking of Barry. He wanted to know if my old man would put him up for the Midday Club. Imagine! When he's never even met him. But I wonder if Barry's very lack of guile might not turn out to be his strongest asset."

"He's so *different*."

"Ah, but that's just it, Jake, old man. That's what you don't see with all your graphs and charts. We live in an age where it's the fashion to break precedents."

"What do you know about my charts?" Jake demanded heatedly. "Have you been looking in my desk?"

"Of course I have," Horace retorted calmly. "As you've been looking in mine. But that's aside from the point. The point is that this firm is properly concerned with its reputation of being a bit on the social side. Having Barry as a partner might balance things out."

Jake turned morosely back to his work, remembering Horace's earlier prediction that the firm would make only one partner that year. And who had earned it more than Jake Platt? Who was more qualified by his industry, his tenure in office, his undisputed position as Clitus Tilney's "fair-haired boy," by the fact that he had never made an enemy, that he was as popular with the office boys as with the partners, that he was handsome Jake, serious Jake, smiling Jake, a fixture in Tower, Tilney who never blinked if asked to work around the clock yet who organized the sports on the firm outing? All the vectors on the partnership graph laid out now on the blotter of his desk pointed to what should occur that Christmas: the happy exclusion of Jake from the long list of those running up to Clitus Tilney's office to be told of their mere annual raises, the breathless hiatus, the final summoning, the twinkle, the hand on the shoulder, the hand in Jake's hand, the explanation, with a gruff chuckle, of why there would be no further talk of raises. And Barry Schlide would get all that? Barry Schlide would take his place and feel the pressure of that near-paternal grip under the puffy shoulder pads of his vulgarly cut coat? Jake was so upset that he did not pick up his telephone until the third ring.

"Oh, Jake," came his master's voice, "this merger of Standard Trust with Bank of Commerce, if it ever comes off, is going to have tax headaches, along with everything else. I think we'd better have a first-class tax man at the meeting on Thursday. Have you anyone to suggest?"

"What about Schlide?"

"Schlide?" There was a faint note of surprise in Tilney's high, smooth tone. "Oh, all right, Schlide. See if you can get him."

"I'll get him all right."

"Good. And Jake?"

"Yes, sir?" He found it perfectly consistent to use this title of address alternately with "Clitus." So, evidently, did Tilney.

"My spies tell me you've been overdoing it. Down here every night last week. I want you to get some rest before the merger talks and go home to that lovely wife of yours. Promise?"

"I promise, sir."

Jake's plan of pushing Barry into the face of the senior partner, for whom he had never directly worked, so that Tilney would see him in all his horribleness and not accept, secondhand, the opinion of the easily flattered tax chief, Mr. Madison, had been conceived in a split second, but looking around the conference in Tilney's office on Thursday morning he felt that he had no

reason to regret it. Tilney, so smooth and big in the
dark blue, almost black suit that fell, creaseless, from
his broad shoulders to his thin ankles, so formidably
cerebral with his wide brow, his long, wide-nostriled
nose and the rimless pince-nez clamped to its tiny
bridge, so authoritative with his thunderous coughs
and habit of slapping a broad silver paper cutter on
the blotter of his desk, loomed over the group of silent
associates like an old bull among yearlings. It was as
simple to see that he had grown out of one of them as
that they, or at least some of them, would grow into
him. But could anything ever come out of, or come *of,*
Barry Schlide? Could anyone fail to note his discrep-
ancy in that chamber: the too light suit, the white tie
with blue triangles, the red beaming face that, instead
of being bent, like the others, over the printed proofs,
was motionlessly erect so that the big drippy eyes could
contemplate with rapture the profile of the senior
partner?

"These bank mergers, gentlemen, always bristle with
problems," Tilney was beginning. "And not the least
of them, to us anyway, is which bank's counsel is going
to end up representing the merged banks. The Standard
Trust boys may be in there rooting for us, but you can
be sure Bank of Commerce is rooting just as hard for
Mason, Winthrop & Sears. That's why we must be on
our toes. Now here's a draft letter that Mr. Madison
has banged out on the tax features of the merger. It
looks pretty good to me, Barry, but I want you to check
it out and then clear it with Mr. Sears."

With a flick of his wrist he sent a long sheet of paper
sliding down the glazed surface of the conference table
to Barry who picked it up gingerly and held it before
him as tenderly as if he were viewing a rare old scroll.

"All I can say," he said after a pause, with a twinkle
in his eye and a shy smile down the table, "is that if
Mr. Madison wrote this letter and . . ."; here he paused
again to broaden his grin, "and if Mr. Tilney approved
it, I doubt if Mr. Schlide is going to find too much
to add."

"That widow's mite is what we pay you for," Tilney
said gruffly, and in the ripple of laughter that went

around the table Barry's guffaw was the loudest of all.

After the conference Jake stayed on in Tilney's office. The latter had risen and moved to the window, and Jake, having scrutinized the broad, dark back for ten cautious seconds, at last made his venture.

"I'm sorry about Schlide, Clitus."

"Schlide?" Tilney was playing with the curtain cord, and his tone was remote. "What's he done?"

"I mean, sorry I suggested him. That business about the letter was a bit thick."

"Oh, that."

Jake knew all the dangers of depreciating a fellow associate behind his back, but there were times when the most obvious maneuver was in fact the subtlest. "Barry's got a heart as big as a mountain and a mind like a steel trap," he allowed, "but he doesn't do things like other people." Here he chuckled and jotted a correction on his proof sheet as though only a small part of his mind was occupied by the subject in discussion. "He told Morris Madison that if he and Margy had another baby, of either sex, they were going to call it Morris Schlide." He paused and felt his breath return when he heard Tilney's grunt of amusement. "I hope he didn't embarrass you with that remark about the letter. He meant it so well."

Tilney turned to look at him oddly. "What do you take me for, Jake? Of course I didn't mind. When have you known me to care about anything but how a man does his job? And can't I count on Barry?"

"Most certainly."

"Then what the hell? Let's get back to work. What do you think of my rider about the Class-A voting stock?"

Jake picked up the rider and fingered it in Barry's gingerly fashion. "If Mr. Tilney wrote it," he said with a simpering smile, "I doubt if Mr. Jake Platt is going to find too much to add."

But this time the maneuver, however subtly obvious, failed. A dry "Cut it out, will you, Jake," was Tilney's sole response.

When he returned to his own office, Jake found Barry waiting to thump him on the back. "I want to thank you, old man, for recommending me to Tilney! It's the first chance I've had to work with him. You've got a blank check from Barry Schlide, my boy, a real blank check! How about you and Leila coming over Saturday night for drinks and dinner?"

"I'm afraid I'm going to have to work Saturday night," Jake muttered. "I'm afraid you may, too."

"Okey-doke! Let's work!"

From then on everything went wrong. In the daily conferences in Tilney's office the center of gravity seemed to be slowly shifting from the big gleaming brow and glittering pince-nez of the senior partner to the ruddy complexion and broad smile of his tax associate. At times they even seemed like a team engaged in a vaudeville act, shouting louder and louder in a desperate effort to amuse their souring audience. If Tilney made a joke, Barry would roar, and roar so long that at last the others, in simple inability to resist the contagion, would begin, however impatiently, to chuckle, which would have the effect of setting Barry, at last subsiding, off again. Tilney, unaccountably, seemed to find it all very amusing. Sometimes he would frown and grumble: "Let's cut the clowning and get on with it," but his admonition would be lost in the high scream of Barry's renewed laughter which in turn would start off the whole conference table until Tilney, helpless, shrugging, with eyes raised to the ceiling, would succumb again to the wave himself. Even Jake would have to laugh, which at least had the advantage of making his tears of anger seem their opposite.

Barry's response to Tilney's ideas was as violent as to his jokes. The least opinion of the older man gave rise to whistles and cluckings, and the smoke-filled air of the chamber was made even thicker by a flurry of comments such as: "By cricky, I wish I'd said that!" or "Let's go home, boys, and let the boss finish" or "Where was Mrs. Schlide's little boy Barry when the brains were parceled out?" It was true that in the beginning Tilney had looked embarrassed, at times even cross, but now he would grin and play the game and even, to the delight of his brash admirer, make sarcastic rejoinders. "Go to the head of the class,

Barry!" he would exclaim when the latter had hit upon a solution, or, "Jake, give Barry another gold star!" It was only too evident that the more he saw of Barry, the more he liked him, and that Jake's little plan was having precisely the opposite effect of what he had intended.

Wherein had he failed? Certainly not with Barry, who was behaving more repulsively than Jake could have dared hope. No, he at last concluded bitterly, he had failed to realize that Tilney had aged, that he would now forgive the grossest obsequiousness, submit to the most cringing flattery, so long as he could maintain his little fantasy of strutting, a combination of Mr. Pickwick and Joseph H. Choate, a Christmas card figure of Dickensian glow and cheer, before an audience of perpetually applauding Cratchits. Surely in the history of every law firm there had to be a moment, a hovering moment when time paused and when the decision was half consciously made to go on growing or to decline instead into a parasitic existence, like that of the larva of the desert wasp feeding on a paralyzed spider, living on captive clients, on drawn-out estate administrations, on old trust accountings and odd bits of unsettled litigation. And Jake began to wonder sorely if that moment had not come for Tower, Tilney & Webb.

His friend Horace Mason did little to encourage him.

"Have you heard about Standard Trust?"

"You mean the merger?"

"No, of course, everyone knows about that. Have you heard who's going to be counsel to the new bank? Mason, Winthrop & Sears!"

Jake arranged his features quickly to give Horace the least satisfaction. "I find that a bit difficult to credit."

"I had it from the senior partner there," Horace said loftily.

"The wish, no doubt, was *father* to the thought."

Horace went out to spread his news among the more credulous, and Jake was left to contemplate the bleak possibility of the firm without its biggest client. Tower, Tilney without Standard Trust! Why, it was like Davis,

Polk without Morgan's! Or Milbank, Tweed without the Chase! He was positively shocked now at the wickedness of Lorelei partners who induced young men to sweat out their young years only to be sucked under the tide of failure in the waterlogged barge of heavy overhead and shrinking fees. But could he be sure? Law firms were very deceptive. There was Mason, Winthrop & Sears, for example, which had been described as "skidding" for a quarter of a century. It was often possible that some old corporate client, a bank or trust company, whether through inertia, nepotism or failure to comprehend the inadequacy of the legal services, would remain faithful through the bad years until the firm, like the human body replacing old tissue with new cells, had substituted young and abler men for the fumbling practitioners of yesteryear.

Nothing in Jake's legal training, however, was conducive to mere idle speculation. When there was something to find out, he could be a man of action, and he knew that the only way to make a true count of the firm's pulse was to make a survey of the correspondence files of the partners. It was a difficult, complicated, even a distasteful task, but Jake knew what he owed to his family, his career and himself. On Saturday the file room was normally free of the big, bony presence of the suspicious and insinuatingly familiar Miss Gibbon, one of those "treasures" of old law firms, and under the more relaxed supervision of her younger assistant, Miss Fenton, invisible behind the spread pages of the *Journal-American*. Here Jake, seated in a corner protected by a barricade of bound registration statements, went to work, starting with the files of the most junior partner, and working up. As the hours passed, he learned many interesting things. He learned that Mr. Tyler had been in psychoanalysis for two years and that Mr. Todd had employed a detective to watch his wife. He learned that Mr. Rogers was flirting with a corporate client, unbeknownst to his partners, in the hope of becoming its president, and that Mr. Tower had suggested to a rich old aunt that she name him, rather than Clitus Tilney, executor of her will. The income tax returns showed a disproportionately large percentage of the firm's profits going to the older partners and confirmed Jake's suspicion of the disintegrating increase of selfish interests and decline of the team spirit so necessary to any large organization. But the clinching discovery came at the very end of his search, in the last letter of the senior partner's file . . .

"What are you doing with Mr. Tilney's correspondence?" It was the rasping voice of Miss Gibbon herself, unaccountably, improperly, present.

Jake turned slowly and stared up at her expressionlessly. "I'm not accustomed to being spied on, Miss Gibbon."

Her angry darting eyes flickered wtih momentary doubt. Jake knew that for some reason this gnarled, grey, wide-bottomed, popular old creature had never responded, in the way of the other office women, to his blond, clean looks. There must have been something unwholesome behind the parade of her own fidelity to Tower, Tilney to make her nose so sharp.

"I wasn't spying," she grumbled. "I was looking for Mr. Tilney's correspondence. Nobody's supposed to read a partner's personal files, not even another partner. Did he say you could?"

"I suggest you ask *him* that," Jake said coolly and turned back to resume his study of the file. There was a pause, a breathing and a rustle behind him evocative of her indecision, and at last the sound of retreating heels. His bluff had worked; she would never tell Tilney, and if she did, excuses abounded. The important thing was that the letter now under his eyes, addressed to Mr. Mason, of Mason, Winthrop & Sears, contained the recommendation, in the now "likely contingency" of Mr. Mason's firm being chosen counsel to the merged banks, that it take over certain associates of Tower, Tilney who were expert in Standard Trust matters. And the list of "experts" so to be saved from the wreck was headed by the name of Barry Schlide! When Jake slapped shut the file and strode down between the long rows of green cabinets to toss it boldly on Miss Gibbon's desk, he had already decided on his resignation.

Leila proved surprisingly difficult to convince. In

the perverse way of women her enthusiasm for the firm seemed to intensify as his own waned. For the first time in all their discussions of his legal career he had the uneasy sense of her undivided attention.

"But how do you know that Standard Trust will change its lawyers?" she demanded, cross-legged in green velvet pants as she bent intently over the bowl of peas that she was shelling. "How do you know it's not all just a rumor?"

"Because I read about it in Mr. Tilney's correspondence."

"What on earth were you doing reading his correspondence?"

"He asked me to help him on a personal matter."

"Do the partners do that?"

"Why not? We're the hired help, that's all."

"What kind of a personal matter?"

"Oh, just an income tax deduction."

"Why didn't he go to the tax department?"

There were a dozen ways that he could have foiled her, but he was angered at the obvious distrust in her tone. "All right, I went into his files to find out about the merger. What's wrong with that?"

"Jake Platt! You old snoop!"

Her tone was sharper than her words, and there was a gleam of old suspicions in her frankly staring dark eyes, a note of "So you *are* that sort, after all."

"May I remind you that I have a career to look after?" he asked irritably. "May I remind you that I have a wife and child who depend on it?"

"Oh, don't put it off on Jock and me. If you're going to snoop, snoop for yourself."

"Honestly, Leila, it's high time you came out of dreamland. You can't expect the partners in Tower, Tilney to come to *me* and tell me they're on the skids. Chances are they don't know it themselves."

"Then you ought to tell them!"

"Are you quite mad?"

"Why is that mad? Why shouldn't you go to Mr. Tilney, who's done so much for you, and tell him frankly about your fears for the firm? Maybe you and he could work out some system to save it."

Jake covered his face with his hands and uttered a low groan. "Because that isn't the way life is," he was murmuring, but he stopped. What was the use? "Anyway, it's too late. You can't arrest that kind of rot once it's started."

"All you can do is leave the sinking ship, is that it?"

Their eyes met in a stare that was suddenly grim.

"That's right."

"Does your decision to be a rat mean that I must be a rat's wife?"

Jake knew that the satisfactions which they derived from this kind of argument were not worth the damage it did to their relationship. He closed his lips very tightly and nodded his head slowly as he counted to ten. "You must do as you see fit, my dear. I'm only trying to be a good husband and father."

The following night he did not come home but worked until dawn at the office, arranging his matters and calculating the time that it would take him to complete each. It was the only way he knew of reorienting his thoughts and emotions after the tumultuous invasion of the irrational as represented by his wife. It seemed a pity that a man could not find even in his home life a chance to relax from the ceaseless hypocrisy which the whole world demanded, but so it was. Remorselessly, other humans, males and particularly females, required that he should toe every minute, every second even, the line of fatuity that was to them more than an imagined line, that was to them, presumably, a saving granite wall that hemmed out a thrusting jungle of horror. If one had the ill chance to be born a freak or a Mowgli, and to understand the jungle, one had to spend a lifetime persuading one's fellow monkeys (for what else were they?), despite their screams and chattering, their flung coconuts and scampering up and down the trees, that they weren't in the wilderness at all, that they were confined instead in a nice, neat, cozy zoo where their cages would be cleaned in the morning and where they would be fed at noon. But it made life a weary business for the freak.

At half past eight Barry Schlide burst into his room with a red beaming face full of news. "Say, Jake, what do you *know?* I've got the hot dope on the Standard-Commerce merger!" He paused as he took in Jake's unshaven and haggard appearance and whistled. "Hey, haven't you been home?" When Jake simply shrugged impatiently he went back to his news. "You want to hear the hot dope?"

"You mean about Mason, Winthrop representing them?"

"Mason, Winthrop, my eye!" Barry cried in triumph. "Do you think old Clitus was going to let them get away with *that?* Not on your life, kid. This is old Tilney's finest hour. Towney, Tilney will be retained as counsel to the new Standard Bank of Commerce."

Jake's stare was now all that even Barry could have wished. "How do *you* know?"

"Oh, a tiny, tiny bird," Barry responded with his widest grin. "A tiny bird called Clitus Tilney."

"He told you?"

"None other."

"But why? What have you to do with it, unless . . ." Jake stopped. Very definitely, he could not endure to be told of Barry's partnership by Barry.

"Unless, exactly," Barry concluded for him. "Unless I have a place in the merger. Which it so happens that Yours Truly does." Barry puffed out his chest and put one hand over his heart and the other in his hip pocket in what was supposed to be a Napoleonic stance. "You have the privilege of seeing before you the new head of the pension trust department of the Standard Bank of Commerce!"

Jake rose shakily to take the now proffered hand. "You mean you're leaving us? Well, that's terrific, old man, and it's one hell of a fine job, but what about here?" He gripped Barry's shoulder in a sudden surge of friendly feelings.

"Here? What do you mean, here?"

"I mean your chances of being a partner."

Barry's smile exploded into one of his happy, boisterous laughs. "Are you kidding? Mrs. Schlide's little boy from Queens amid all the Towers and Tilneys? Do I look like the Social Register type?"

"As a matter of fact, only five of the partners are in the Social Register."

"Oh, only five?" Barry's laugh might have been as good-natured as ever, but the hint of mockery in his eyes showed that he had noted the depth of information which Jake had allowed himself to uncover. "Well, I'm betting on you to make it six!"

"I'm not in the Social Register."

"You will be, old boy, don't worry. And I'll be rooting for you all the way!"

"But Barry," Jake protested, in bewilderment, "if you felt that way about the firm, why did you come here in the first place?"

"For the resale, my friend, for the resale. And didn't it work?"

An hour and a seeming lifetime later, when Jake had received the long-awaited, the ceased-to-be anticipated, the altogether incredible summons to Clitus Tilney's office, after the usual banter about his exhausted appearance, the usual orders to go home immediately to shave, to rest, to forget work, after the offer, premised with sudden seriousness and contracted brow on the expansion that would be required by the new legal work resulting from the merger, the offer that was simply what one had lived for—the offer that in its very making, carried the germ, already recognizable, of a lifetime of anticlimax—the offer to become a partner in Tower, Tilney & Webb, sitting back weakly in his chair and inhaling a cigarette that was dizzying at this time before sleep or food, heard himself asking: "And what, sir, if I may ask, about Barry?"

"Barry? Barry Schlide? Well, I guess we needn't worry about Barry. I've fixed him up with a fine job in the new bank."

"So he told me. But did he have no chance here?"

"Barry?" Tilney seemed to multiply his interrogation infinitely by his third query of the name, an interrogation that made him and Jake seem like two figures scampering down the long echoing corridor of all that had to be taken for granted, away from the poor capering clownish outline, dimmer and dimmer as they left it behind, of Barry Schlide. "Barry's all very well, of

course—a first class tax mind—but Barry's not for us.
He just isn't the type. Surely, Jake, you know that as
well as I."

"Because he didn't go to Harvard?"

"Harvard? What in the deuce does Harvard have
to do with it?" Tilney demanded impatiently, as if
distressed to find, in the first minutes of a new relationship which was supposed to ease communication,
that such things had still to be explained. "Schlide
doesn't have the personality for our kind of firm. Can
you see what would happen if he pulled one of those
corny jokes on old Miss Johanna Shepard? Or if he
talked to the crowd at East Coast Railways about Mrs.
Schlide's little boy Barry? You know the facts of life,
Jake."

"It seems a pity. He means so well."

"Well, did you and I make the world? Now stop
worrying about Barry Schlide and get yourself home
and shaved and rested and take that pretty wife of
yours out to dinner tonight and tell her your good
news over a bottle of champagne. Okay?"

Jake, weary as he was, walked all the way up to
Stuyvesant Town, and it seemed to him that the gleam
of sunlight on the sapphire blue of the East River was
as cold as the twinkle in the senior partner's eye.

POWER OF BEQUEST

RUTHERFORD TOWER, although a partner, was not the Tower of Tower, Tilney & Webb. It sometimes seemed to him that the better part of his life went into explaining this fact or at least into anticipating the humiliation of having it explained by others. The Tower had been his late Uncle Reginald, the famous surrogate and leader of the New York bar, and the one substantial hope in Rutherford's legal career. For Rutherford, despite an almost morbid fear of clerks and courts, and a tendency to hide away from the actual clients behind their wills and estates, had even managed to slip into a junior partnership before Uncle Reginald, in his abrupt, downtown fashion, died at his desk. But it was as far as Rutherford seemed likely to go. There was nothing in the least avuncular about Uncle Reginald's successor, Clitus Tilney. A large, violent, self-made man, Tilney had a chip on his shoulder about families like the Towers and a disconcerting habit of checking the firm's books to see if Rutherford's "Social Register practice," as he slightingly called it, paid off. The junior Tower, he would remark to the cashier after each such inspection, had evidently been made a partner for only three reasons: because of his name, because of his relatives, and because he was there.

And, of course, Tilney was right. He was always right. Rutherford's practice didn't pay off. The Tower cousins, it was true, were in and out of his office all day, as were the Hallecks, the Rutherfords, the Tremaines, and all the other interconnecting links of his widespread family, but they expected, every last grabbing one of them, no more than a nominal bill. Aunt Mildred, Uncle Reginald's widow, was the worst of all, an opinionated and litigious lady who professed to care not for the money but for the principle of things and was forever embroiled with landlords, travel agencies, and shops. However hard her nephew worked for her, he could never feel more than a substitute. It was Clitus Tilney alone whose advice she respected. Rutherford sometimes wondered, running his long nervous fingers over his pale brow and through his prematurely grey hair, if there was any quality more respected by the timid remnants of an older New York society, even by the flattest-heeled and most velvet-gowned old maid, than naked aggression. What use did they really have for anyone whom they had known, like Rutherford, from his childhood? He was "one of us," wasn't he—too soft for a modern world?

The final blow came when Aunt Margaretta Halleck, the only Tower who had married what Clitus called "real money," and for whom Rutherford had drawn some dozen wills without fee, died leaving her affairs, including the management of her estate, in the hands of an uptown practitioner who had persuaded her that Wall Street lawyers were a pack of wolves. The next morning, when Rutherford happened to meet the senior partner in the subway, Tilney clapped a heavy hand on his shrinking shoulder.

"Tell me, Rutherford," he boomed over the roar of the train. "Have you ever thought of turning yourself into a securities lawyer? We could use another hand on this Smilax deal."

"Well, it's not a field I know much about," Rutherford said miserably.

"But, man, you're not forty yet! You can learn. Quite frankly, this Halleck fiasco is the last straw. I'm not saying it's anyone's fault, but the family business isn't carrying its share of the load. Think it over."

Rutherford sat later in his office, staring out the window at a dark brick wall six feet away, and thought gloomily of working night and day on one of Tilney's securities "teams," with bright, intolerant younger men who had been on the *Harvard Law Review*. The telephone rang, startling him. He picked it up. "What is it?" he snapped.

It was the receptionist. "There's a Colonel Hubert here," she said. "He wants to see Mr. Tower. Do you know him, or shall I see if Mr. Tilney can see him?"

It was not unusual for prospective clients to ask for

"Mr. Tower," assuming that they were asking for the senior partner. Rutherford, however, was too jostled to answer with his usual self-depreciation. "If I were the receptionist," he said with an edge to his voice, "and somebody asked for Mr. Tower, I think I'd send him to Mr. Tower. But then, I suppose, I have a simple mind."

There was a surprised silence. "I'm sorry, Mr. Tower. I only meant—"

"I know," he said firmly. "It's quite all right. Tell Colonel Hubert I'll be glad to see him."

Sitting back in his chair, Rutherford immediately felt better. *That* was the way to deal with people. And, looking around, he tried to picture his room as it might appear to a client. It was the smallest of the partners' offices, true, but it was not entirely hopeless. If his uncle's best things, including the Sheraton desk, had been taken over by Mr. Tilney, he at least had a couple of relics of that more solid past: the large framed signed photograph of Judge Cardozo in robes, and his uncle's safe, a mammoth green box on wheels with REGINALD TOWER painted on the door in thick gold letters. The safe, of course, would have been more of an asset if Tilney had not insisted that it be used for keeping real estate papers and if young men from that department were not always bursting into Rutherford's office to bang it open and shut. Sometimes they even left papers unceremoniously on his desk, marked simply "For Safe." Still, he felt, it gave his room some of the flavor of an old-fashioned office, just a touch of Ephraim Tutt.

An office boy appeared at the doorway, saying "This way, sir," and a handsome, sporty old gentleman of certainly more than eighty years walked briskly into the office.

"Mr. Tower?"

Rutherford jumped to his feet to get him a chair, and the old man nodded vigorously as he took his seat. "Thank you, sir. Thank you, indeed," he said.

He was really magnificent, Rutherford decided as he sat down again and looked him over. He had thick white hair and long white mustaches, a straight, large, firm, aristocratic nose, and eyes that at least tried to be piercing. His dark, sharply pressed suit covered a figure whose only fault was a small, neat protruding stomach, and he wore a carnation in his buttonhole and a red tie with a huge knot.

"You are in the business of making wills?" the Colonel asked.

"That is my claim."

"Good. Then I want you to make me one."

There was a pause while the Colonel stared at him expectantly. Rutherford wondered if he was supposed to make the will up then and there, like a sandwich.

"Well, I guess I'd better ask a few questions," he said with a small professional smile. "Do you have a will now, sir?"

"Tore it up," the Colonel said. "Tore them all up. I'm changing my counsel, young man. That's why I'm here."

Rutherford decided not to press the point. "We might start with your family, then. Do you have a wife, sir? Or children?"

"My wife is dead, God bless her. No children. She had a couple of nieces, but they're provided for."

"And you, sir?"

"Oh, I have some grandnephews." He shrugged. "Nice young chaps. You know the sort—married, live in the suburbs, have two children, television. No point in leaving them any money. Real money, I mean. Scare them to death. Prevent their keeping down to the Joneses. Fifty thousand apiece will be plenty."

Rutherford's mouth began to feel pleasantly dry as he leaned forward to pick up a pencil. He quite agreed with the Colonel about the suburbs. "And what did you have in mind, sir, as to the main disposition of your estate?"

"I don't care so much as long as it's spent," the Colonel exclaimed, slapping the desk. "Money should be spent, damn it! When I was a young man, I knew Ward McAllister. I was a friend of Harry Lehr's, too. Newport. It was something then! Mrs. Fish. The Vanderbilts. Oh, I know, people sneer at them now. They say they were vulgar, aping Europe, playing at being dukes and duchesses, but, by God, they had something to show for their money! Why, do you know, I can remember a ball at the Breakers when they had a footman in livery on every step of the grand stairway. Every step!"

"I guess you wouldn't see that today," Rutherford said, impressed. "Not even in Texas."

"Today!" The Colonel gave a snort. "Today they eat creamed chicken and peas at charity dinners at the Waldorf and listen to do-gooders. No, no, the color's quite gone, young man. The color's entirely gone."

At this, the Colonel sank into a reverie so profound that Rutherford began to worry that he had already lost interest in his will. "Perhaps some charity might interest you?" he suggested cautiously. "Or a foundation? I understand they do considerable spending."

The Colonel shrugged. "Only way to keep the money out of the hands of those rascals in Washington, I suppose. Republicans, Democrats—they're all alike. Grab, grab." He nodded decisively. "All right, young man. Make me a foundation."

Rutherford scratched his head. "What sort of a foundation, sir?"

"What sort? Don't they have to be for world peace or some damn-fool thing? Isn't that the tax angle?"

"Well, not altogether," Rutherford said, repressing a smile. "Your foundation could be a medical one, for example. Research. Grants to hospitals. That sort of thing."

"Good. Make me a medical foundation. But, mind you, I'm no Rockefeller or Carnegie. We're not talking about more than twelve or fifteen million."

Rutherford's head swam. "What—what about your board?" he stammered. "The board of this foundation. Who would you want on that?"

The Colonel looked down at the floor a moment, his lips pursed. When he looked up, he smiled charmingly. "Well, what about you, young man? You seem like a competent fellow. I'd be glad to have you as chairman."

"Me?"

"Why not? And pick your own board. If I want a

man to do a job, I believe in letting him do it his own way."

Rutherford's heart gradually sank. One simply didn't walk in off the street and give one's fortune to a total stranger—not if one was sane. It was like the day, as a child at his grandmother's table, when she suddenly gave him a gold saltcellar in the form of a naked mermaid with a rounded, smooth figure that he had loved to stroke, only to be told by his mother that it was all in fun, that "Granny didn't mean it." It had been his introduction to senility. Projects like the Colonel's, he had heard, were common on Wall Street. It was a natural place for the demented to live out their fantasies. Nevertheless, as the old Colonel's imagined gold dissolved like Valhalla, he felt cheated and bitter. Abruptly, he stood up. "It's a most interesting scheme, Colonel," he said dryly. "I'd like a few days to think it over, if you don't mind. Why don't you leave me your name and address, and I can call you?"

The Colonel seemed surprised. "You mean that's all? For now?"

"If you please, sir, I'm afraid I have an appointment."

After the old man had placed his card on the desk, Rutherford relentlessly ushered him out to the foyer, where he waited until the elevator doors had safely closed between them. Returning, he told the receptionist that he would not be "in" again to Colonel Hubert.

That night, Rutherford tried to salvage what he could out of his disappointment by making a good story of it to his wife as she sat knitting in the living room of their apartment. Phyllis Tower was one of those plain, tall, angular women who are apt to be tense and sharp before marriage and almost stonily contented thereafter. It never seemed to occur to her that she didn't have everything in the world that a well-brought-up girl could possibly want. Limited, unrapturous, but of an even disposition, she made of New York a respectable small town and believed completely that her husband had inherited an excellent law practice.

She followed his story without any particular show of interest. "Hubert," she repeated when he had finished. "You don't suppose it was old Colonel Bill Hubert, do you? He's not really mad, you know. Eccentric, but not mad."

Rutherford felt his heart sink for the second time as he thought of the card left on his desk—"William Lyon Hubert." He watched her placid knitting with a sudden stab of resentment, but closed his lips tightly. After all, to be made ridiculous was worse than *anything*. Then he said guardedly: "This man's name was Frank. Who is Colonel Bill?"

"Oh, you know, dear. He's that old diner-out who married Grandma's friend Mrs. Jack Tyson. Everyone said she was mad for him right up to the day she died."

Again his mouth was dry. It was too much, in one day. "And did she leave him that—that *fortune?*"

"Well, I don't suppose she left him all of it," she said, breaking a strand of yarn. "There were the Tysons, you know. But he still keeps up the house on Fifth Avenue. And *that* takes something."

"Yes," he murmured, a vast impression of masonry clouding his mind. "Yes, I suppose it must."

"What's the matter dear?" she asked. "You look funny. You don't suppose you could have been wrong about the name, do you? Are you sure it was Frank?"

"Quite sure."

Buried in the evening newspaper, he pondered his discovery. And then, in a flash, he remembered. Of course! Mrs. Jack Tyson had become Mrs. W. L. Hubert! What devil was it that made him forget these things, which Phyllis remembered so effortlessly? And fifteen million—wasn't that just the slice that a grateful widow *might* have left him?

The next morning, after a restless night, Rutherford looked up Colonel Hubert's number and tried to reach him on the telephone, but this, it turned out, was far from easy. The atmosphere of the great house, as conveyed to him over the line, was, to say the least, confused. Three times he called, and three times a mild, patient, uncooperative voice, surely that of an ancient butler, discreetly answered. Rutherford was obliged to spell and respell his name. He was then switched to an extension and to a maid who evidently regarded the ring of the telephone as a personal affront. While they argued, a third voice, far away and faintly querulous, was intermittently heard, and finally, on the third attempt, an old man called into the telephone "What? What?" very loudly. Then, abruptly, someone hung up, and Rutherford heard again the baffling dial tone. He decided to go up to the house.

When he got out of the cab, he took in with renewed pleasure the great façade. He knew it, of course. Everyone who ever walked on the east side of Central Park knew the eclectic architecture of the old Tyson house, rising from a Medicean basement through stories of solemnified French Renaissance to its distinguishing feature, a top-floor balcony in the form of the Porch of the Maidens. To Rutherford, it was simply the kind of house that one built if one was rich. He would have been only too happy to be able to do the same.

Fortunately, it proved as easy to see Colonel Hubert as it was difficult to get him on the telephone. The old butler who opened the massive grilled door, and whose voice Rutherford immediately recognized, led him without further questions, when he heard he was actually dealing with the Colonel's lawyer, up the grey marble stairway that glimmered in the dark hall and down a long corridor to the Colonel's study. This was Italian; Rutherford had a vague impression of red damask and tapestry as he went up to the long black table at which an old man was sitting, reading a typewritten sheet. He sighed in relief. It *was* the right colonel.

"Good morning, Colonel. I'm Tower. Rutherford Tower. Do you remember me? About your will?"

The Colonel looked up with an expression of faint puzzlement, but smiled politely. "My dear fellow, of course. Pray be seated."

"I wanted to tell you that I've thought it over, and that I'm all set to start," Rutherford went on quickly, taking a seat opposite the Colonel. "There are a few points, however, I'd like to straighten out."

The Colonel nodded several times. "Ah, yes, my will," he said. "Exactly. Very good of you."

"I want to get the names of your grandnephews. I think it advisable to leave them more substantial legacies in view of the fact that the residue is going to your foundation. And then there's the question of executors . . ." He paused, wondering if the Colonel was following him. The old man was now playing with a large bronze turtle—the repository of stamps and paper clips—raising and lowering its shell. "That's a handsome bronze you have there," Rutherford said uncertainly.

"Isn't it?" the Colonel said, holding it up. "I'd like Sophie to have it. She always used to admire it. You might take her name down. Sophie Winters, my wife's niece. Or did she take back her own name after her last divorce?" He looked blankly at Rutherford. "Anyway, she's living in Biarritz. Unless she sold that house that Millie left her. Did she, do you know?"

Rutherford took a deep breath. Whatever happened, he must not be impatient again. "If I might suggest, sir, we could take care of the specific items more easily in a letter. A letter to be left with your will."

The Colonel smiled his charming smile. "I'd like to do it the simple way myself, of course. But would it be binding? Isn't that the point? Would it be binding?"

"Well, not exactly," Rutherford admitted, "but, after all, such a request is hardly going to be ignored—"

"How can we be sure? Do you see?" the Colonel said, smiling again. "Now, I tell you what we'll do. I'll ring for my man, Tomkins, and we'll get some luggage tags to tie to the objects marked for the different relatives."

Rutherford sat helpless as the Colonel rang, and told Tomkins what he wanted. When the butler returned with the tags, he gave them to the Colonel and then took each one silently from him as the old man wrote a name on it. He then proceeded gravely to tie it to a lamp or a chair or to stick it with Scotch tape to the frame of a picture or some other object. Both he and the Colonel seemed quite engrossed in their task and entirely unmindful of Rutherford, who followed them about the study, halfheartedly writing down the name of the fortunate niece who was to receive the Luther

Terry "Peasant Girl" or the happy cousin who was to get the John Rogers group. By lunchtime, the study looked like a naval vessel airing its signal flags. The Colonel surveyed the whole with satisfaction.

"Well!" he exclaimed, turning to Rutherford. "I guess that's that for today! All work and no play, you know. Come back tomorrow, my dear young man, and we'll do the music room."

Rutherford, his pockets rustling with useless notes, walked down Fifth Avenue, too overwrought to go immediately back to the office. He stopped at his club and had an early drink in the almost empty bar, calculating how long at this rate it would take them to do the whole house. And what about the one on Long Island? And how did he know there mightn't be another in Florida? It was suddenly grimly clear that unless he managed to get the Colonel out of this distressing mood of particulars and back to his more sweeping attitude of the day before, there might never be any will at all. And, looking at his own pale face in the mirror behind the bar, he drew himself up and ordered another drink. What was it that Clitus Tilney always said was the mark of a good lawyer—creative imagination?

At his office, after lunch, he went to work with a determination that he had not shown since the Benzedrine weekend, fifteen years before, when he took his bar examinations. He kept his office door closed, and snapped "Keep out, please!" to each startled young man who banged it open to get to the real estate safe. He even had the courage to seize one of them, a Mr. Baitsell, and demand his services. When Baitsell protested, Rutherford asserted himself as he had not done since his uncle's death. "I'm sorry. This is emergency," he said.

Once obtained, Baitsell was efficient. He dug out of the files a precedent for a simple foundation for medical purposes and, using it as a guide, drafted that part of the will himself while Rutherford worked out the legacies for the grandnephews. This was a tricky business, for the bequests had to be large enough to induce the young Huberts not to contest the will. There were moments, but only brief ones, when he stopped to ponder the morality of what he was doing. Was it *his* responsibility to pass on the Colonel's soundness of mind? Did he *know* it to be unsound? And whom, after all, was he gypping? If the old man died without a will, the grandnephews would take everything, to be sure, but everything minus taxes. All he was really doing with his foundation was shifting the tax money from the government, which would waste it, to a charity, which wouldn't. If that wasn't "creative imagination," he wanted to know what was! And did anyone think for a single, solitary second that in his position Clitus Tilney would not have done what he was doing? Why, he would probably have made himself residuary legatee! With this thought, Rutherford, after swallowing two or three times, penciled his own name in the blank for "executor" on the mimeographed form he was using.

The following morning at ten, Rutherford went uptown with his secretary and Mr. Baitsell to take the Colonel, as he now knew was the only way, by storm. While the other two waited in the hall, he followed the butler up the stairs and down the corridor to the study. Entering briskly, he placed a typed copy of the will on the desk before the astonished old gentleman.

"I've been working all night, Colonel," he said, in a voice so nervous that he didn't quite recognize himself, "and I've decided that it doesn't pay to be too much smarter than one's client—particularly when that client happens to be Colonel Hubert. All of which means, sir, that you were right the first time. My scheme of including in the will all those bequests of objets d'art just isn't feasible. We'll accomplish the same thing in a letter. And in the meanwhile here's your will as you originally wanted it. Clean as a whistle."

The Colonel watched him, nodding vaguely, and fingered the pages of the will. "You think it's all right?"

"Right as Tower, Tilney & Webb can make it," Rutherford said, with the smile and wink that he had seen Clitus Tilney use.

"And you think I should sign it now?"

"No time like the present." Rutherford, who had

been too nervous to sit, walked to the window, to conceal his heavy breathing. "If you'll just ring for Tomkins and ask him to tell the young lady and gentleman in the hall to come up, we'll have the necessary witnesses."

"Is Tomkins covered all right?" the Colonel asked as he touched the bell beside him.

"He's covered with the other servants," Rutherford said hastily. "In my opinion, sir, you've been more than generous."

The witnesses came up, and the Colonel behaved better than Rutherford had dared hope. He joked with Baitsell about the formalities, laughed at the red ribbon attached to the will, told a couple of anecdotes about old Newport and Harry Lehr's will, and finally signed his name in a great, flourishing hand. When Rutherford's secretary walked up to the table to sign her name after his, he rose and made her a courtly bow. It was all like a scene from Thackeray.

In the taxi afterward, speeding downtown, Rutherford turned to the others. "The Colonel's a bit funny about his private affairs," he told them. "As a matter of fact, I haven't even met his family. So I'd rather you didn't mention this will business. Outside the office *or* in."

Baitsell looked very young and impressed as he gave him his solemn assurance. He then asked, "But if the Colonel should die, sir, who would notify us? And how would the family know about the will?"

"Never mind about that," Rutherford said, with a small smile, handing him the will. "I don't think the Colonel is apt to do very much dying without my hearing of it. When we get to the office, you stick that will in the vault and forget it."

It was risky to warn them, of course, but riskier not to. He couldn't afford to have them talk. There was too much that was phony in the whole picture. He had no guaranty, after all, that the Colonel had either the money or the power to will it. It was the kind of situation where one had to lie low, at least until the old man was dead, and even after that, until it was clear that one had the final and valid will. How would he look, for example, rushing into court to probate the document now under Baitsell's arm if the family produced a later will, or even a judicial ruling that the old man was incompetent to make one? Would he not seem ridiculous and grabby? Or worse? And Clitus Tilney! What would *he* say if his firm was dragged into so humiliating a failure? But no, no, he wouldn't even think of it. He could burn the will secretly, if necessary; nobody need know unless—well, unless he won. And his heart bounded as he thought of the paneled office that Tilney would have to assign to the director of the Hubert Foundation.

A new office was only the first of many imaginative flights in which he riotously indulged. He saw himself dispensing grants to universities and hospitals, called on, solicited, profusely thanked. He calculated and recalculated his executor's commissions on increasingly optimistic estimates of the Colonel's estate. In fact, his concept of the old man's wealth and his own control of it, the apotheosis of Rutherford Tower to the position of benefactor of the city, *the* Tower at long last of Tower, Tilney & Webb, began, in the ensuing months, to edge out the more real prospect of disappointment. The fantasy had become too important not to be deliberately indulged in. When he turned at breakfast to the obituary page, he would close his eyes and actually pray he would not find the name there, so that he would have another day in which to dream.

When the Colonel did die, it was Phyllis, of course, who spotted it. "I see that old Colonel Bill is dead," she said at breakfast one morning, without looking up from her newspaper. "Eighty-seven. Didn't you say he'd been in to see you?"

For a moment, Rutherford sat utterly still. "Where did he die?" he asked.

"In some lawyer's office in Miami. So convenient, I should imagine. They probably had all his papers ready. Why, Rutherford, where are you going?"

He didn't trust himself to wait, and hurried out. In the street, he bought copies of all the newspapers and went to a Central Park bench to read them. There was little more in any of the obituaries than the headlines:

"Former Army Officer Stricken" or "Husband of Mrs. J. L. Tyson Succumbs." He could find nothing else about the Miami lawyer. After all, he reasoned desperately as he got up and walked through the Mall, wasn't it only natural for the Colonel to have Florida counsel? Didn't he spend part of the year there? But, for all his arguments, it was almost lunchtime before he gathered courage to call his office. His secretary, however, had to report only that Aunt Mildred Tower had called twice and wanted him to call back.

"Tell her I'm tied up," he said irritably. "Tell her I've gone to the partners' lunch."

For, indeed, it was Monday, the day of their weekly lunch. When he got to the private room of the Down Town where they met, he found some twenty of them at the table, listening to Clitus Tilney. Rutherford assumed, as he slipped into a chair at the lower end of the table, that the senior partner was telling one of his usual stories to illustrate the greatness of Clitus and the confounding of his rivals. But this story, as he listened to it with a growing void in his stomach, appeared to be something else.

"No, it's true, I'm not exaggerating," Tilney was saying, with a rumbling laugh. "There are twenty-five wills that they know of already, and they're not all in by a long shot. Sam Kennecott, at Standard Trust, told me it was a mania with the old boy. And the killing thing is, they're all the same. Except for one that has forty-five pages of specific bequests, they all set up some crazy foundation under the control of—guess who —the little shyster who drew the will! Sam says you've never seen such an accumulation of greed in your life! In my opinion, they ought to be disbarred, the lot of them, for taking advantage of the poor old dodo. Except the joke's on them—that's the beauty of it!"

Rutherford did not have to ask one of his neighbors the name of the deceased, but, feeling dazed, he did. The neighbor told him.

"Did any of the big firms get hooked?" someone asked.

"Good Lord, we have *some* ethics, I hope!" Tilney answered. "Though there's a rumor that one did. Harrison & Lambert, someone said. Wouldn't it be wonderful?" Tilney's large jowls positively shook with pleasure. "What wouldn't I give to see old Cy Lambert caught like a monkey with his fist in the bottle!"

Rutherford spoke up suddenly. His voice was so high that everyone turned and looked at him. "But what about the man with the *last* will?" he called down the table to Mr. Tilney. "Why is it a joke on him?"

"You mean the man in Miami?" Tilney said, flashing at Rutherford the fixed smile of his dislike. "Because the old guy didn't have that sort of money. Not foundation money. The big stuff was all in trust, of course, and goes to the Tysons, where it should go."

Rutherford concentrated on eating a single course. It would look odd, after his interruption, to leave at once. When he had emptied his plate, he wiped his mouth carefully, excused himself to his neighbors, and walked slowly from the room.

Back at the office, however, he almost dashed to Baitsell's room. Closing the door behind him, he faced the startled young man with wild eyes. "Look, Baitsell, about that will of Colonel Hubert's—you remember." Baitsell nodded quickly. "Well, he died, you see."

"Yes, sir. I read about it."

"Apparently, he's written some subsequent wills. I think we'd better do nothing about filing ours for the time being. And if I were you I wouldn't mention this around the office. It might—"

"But it's already filed, sir!"

"It's *what?*"

"Yes, sir. I filed it."

"How could you?" Rutherford's voice was almost a scream. "You haven't had time to prepare a petition, let alone get it signed!"

"Oh, I don't mean that I filed it for probate, Mr. Tower. I mean I filed it for safekeeping in the Surrogate's Court. *Before* he died. The same day he signed it."

Rutherford, looking into the young man's clear, honest eyes, knew now that he faced the unwitting agent of his own devil. "Why did you do that?" he asked in a low, almost curious tone. "We never do that with wills. We keep them in our vault."

"Oh, I know that, sir," Baitsell answered proudly. "But you told me you didn't know the relatives. I thought if the old gentleman died and you didn't hear about it at once, they might rush in with another will. Now they'll find ours sitting up there in the courthouse, staring them right in the face. Yes, sir, Mr. Tower, you'll have to be given notice of every will that's offered. Public notice!"

Rutherford looked at the triumphant young man for a moment and then returned without a word to his own office. There he leaned against Uncle Reginald's safe and thought in a stunned, stupid way of old Cy Lambert laughing, even shouting, at Clitus Tilney. Then he shook his head. It was too much—too much to take in. He wondered, in a sudden new mood of detachment, if it wasn't rather distinguished to be hounded so personally by the furies. Orestes. Orestes Rutherford Tower. His telephone rang.

"Rutherford? Is it you?" a voice asked.

"Yes, Aunt Mildred," he said quietly.

"Well, I'm glad to get you at last. I don't know what your uncle would have said about the hours young lawyers keep today. And people talk about the pressure of modern life! Talk is all it is. But look, Rutherford. That blackguard of a landlord of mine is acting up again. He now claims that my apartment lease doesn't include an extra maid's room in the basement. I want you to come right up and talk to him. This afternoon. You can, can't you?"

"Yes, Aunt Mildred," he said again. "I'm practically on my way."

THE SINGLE READER

NONE of his law partners or clients, or even the friends who considered themselves closest to him, knew the secret of Morris Madison. They saw the tall, thin, smooth, urbane tax expert, at the height of his career in his early fifties, the thick, greying hair parted in the center and rising high above a tall forehead, the long, strong, firm nose and the long oblong face, the melancholy but un-self-betraying eyes. They heard the soft, precise voice, the slow, clear articulation; they marveled at the ease with which he could explain the thorniest tax principle and at the profundity of his general information, from politics to social gossip. Morris, they all agreed, was not only the ideal extra man for the grandest dinner party; he was the perfect companion for the Canadian fishing trip. But they had no idea that he was a dedicated man. They suspected all kinds of lacks in his life, besides the obvious ones of a wife and children, and in the free fashion of a psychiatrically minded era they attributed his reserve and good manners to every kind of frustration and insecurity. But none of them suspected that he had a passion.

He kept a diary. He had started it twenty-five years before, when his wife had left him, a horsy country girl who had never relaxed her attitude that the city was full of "snobs and toadies" of whom her husband was one of the worst. Madison had resented her for a year; then in his mind he had forgiven her; ultimately he had even admitted that he might have mishandled her. He had taken her too seriously, too literally, too reasonably. She had wanted domination rather than understanding. The only person who cared about understanding was himself. And for himself he started a diary.

How he could have lived without it in the years that followed, he would not have known. As a rising young lawyer and a single man he was at everybody's mercy. The wives of the older partners expected him to fill in at their dinner parties and listen respectfully to widows and matrons who talked about their servants and children. Clients with personal problems, knowing that he had no family, felt entitled to help themselves to his nights as well as his days for greater self-revelation. Married friends in domestic trouble poured out their woes to him, ostensibly to profit from his experience, but actually for the heady delights of indiscreet confession. Single women regarded him as fair game for every imaginable confidence, and even happy husbands in summertime, when their wives were at the seashore, sought out the congenial company of "old Morris" to relate to him, in alcoholic profusion at the bars of their clubs, the business worries that no sensible spouse would dream of listening to. It began to seem to Madison, in the words of Emily Dickinson, that "all the heavens were a bell and being but an ear" and that the only way for him to talk was to talk to himself.

At first the diary was, naturally enough, primarily the vehicle for his resentment. His circle of acquaintance appeared in it in all the banality of their unsolicited communication, with huge heads and eyes and bigger mouths; their talk was lampooned rather than reported. But on a reading at the end of its first year Madison had been struck by the fact that the most illuminating passages were those where he had dryly set down scenes and conversations that had not seemed of particular interest at the time. For example, a lunch with Clitus Tilney in which the latter had discussed his own prospects of partnership in the firm contained in a dozen lines the very portrait of downtown ambition. Madison now became more selective in his entries. His ears were alerted for the right confidence, the right complaint, even the right phrase that would convey the essential quality of the speaker. And as his people began to breathe and chatter like themselves in his pages, he realized the first great joy of re-creation.

He began to raise his sights. He decided that he wanted to paint a picture of life in New York for a subsequent generation. He began to note the razing of buildings and the erection of new ones. He watched ticker tape parades and dined in the newest restaurants.

He marked fashions and fads and even attended fires.
He read exhaustively in the great diarists of the past,
Pepys, Evelyn, Saint-Simon, and paid many visits to
the New York Historical Society to pore over the un-
published pages of Mayor Hone. His conservative
friends were surprised to find themselves deserted for
Elsa Maxwell's frolicsome balls, as was café society
in turn to find itself abandoned for the dullest bar association dinners. Madison would leave a reception at
the Archdiocese to go to a late party at Mrs. Cornelius
Vanderbilt's and slip away from there to a gathering
at Sardi's. He was widely regarded as a snob, but it was
rare for two people to agree on what kind.

Inevitably, he came to think of his people as they
would one day appear in his diary. If a judge was rude
to him while he was arguing a case, if a government
official was quixotic or arbitrary, Madison would reflect with an inner smile that they were marring their
portraits for posterity. Yet he took great pains to avoid
the prejudices which he suspected even in his idol,
Saint-Simon. Most of the people whom he knew, like
many of Saint-Simon's, would survive to posterity only
in his own unrebuttable pages. If he succumbed to the
temptation of "touching them up," of making them
wittier or nastier or bigger or smaller than they were,
nobody in a hundred years would be any the wiser.
But his work would have become fiction, and he had no
intention of being a mere novelist.

When he was fifty-three, the great set of red morocco
on the shelves of his cedar closet totaled more volumes
than the years of his age, for there were sometimes
three or four to a single year. The diary was now in-
satiable. It not only demanded its daily addition; it
demanded footnotes, appendices, even illustrations.
Madison found that he spent as much time editing it
as he did writing it, but the former task had the advantage of requiring a constant rereading of his work,
a constant reabsorbing of his own glowing, crowded,
changing picture of the city, now a Bruegel, now a Ho-
garth, now a quiet, still Vermeer. Was it not as near as
he might ever come to the joys of having an audience?
Friends were surprised to find him asking for snap-

shots of themselves or of their deceased relatives or even of long destroyed houses. They decided that he was becoming sentimental with age. His dinner partners were sometimes piqued to find the "perfect listener" interrupting their confidences with such questions as: "Do you happen to remember what year your father sold the house in Seventieth Street?" or "Is it true that your Aunt Gisèle refused to swim in a pool if there were men in it?"

But only Clitus Tilney seemed to suspect the existence of an avocation. At lunch one day at the Down Town Association, Tilney rubbed his cheeks, his elbows on the table, for several long silent moments, reminding Madison of a great sleek lazy bear, bored in a zoo.

"Morris, do you know something?" he began, folding his hands on the table and contemplating them with an air of mild surprise. "I worry about you. Oh, I know, downtown we never talk personally. We live and work, cheek by jowl, year after year, and never know a thing about each other. And never seem to want to, either. But once in a while I have to break that rule. With people I like, anyway. And I like you, Morris. But if you don't want to hear me, just tell me to shut my big mouth."

"No, please, Clitus. I'd love to hear you."

"That's what you always say: 'I'd love to hear you.'" Tilney shook his large head as if Madison's response were the very symptom that most troubled him. "But anyway. I've never had a doubt that, after my own, yours was the best legal head in the office." He smiled to show that his boast was humorous. "Yet you and I both know that we can go just so far in life as lawyers. We don't kid ourselves. I'm a securities expert, and you're a tax wizard. We've mastered our respective fields of gimmickry. But that's not enough for us. Rutherford Tower can be perfectly happy with his wills and trusts, and Waldron Webb with his lawsuits. But you and I . . . well, our souls need more."

"What does your soul need, Clitus?"

"There you go again, throwing the ball right back

at me. Will you hang on to it a moment, for pity's sake? I want to talk about *you*."

Madison stirred uneasily. "But I could answer better if you told me first."

"Oh, very well," Tilney answered with an impatient shrug. "Only you know it, anyway. I've got the Washington bug. Ever since I had that job with Bob Lovett. And sometimes I even think I'd like to go back to Ulrica and teach."

"The firm will never let you go."

"Ah, well," said Tilney with a sigh, "that's another matter, isn't it? But to get back to you. You see? I can be very persistent. I've noticed in the past year that you've delegated more work."

"Is that a reproach?"

"Not in the least, my dear fellow. You know how I feel about that sort of thing. If a man can't delegate most of his work at fifty, he's either a dunce or a Napoleon. No, I'm wondering what you *do* with your life. Do you have any hobbies? Are you a Sunday painter? Or do you simply gaze at the sky and think great thoughts?"

The bantering tone of Tilney's question did not in the least conceal its genuine friendliness and concern. Madison was surprised to feel, for the first time in many years, that sharp pricking little urge to confide in another human. As he gazed back into his partner's sympathetic grey eyes, he moistened his lips and after a silence that was beginning to be embarrassing, began: "Well, as a matter of fact, I have what you might call a hobby—"

But he stopped. He stopped, frozen, on the edge of this new precipice. Talk about his diary? It was appalling; it was unthinkable. He shook his head quickly several times, as if to awaken himself. "It's my social life," he concluded lamely.

"Great Scott, man!" Tilney exploded. "You don't mean to sit there and tell me that all you care about is to dress up in a monkey suit and exchange banalities with stupid women?"

Madison wondered if he had ever wanted anything so much as he now wanted to have Tilney read the diary. But it was out of the question. Tilney would have been scandalized at the entries about his partners and clients, about the innermost workings of the firm, about Tilney himself. Besides, his personality was too powerful. Even if he *liked* the diary, in some bullying fashion he would try to put his own stamp on it.

"I take a broader view of social life than you do, Clitus," Madison said meekly. "To me it's more than a matter of monkey suits and stupid women. I like to think I'm observing a microcosm of the world. Everything, you know, can be contained in everything else. Isn't it a question of the power of one's lens?"

"I suppose it is, of course," Tilney said gruffly, and, giving up, he turned the conversation to office matters.

Madison discovered in the weeks that followed that the seeds which Tilney had so officiously scattered were growing with tropical speed into the jungle of his own uneasiness. His evening delight of dipping into the old volumes of the diary was now curtailed by the most agitating speculations. What would Tilney think of it? What would his other partners think? What would his ex-wife, long since remarried and contentedly living in Pasadena? Would they laugh? Or would they be impressed? Even dazzled? Was it enough to be thought all one's life a mere clever lawyer and diner-out and only to be posthumously appreciated at one's true worth? If there were no life hereafter, what would it gain him to have his diary acclaimed? Madison began to feel that he had to have at least one reader. At least one judge in his lifetime. But whom? Nobody seemed to have just the right qualifications. They were all too close to him or too distant, too ignorant or too terrifyingly knowing, too kind or too malicious. He started thumbing the Social Register and ended with the Manhattan Directory.

There was, however, one name that reoccurred on every list that he jotted down, and that was Aurelia Starr. Mrs. Starr was a widow, without children or other visible appendages, a few years younger than himself, with a small but adequate income, a trim and well-clad figure, who managed, for the proverbially unwanted extra woman, to get herself asked out nearly as widely as Madison himself. She was very decorative, with her dark, sleek hair, her long eyebrows rising to her temples, her widely parted blue eyes, her straight Egyptian nose. She might have had some of the elegance of a Nefertiti had she not trembled with an American widow's insecurity. But Aurelia, for all her nervous charm, was "safe." She was supposed, like all the unattached of her sex, to be after a husband, but she was so kind, so considerate, so understanding, such a good sport, that no man felt there was any danger of a dinner-table flirtation being taken too seriously. It was probably for just this reason that poor Aurelia had not rewed. Like Madison himself she was too good a listener.

When he sat beside her at dinner the next time, in the penthouse of a theatrical designer, he for once had no eyes or ears for the other guests. All he could think of, as he listened to her quiet, tense, pleasant chatter, was the question of showing her the diary. When the party was over, he took her home in a taxi, and she asked him up to her apartment for a drink. It was the kind of invitation that as a prudent single man he ordinarily declined, but now he hesitated.

"Oh, do come up, Morris," she urged him. "You and I meet and talk so often, and I love it, of course, but what do we ever really *say?* What do any of us ever really say in social life? Couldn't we try to talk for once, just you and me?"

"We could try."

In her tiny white and gold living room, that gloried in an Aubusson rug and Hubert Robert panels, he took a long draft of whiskey and relaxed.

"It's true that people talk banalities at parties," he agreed. "They like it that way. They think any real communication would be too much work. And then they complain of loneliness." He snorted in derision.

"Are you never lonely?"

"I think I can honestly say I'm not."

Aurelia laughed. "You sound very superior. With whom do *you* communicate? Or don't you?"

"I communicate with the future."

When she paused to consider this, he hoped that she would not try too hard to be sympathetic. But she was simplicity itself. "And how do you do that?"

"By keeping a diary. Or a journal. I'm not sure which you'd call it."

"I can see the advantage to *you*. But how does the poor future get its word in?"

"That's exactly what I was going to ask you. How can I arrange to let it?"

She mused. "Does it go back far, your diary?"

"Twenty-five years."

"My goodness. And it's complete?"

"As you can't imagine."

"Oh." She seemed to be looking through him, her lips apart, as if she could dimly make out those red volumes in the cedar chest. "And now you want someone to see it. For an opinion? Do you want a historian or a professor of literature?"

"Hardly. I think I just want someone to tell me if it's . . ." He paused to swallow and moisten his lips. "Well, if it's real. I mean, if it really exists. I sometimes wonder. But I think I've found the person who can tell me. Do you suspect who it is, Aurelia?"

"Of course I do! But I'm doubling back and forth in my tracks. I'm scared stiff! Why should *I* be the one so honored?"

"Because you never appear in it." He had not realized that this was so until the second before he said it, and immediately he understood that it might hurt her. "I don't mean by that that there's nothing to say about you. I mean that I must have always planned that you should be my reader."

"But I can't!" she protested, and the way she touched her middle fingers to the ends of her long eyebrows conveyed some of her tenseness. "It's not simply that I'm scared of such a responsibility. I think you're making a mistake. Once it's shared it isn't really a diary any more. There wouldn't still be that special intimacy between you and it. Be careful how you play with that!"

"Oh, but I *know*," he exclaimed. "This has been no light decision, believe me. You should be very proud. My diary and I are choosy!"

"I *am* proud, dear Morris. But I'm not foolhardy."

Nor was she. He was baffled and at length irritated to find that he could not move her. The most that he could obtain was her promise to discuss it on another occasion, and to do this he took her out for dinner the following week in a new Javanese restaurant. Aurelia had quite recovered her equanimity and was able to talk about the diary in a lively, even a facetious manner. She asked him all kinds of questions and seemed particularly fascinated by the mechanical details of its typing and storage. He told her about the safe deposit vault where one copy was always kept and described his plans for its posthumous publication and the trust to effect them that he had established in his will.

"But we can't talk all evening about my diary," he interrupted himself, with perfunctory courtesy, when the dessert was placed on the table.

"You mean you'd rather talk about mine?"

"Do you keep one?" The sudden sharpness of his tone reflected the instant crisis of his jealousy. "But of course you do! It's too obvious. How could I not have guessed it?"

"It's just a line-a-day."

"Just a line-a-day!" he retorted with a snort. "But, obviously, you love it. Obviously, you have visions of it being published."

"Oh, Morris," she protested laughing. "You're too absurd!"

"Am I?" His tone was almost plaintive. "I see it all too clearly. Your diary will come out the same year as mine and put it completely in the shade. Oh, I can read those reviews as if they were written on that wall! 'Although Mrs. Starr may not have the thoroughness of Mr. Madison, neither does she have his pedantry. Hers is the woman's hand, the light touch that illuminates her era. The universities and the scholars will undoubtedly be grateful for Mr. Madison's painstaking observations, but for that train trip, for that hospital gift, or even for reading aloud at the family hearth, we recommend Aurelia Starr.' "

"My dear friend, I promise you my diary is simply

to keep track of dentist appointments and cleaning women." Aurelia had stopped laughing and was serious again. "I'm in no way a writer. I like to talk. And, like a mirror, to reflect."

"What do you reflect?"

"Well at the moment, you. Or perhaps your diary. I'm not always quite sure which. I'm like a confidant in a French tragedy. I may not exist when the hero's offstage, but he tells me his thoughts. Or maybe just the ones that aren't worthy of his diary. I wouldn't have the presumption to compete with *yours*."

She was very elusive, but she was equally charming. Their dinner was repeated the next week and then the following and soon become a Friday night habit. It was agreed that neither would accept another invitation, no matter how exalted, for that evening. Madison had never enjoyed the regular companionship of a sympathetic woman, and he was beginning to understand what he had missed. They discussed other things besides the diary, yet it continued to have significance in their relationship as a starting point, a link, as the leitmotif that symbolized their rare intimacy. Aurelia always raised her first cocktail of the evening with a little nod across the table that meant she was drinking to it.

At times he would think back ruefully over the crowded years in which he had lived so constantly with people, so rarely with friends, and wonder if he had not wasted his life by being so private. But then it would strike him that he could never have met another Aurelia, for Aurelia was unique. She seemed to have no self at all. She listened; she laughed; she sympathized, and when she talked it was always about the subject that he had raised. He had never imagined that another human could be so intuitively understanding.

"You realize, of course, that you're spoiling me horribly," he pointed out. "Shouldn't we ever talk about your life?"

"I don't have one. Or rather, this is it."

"But you make me feel such a fatuous ass!"

"Do I? I'm sorry."

"Not really, of course. Only when I stop to think what an egotist I'm becoming."

"Don't." She was very clear about this. "My theory has nothing to do with egotism. I simply believe that communication can only exist between a man and a woman and then only when the man takes the lead. Don't worry about me. I think I'm doing rather nicely."

One result of their friendship was that his diary entries were becoming shorter and more matter-of-fact. He knew now that Aurelia would ultimately consent to read it, and his words no longer flowed when subject to her imagined scrutiny. It was like writing with her looking over his shoulder. This was not because he thought of her as necessarily critical; it was more that he could not imagine, well as he now knew her, just what her reaction would be. Once he went so far as to insert a flowery compliment to her in his description of one of their dinners, but he then ripped out the page. Perhaps as a diarist he needed a vacation. Perhaps he needed to do less observing and more thinking. For the first time in twenty-five years he let a week go without a single entry. He was conscious at night of that neglected cedar closet from which he could imagine a must of reproach emanating, but he resolutely turned over in his bed, saying aloud: "You've had the best years of my life. It's time you let *me* do a little living."

Matters came logically to a head one early spring afternoon on a bench under the rustling trees of Bryant Park after a matinee of *Tristan and Isolde*. When Aurelia told him it was her favorite opera, he accused her jokingly of harboring a secret death wish.

"It's better than being dead, anyway," she retorted. "You, my dear, are dead and living in a downy heaven where you see your published diary having the greatest success imaginable."

For once she had gone too far. "It seems to me that I live very much in the world," he said gruffly.

"Yes. As a spy."

"You say that because you know I keep a diary," he protested. "People always assume that whatever a man does, he does at the expense of something else. I guess there's only one way a diarist can persuade a beautiful woman that he's more than that."

She looked up quickly. "Oh, Morris," she warned him.

"Only one," he reiterated, firmly, his eyes fixed upon her.

"Be careful."

"What are you afraid of?"

"That you're going to propose to me!"

Madison was so startled that for a moment he could do nothing but shout with laughter. "But that's exactly what everyone thinks you want!" he cried. "The world is always wrong, Aurelia."

"The world is always libelous," she said, flushing.

"Oh, my dear, forgive me. Forgive me and marry me!"

Her face immediately puckered up into what struck him as a curious blend of gratification and near panic. She looked like a child who wanted to cry and couldn't.

"Do you mean it?"

"Of course I mean it."

"Do you swear?"

"I swear! By . . . by my diary!"

Aurelia's countenance cleared at this; already she resumed her mask. "My goodness, as serious as that? Then you must give me time."

"Time for what?"

"Well, for one thing, to read the diary."

"*All* of it?"

"That won't be necessary. Give me one early volume and one in the middle and . . . the current one."

Madison looked at her suspiciously. "You want to read where you come in?"

"What woman wouldn't?"

"You'll be disappointed. There's very little about you."

"Ah, but that's just what I want to see!"

That night, perched on a high stool in the big cedar closet, Madison pulled volume after volume from the shelves and skimmed their pages. The mild pique occasioned by Aurelia's failure to accept him right away

vanished with the exuberance of choosing the volumes
for her inspection. There was no longer any real question of the outcome; he could trust his faithful diary to
plead his cause. And the thrill of thinking of her reading his choicest pages! It made for a giddy night. As a
sample of his early work he picked the volume that
covered the winter months of 1936. He had been working night after night on a big tax case, which gave to his
entries a wonderful unity of mood. Madison liked to
conceive of his diary pictorially, and this volume
seemed to him a Whistler nocturne, with its dull grey
foggy atmosphere of exhausting work, streaked here
and there with the golden flashes of ambition. For the
middle period he chose a little gem of a divorce story
in high circles with which he had been professionally
involved. And for the last . . . well, of course, he had
to be honest and submit the latest volume, though he
hated to have Aurelia end on a flat note. He dated
the blank page following the final entry and wrote: "My
diary is to have its first reader. May she and it be
friends!"

The next Friday night they were to meet as usual
at their restaurant, and Madison, who arrived first,
ordered a cocktail to dull the edge of his now almost
unbearable excitement. As he was raising the glass to
his lips, however, he saw Aurelia crossing the room
towards their table, carrying the three red volumes
which he had sent to her. He noted with instant dismay
that she looked pale and haggard, as if she had not
slept in two nights, and her eyes avoided his as she
slipped into his seat. She pushed the books towards
him, without a word, and he placed them carefully on
the bench beside him.

"Is something wrong?"

"Oh, Morris, my friend, I don't know how to tell
you. Please order me a drink. No, let me have yours."
She took his glass and drank from it quickly. "I can't
stay for dinner. I'm all done in. I'm going to bed. I only
came to return the books. I know how precious they
are."

"Are you ill?"

"No, just tired."

"Was my poor diary so tedious?" he asked, with death in his heart.

She took another sip of his cocktail. "I tell you what," she said abruptly. "I'll have my little say, and then I'll be off." She paused, and when she spoke again there was a tremble of deep feeling in her voice. "Dear Morris, I hope that you and I will always be the best of friends. But I cannot marry you."

"Because of the diary?"

"Because of the diary."

"Is it so terrible?"

She seemed to consider this. "It's a monster," she said in a hushed, low tone. Again she paused and then relented a bit. "Though I suppose there's nothing wrong with a monster if you don't happen to be on its bill of fare."

"And you are?"

"Oh, my dear, you should know that. Don't you send a tribute of men and maidens each year to the labyrinth? No, I'm *serious,* Morris," she exclaimed when he smiled. "You've created a robot! He's grown and grown until you can no longer control him, and now he's rampaging the countryside. I dared to face him. I tried to give you time to get away. I was even able to stand him off a while. But now my stones are gone, and Goliath is stalking towards me!"

"How fantastical you are. Really, Aurelia, I wouldn't have thought it of you. You've seen for yourself that the entries stop with our friendship. If anyone's won, it's you."

"But I tell you I'm out of ammunition!" she exclaimed shrilly. "I have to take my heels while I can. For don't think Goliath wouldn't get his revenge for all those missing entries. I should be made his slave, like you. I should be harnessed and put to work. After all, he has missed the woman's touch, hasn't he? The woman's point of view? Isn't that the one thing he needs. Didn't Pepys have a wife? Wasn't there a Mrs. Saint-Simon?"

"There was a duchess," Madison said dryly.

"Exactly. And your diary wants a Mrs. Madison. But it won't be me. And if you're wise, Morris, it won't be anyone. You and your diary can be happy together. But I beg of you, don't listen to it when it points its long, inky finger at another human being!"

Madison was beginning to wonder if she was sober. "You must think me demented."

"Well, I don't suppose you'd burn down New York to make a page for your diary." She laughed a bit wildly. "After all, you might burn the diary with it. But, no, you have copies in a vault, don't you?" Here she seemed at last to remember herself, and she placed a rueful hand on his. "Forgive me, my dear, for being so overwrought. Let me slip away now and get a good night's sleep. I'll take a pill. And next week we'll talk on the telephone and see if we can't put things back on the nice old friendly basis."

"Aurelia—"

But she was gone. She was hurrying across the room, between the tables, and he had actually to run to catch up with her, clutching his three volumes.

"Aurelia," he cried in a tone that made her turn and stare. "Wait!"

"What is it, Morris? What more is there to say?"

"You haven't told me what you *think* of the diary."

She seemed not to comprehend. "I haven't?"

"I mean what you think of it *as* a diary."

"Oh." She treated this almost as an irrelevance. "But it's magnificent, of course. You know that."

"It's just what I *don't* know! It's just what I've spent the past several months trying to find out!"

"Oh, my dear," she murmured, shaking her head sadly, "you have nothing to worry about *there*. It's luminous. It's pulsating. It's unbelievable, really. I doubt if there's ever been anything like it. Poor old Saint-Simon, his nose *will* be out of joint. Oh, yes, Morris. Your diary is peerless."

She turned again to go out the door, and he let her go. For a moment he stood there, dazed, stock-still by the checkroom, until the headwaiter asked him if he wished to dine alone. He shook his head quickly and went out to the street to hail a taxi. It was only seven-thirty; he still had time to dine at the Century Club. When he got there, he hurried to the third floor

and glanced, as he always did, through the oval window
to see who was sitting at the members' table. There
was an empty seat between Raymond Massey and Ed
Murrow. Opposite he noted the great square noble
face and shaggy head of Learned Hand. He must have
just finished one of his famous anecdotes, for Madison
heard the sputter of laughter around his end of the
table. It would be a good night. As he glided forward
to take that empty seat he knew that he was a perfectly
happy man again.

THE REVENGES
OF MRS. ABERCROMBIE

MRS. ABERCROMBIE would have been with Tower, Tilney & Webb, come December, a grand total of forty years and was scheduled to be retired in the spring on her sixty-fifth birthday, when she and Mr. Abercrombie, an already pensioned accountant, planned to move to a new ranch house at a prudent distance from the beach in Montauk. Mr. Abercrombie, who found his rambles in Prospect Park, even with the zoo, inadequate to fill the long Brooklyn mornings and afternoons, looked forward to the change, but his wife was less enthusiastic. Where would she find, along the windy dunes of Long Island, the special consideration, the almost awesome isolation, which she enjoyed as secretary of the Tower Estates and treasurer of the Tower Foundation, known to all the office staff as the amanuensis of the late senior partner and surrogate, Reginald Tower?

Mrs. Abercrombie liked to think that she looked the part that she liked to play, and to some extent she did. Her slow, rolling gait gave to her broad figure, as it progressed down the corridors, and to her square chin, her high, broad brow, her crowning pompadour of silky grey, some of the dignity of a capital ship proceeding into harbor on a choppy sea but nonetheless ready, with sailors in white manning the rail, to render honors to the local commander. Her small office contained only a desk, two chairs and a large, mahogany framed photograph of Surrogate Tower in his robes, but she had it all to herself, and on the opaque glass door appeared, in gold lettering, the words "Tower Estates," followed by "Mrs. Abercrombie, Secretary." The next office was occupied by Rutherford Tower, whose nervous manner and furtive eyes seemed constantly to apologize for any presumption in sharing the last name of his deceased uncle. Mrs. Abercrombie could see only a parody of the Surrogate in his long, sallow features, and she particularly minded his habit of setting his teeth, because he did so only when he was frightened and not, like his uncle, when he was crossed. His teeth were set with a particular rigidity one morning, a month before Christmas, when he called her in to discuss tax returns.

"Mr. Tilney's on one of his efficiency rampages," he began gloomily. "He seems to think all the income tax returns should be prepared by the tax department."

"Surely not mine?"

By "mine" Mrs. Abercrombie meant those of Rutherford Tower's uncle's family. Indeed, the preparation of these, plus the processing of law students' applications for Tower Foundation grants, constituted her principal activities in the firm.

"Even yours, I'm afraid." He looked up at her with the abrupt, sullen defiance of the timid. "Even Aunt Mildred's."

"I don't think Mrs. Tower would want anyone else prying into her personal affairs. I have *always* done her returns."

"Well, it seems she was at dinner at the Tilneys' the other night and agreed to the whole thing. Tilney told her you couldn't be expected to keep up to date on every last tax wrinkle."

His words were a bleak reminder of the desolating disloyalty of people like Mrs. Tower. It was all very well to warm oneself in the sunshine of their benignant smiles on those rare visits downtown to sign a will, to cut a coupon, to make a tax-free gift, or to be lulled by their smooth, firm, complimentary voices on the telephone—"Dear Mrs. A, would it be a terrible imposition to ask you to address my Christmas cards this year?"—but one always knew, in a drafty little corner of one's heart, that one did not really exist for them, that at dinner tables covered with thin-stemmed wineglasses and silver candelabra they would betray one to the Tilneys of this world, for a snicker, let alone a laugh.

"I think, if you don't mind my saying so, Mr. Tower, that you make a mistake to let Mr. Tilney take over the running of your department. Of course, I understand that as senior partner he has a general responsibility for the firm. But surely that doesn't include all the details. Surely, it behooves you to stand up for your own!"

"I do my best, Mrs. A.," he replied with an ashy little smile. "But Tilney's always shouting about people not pulling their weight."

"The Surrogate used to say," Mrs. Abercrombie retorted in the high, cheerful, rippling tone, like the crest of a fast moving breaker, that she used in invoking her late employer's title, "that one couldn't evaluate an estate practice over one year, or even two or three. But he maintained that if one took a sufficiently long view, one would find it was estates that paid the rent!"

"Well, until you can convince Mr. Tilney of that, I am afraid we must do as he says."

Mrs. Abercrombie stood motionless for a heavy moment; then, without a word, she slowly turned to depart. But she did not fool herself. The dignity of her exit hardly covered her sweeping defeat in the matter of the tax returns. For years now, in fact, even since before the beloved Surrogate's death, she had viewed with an increasingly critical eye what Clitus Tilney was doing to the firm. As a young woman she had come into an office that still had some of the aroma of the days of the great individualist lawyers, those driving, nervous men who had cleaned out of the practice of law the windy court oratory of a Websterian age and substituted the machinelike chatter of corporate meetings, dry, snappish authoritarian men who, for all that, had had distinction as well as arrogance, manners as well as testiness, who had believed in being gentlemen as well as lawyers, who had collected paintings, built great houses, loved old wines. They might have driven their staffs unmercifully, but their offices had had charm: safes that did not open, or to which everyone had the combination, receptionists who were burly, storytelling, retired cops who shouted at clients, and tea served to everybody at five in big, dark comfortable libraries. There were no silvery bells to summon people to the telephone, no honey-toned switchboard operators, no "office organization" pamphlets, no memoranda from headquarters on little points of procedure, no office parties or "outings" to improve morale. And now? Well now they might as well move to Madison Avenue and have done with it!

Mrs. Abercrombie lunched that day with Mrs. Grimshawe, head of stenographic. Her relations with the staff were governed by three simple rules. To the new girls and office boys she merely nodded, if she happened to pass them in the corridor. With those who had been employed five years or more she occasionally chatted, seated in her corner armchair in the recreation room. With a few intimates, of high position and long tenure of employment, she lunched and permitted the use of Christian names. Of the latter group Lois Grimshawe was certainly closest to her, yet Mrs. Abercrombie had always ruefully to acknowledge that Lois, for all her sympathy and sharing of complaints, had manifested a distinct tendency to compromise with the Tilney administration. She had dyed her hair and divorced her husband, and Mrs. Abercrombie even suspected that the morning headaches of which she complained were not always the result of her vaunted insomnia.

At lunch Mrs. Grimshawe always had a martini, while her friend had a small dry sherry, but that day she suggested a second round.

"I'm sorry, Annabel," she said a bit snappishly, in answer to Mrs. Abercrombie's stare. "I'm feeling nervous today. I can't seem to concentrate on anything I'm doing."

"I wonder if a second cocktail will help that."

"It calms me down. It's all very well for you to be superior with a quiet room to yourself and the same things to do every day. I'd like to see you in that stenographic pool coping with twenty-five giddy girls who can think of nothing but lipstick and dates!"

Mrs. Abercrombie knew perfectly well that Lois Grimshawe was proud of her high position in the new scheme of things. She was like a collaborating member of a dispossessed nobility who sneers at the People's Army while secretly exulting in his commission. Mrs. Abercrombie knew how to deal with such pride.

"I know how difficult it must be for you, Lois," she said in a soothing tone. "Believe me, you will have all my sympathy. You're the one who gets the real worm's-eye view of the Tilney system. The clients may be impressed by the smooth efficiency of the outer office, but it's you who see the chaos behind it all."

"I'll have you know, Annabel, there's no chaos in *my* department!"

"Of course, I don't mean it's your fault, my dear."

"If there were chaos, it *would* be my fault."

"We all do our best, I'm sure," Mrs. Abercrombie said enigmatically as she raised her near-empty glass of sherry to her lips. In the silence that followed her final sip Mrs. Grimshawe gathered the courage to jettison the rattling piece of news for which she had wanted the binding chords of a second martini.

"I'm afraid Miss Bruney is going to be added to that chaos."

Mrs. Abercrombie started. "Miss Bruney?" she demanded. *"My* secretary?"

Of course she knew perfectly well and knew that Mrs. Grimshawe knew, that Miss Bruney was Rutherford Tower's secretary, but by dint of long encroachment, now amounting to a kind of eminent domain and having started from a simple plea for "a couple of letters a day," she had succeeded in pre-empting a good half of Miss Bruney's time.

"She's being transferred to the stenographic pool. I had a memo this morning from the boss himself."

"But *I* trained Miss Bruney!"

"Tell that to Tilney."

"What perversity makes that man interfere with things that don't concern him? This is the second time today!"

"Not a sparrow falls but he notices," Mrs. Grimshawe said somberly.

"Well, here's one sparrow that may be going to tumble right out of his nest!"

"You don't mean you'd resign?"

"I mean," Mrs. Abercrombie said grandly, "that there must be some limit to the quantity of humble pie that even an old and faithful servant can be obliged to consume."

"Annabel!" exclaimed Mrs. Grimshawe, her resentment dwindling now before her genuine concern. "Remember your pension. All you have to do is wait for the spring. Don't rock the boat now, dearie. Nothing's worth that!"

"If God Tilney chooses to cut off my pension, after forty years of faithful service, then God Tilney will do so."

"Let's not go to extremes." Mrs. Grimshawe's tone was sharp and practical. "You know what I'd do if I were you? I'd go to Mr. Tilney myself and tell him my problem. Everyone knows that he kicks Mr. Tower around. But you're something else again. I wonder if Tilney would make quite so many changes if he had to deal directly with you. Let me call Marjorie Clinger this afternoon and make an appointment."

Mrs. Abercrombie was at once struck with the idea and relieved not to have to make the first overture to the senior partner's secretary. For Miss Clinger was the very symbol of the Tilney era; she had a reputation for miraculous efficiency and seemed to live for her work. She was one of those large, pretty, modern old maids who seem to freeze at forty into a perpetual pantomime of eye rolling and good-natured, half rueful jokes about their own virgin status. She treated everyone, from Mr. Tilney down, with the same slangy familiarity, and was even supposed to be invited to cocktail parties in the home of partners. Mrs. Abercrombie found this all very unfitting. It was true that she herself had been invited to the Surrogate's at "Number Nine," as the house on Seventieth Street had been called, but only on New Year's Day for a glass of hot mulled wine.

"Lois tells me you want to see the boss," Miss Clinger told her on the telephone later that afternoon. It was like Miss Clinger to start right off that way, without even announcing herself, as soon as Mrs. Abercrombie had picked up the instrument. "It must be mental telepathy because he wants to see *you*. Why don't you come up in half an hour, and I'll see if I can squeeze you in between appointments?"

"Perhaps you will be good enough to ring me when he's ready. I can come right up."

"No, no, that never works. The only way to catch Tilney is to crouch outside his door and pounce when you see the chance!"

Offensive though she found such a procedure, Mrs. Abercrombie had to submit, and an hour later she found herself literally propelled, by the push of Miss Clinger's palm between her shoulderblades, into the smiling, smoking presence of the big, long-nosed, high-browed senior partner who was calling out to her in his loud, amiably mocking tone: "Well, well, Mrs. Abercrombie, it's good to see you! How is everything going in the great world of philanthropy?"

"Satisfactorily, I trust, sir. We're very busy." She noted that she had not been asked to sit.

"Philanthropy is the greatest thing in the world," Mr. Tilney continued airily, "but unhappily we can't all be foundations. At least law firms can't. We're in the grubby business of trying to make an honest buck. And the cost of overhead, Mrs. Abercrombie, is something that no lawyer can any longer afford to ignore. Gone, gone are the dear old days when you could fill up your stenographic department with trained girls at twenty dollars a week. We must take what we can get and grab what we can grab. Which is why I've had to grab Miss Bruney. I hope you'll understand."

"I suppose I can train another girl. It will take time, but I suppose I can do it."

"But that's just it, my dear Mrs. A, why take the trouble? I'm told that the volume of Mr. Tower's work doesn't warrant a full-time secretary. We thought that you might pitch in and lend us a hand. How about it? Could you take care of him?"

"Me, sir? You mean that I should take . . . that I should take Mr. Tower's *dictation?*"

"Does that astound you?"

"Well, I haven't done that kind of work . . . for years."

"But Mr. Tower, the *real* Mr. Tower, used to tell us

you had the fastest shorthand in the office. Surely, you haven't lost it all?"

"Perhaps not all," Mrs. Abercrombie said hesitantly.

"Oh, I'm sure not," the senior partner went on confidently. "It wasn't all that long ago. And how in awe we all used to be of you, Mrs. A! Do you remember that day I came in looking for a job, with hayseeds in my hair, and you tipped me off on how to handle the old man? I'll never forget it!"

Mrs. Abercrombie was touched. "I remember it very well. The Surrogate always said you were a go-getter. He was very proud that he was the one who'd 'spotted' you."

"And he spotted you, too, didn't he?"

"I guess he did, at that."

"Of course he did. So two old Tower 'spottees' should help each other out, don't you think? After all, it's only until spring, and then you'll be free of the lot of us. Take care of Mr. Tower till then, won't you?" Mr. Tilney glanced at a printed proof on his desk and then reached over to pull it nearer, presumably to resume the day's work. "Oh, and Mrs. A," he added, looking back at her as if it was she and not he who was concluding the interview, "I hope you're planning to attend the office Christmas party this year. We're all very much aware that it's your fortieth anniversary—fortieth, it's hard to believe isn't it?—you look no older than the day I first walked in here—and we've planned a little presentation."

"Well, that's very nice, I'm sure. Thank you, Mr. Tilney."

"Thank *you*, Mrs. A!"

And everything would have been all right; everything would have been, in fact, quite "dreamy," to use Lois Grimshawe's favorite adjective, except for one wretched little circumstance. As Mrs. Abercrombie passed between the two desks, in the anteroom outside his office, of Miss Clinger and Mr. Webb's secretary, she distinctly saw out of the corner of her eye, the former lean forward over her typewriter to cast a quick wink behind her back. So that was it, she breathed to herself as she quickened her pace, as if to flee from the smothered giggle that might follow before she was out of earshot. She had been fixed. She, Annabel Abercrombie, had been "coped with," a poor old shabby piece of baggage which could, with some extra string, be used for one final load, one last trip. And if it burst in the station and cast its goods shamefully over the platform, what did it really matter? It was only the junk bag, anyway.

It was inevitable under the circumstances—and she was even a bit ashamed of it herself—that the first person to test the force of her resentment should be Rutherford Tower. He had certainly never asked, poor man, that Mrs. Abercrombie should replace Miss Bruney; he was simply the baser nature that had come within the pass of mighty opposites. When Mrs. Abercrombie came in the next day and sat sedately down for the morning's dictation, a good forty minutes after his ring (forty minutes, she claimed, that were necessarily dedicated to his aunt's mail) and held up her pad as if it were some strange, faintly comic gadget that she had never seen before, he kept his eyes directed down at the desk to avoid the embarrassment of revealing either his irritation or his timidity. Whenever Mrs. Abercrombie asked him to repeat a word or phrase, which was frequent, he would do so with a loud, clear, patient articulation of each syllable. "I'm not deaf yet, you know," she reminded him cheerfully, and then, when he had recommenced dictation and was going too fast, she would hold her pencil suspended until he had finished a paragraph and lost forever his beginning before observing: "I'm afraid I shall have to ask you to go over that again." If he dared so much as give an answering cough to show his dismay, she would follow up with: "Now, now, Mr. Tower, this isn't some sort of a speed contest, is it?" and settle back in her chair with a rumbling laugh. But the simplest way, she soon found out, to bring him to the slippery edge of distraction was to find a piece of Tower Foundation business to place ahead of every letter or document that he had dictated. If he loomed up in her doorway after lunch, with a hunted look, to ask if the letter to Standard

Trust Company which he had given her at ten o'clock
was ready, she would reply, with a mocking shake of
her head and a serene smile: "Ready? Why, bless you,
I haven't even started it. Do you realize I have *six*
more students' applications to finish before I can
even get to the memos you gave me yesterday?" It
might have been a bit hard on him, but was not the
whole catastrophe attributable to his cowardice? Why
did he not stand up for his rights? Had not his Tower
ancestors been leaders of the bar when the Tilneys
were selling newspapers in the streets of Ulrica?

But it was Tilney himself, of course, and not Tower
who would have to bear the full force of her reproach,
and she had selected the Christmas party as the occasion for this. After receiving her gift she would undoubtedly be asked to say a few words, and then she
would be able to point up the contrast between the
gracious past and a present without values, between
the polished but profound gentleman scholars of yesteryear and the legal hucksters of today. She would not
do it crudely, or even bitterly. She would do it with a
high, dry, faintly wistful humor, with little smiles cast
about among the partners, smiles that would contain
in addition to a proper gratitude and affection, the least
hint of reproach, forgivable in a long-faithful servant,
at their lowered standards and an invocation to remember the splendid old things that had made the firm great.
It would be dignified, tasteful, moving—and devastat-
ing. It would give Clitus Tilney a lesson that even his
bland capacity for wishful thinking would not quite be
able to brush off. She spent her evenings now compos-
ing the speech and trying portions of it out on Mr.
Abercrombie, who was never to have the good fortune of hearing the finished version as the Christmas
party was strictly limited to the office. He listened with
his usual pipe and his usual patience, but he ruffled her
by suggesting that she "sugar" it up with a sprinkle
of Yuletide spirit.

"Why not come right out and ask me to recite 'The
Night Before Christmas'?" she asked frostily. "After all,
it would be perfectly appropriate. The Surrogate used

to say that it was his grandfather who had suggested the names of the reindeer to Mr. Moore."

The finished draft, which her husband had found too sarcastic and she too mild, she began to have misgivings about on the day of the party itself. She had never taken much notice of these parties, at least since the Surrogate's day when he had used to open them with a lively and merry address, full of sly references to the younger lawyers, congratulating some for their past year's industry and exhorting others, though always with a Christmas twinkle in his eye, to greater efforts in the year to come. Mrs. Abercrombie in recent years had usually stayed but half an hour, sitting apart with Mrs. Grimshawe and consuming a small glass of ginger ale and a single watercress sandwich. When she took her leave she made her farewells only to Messrs. Tilney and Webb, the two senior partners, unless she happened to pass close to Rutherford Tower in which event she would shake hands with him as well. But this year, when she saw the office slowly assembling in the stenographic department where the party was held, and realized, as indeed was manifest in the splendid orchid that drooped from her shoulder and which had been sent by Tilney himself, that she would have to address that multitude, she became suddenly tense.

The desks had been pushed back to make a circular area for dancing in the center of which a lone accordionist was playing "White Christmas." On top of the green file cabinets that jutted out from the walls various decorations had been strewn: small trees, paper hats, a sleigh with a Santa Claus and rather too many big red tissue-paper bells. Plates of hard-boiled eggs and turkey sandwiches covered Mrs. Grimshawe's desk, and on a long table with a green cloth cover the office boys mixed bourbon and ginger ale. It was generally supposed among the partners that the girls had a "field day" getting the place ready and that it was only right to let them have one afternoon a year in which they could turn a dreary masculine world into something more festive. But Mrs. Abercrombie knew better. Everybody was bored by the party. As the wise old Surrogate used to say, "We have to give the damn thing, not because anyone likes it, but because if we don't, they'll call us Scrooge & Marley." Looking about the room, Mrs. Abercrombie concluded that it was more than ever like a children's party. The lawyers crowded together on one side of the bar, the girls on the other. A respectful group of the former listened to Mr. Webb's jokes. Mr. Tilney alone circulated, beaming to left and right. After the first forty minutes some of the younger stenographers started dancing with each other. Mrs. Abercrombie, realizing at last to the full that these were the people who would hear her speech, felt the sagging weight of depression in her legs and stomach.

"What's that you're drinking, Lois?" she asked.

"Vodka, dearie. And it's just the thing for you. Let me put a swig in your ginger ale."

Mrs. Abercrombie allowed her to give her a swig and, after she had finished it, she allowed her to go to the bar to get her an even stiffer one. Perhaps it was indiscreet, but on the whole she thought not. She felt better already, and quite a bit better when she was halfway through her second. The depression inside remained, but it was lighter. In fact, it was not altogether disagreeable. She felt less irritated as she thought of the shabby present, more resigned, more philosophical. She even felt a swelling in her heart of something like affection for the good old firm that had planned to honor her that day.

"I'll bet that's better now, isn't it?"

"Yes, Lois, I think it is. I honestly think I can say it is."

"That's one thing we owe the Russians, anyway."

Mr. Tilney now raised a long arm over his head, and silence followed a ripple of warning buzzes to the corners of the room.

"Ladies and gentlemen of Tower, Tilney & Webb, if you please, if you please!" he exclaimed, and when the room was still he continued, in the leisurely, stately manner of one who knows that interruption is impossible and applause to be assumed: "It is once again my happy privilege to wish you all the greetings of the season."

As he went on, smiling in the direction of each

person to be honored with an individual greeting, Mrs. Abercrombie lost track of his words. She had fallen into a listless reverie, with a sense of being surrounded by snow, infinite snow, great silent soft banks of snow on the ground and more snow still descending, relentlessly, in slanted lines. It was the vodka, she vaguely supposed, and the vision which it had evoked of old Russia and now of temples with strange cupolas and men in fur hats in sleighs and grand duchesses in court dress with tiaras as they appeared in the illustrations of court memoirs at her lending library. But it was all suddenly blotted out by a present of marching feet, millions of marching feet, and rude laughs and horrid rough men and the ghastly vision of the poor czarina and her lovely daughters slaughtered in that cellar. And it seemed to Mrs. Abercrombie as she gazed about the room that the green file cabinets poking their sharp corners out from under the absurd incongruity of the hastily assembled, jerry-built pile of Christmas decorations were like the guns and rockets of Soviet military might poking their barrels and noses out from under angels' robes and doves of peace in a cartoon that mocked the sincerity of Russia's aversion to war. She was shocked by the sudden rude poke that Mrs. Grimshawe gave her.

"Annabel," the latter whispered fiercely, "he's talking about you."

And so he was.

"Mrs. A was my first impression of Tower & Strong, as the firm was then somewhat formidably named," he was saying, and his cold, friendly eyes were turned on Mrs. Abercrombie with a twinkle. "I had come down to New York, fresh out of law school, and was trembling at the prospect of my interview with Judge Tower. Mrs. A came out to meet me in the lobby, took in my situation in a moment and smiled a merciful smile. 'Just remember,' she warned me gently about her boss, 'we hate F.D.R., we hate the NRA; we think McKinley was the last great American, and we lunch promptly at twelve-fifteen.' "

The roar of laughter that followed this startled Mrs. Abercrombie, and she gazed about, frightened, at the suddenly raucous throng. And then everything went very fast, and Mr. Tilney was praising her for four decades of devotion and people were clapping as loudly as if their hands were wooden slats, and Mr. Tilney was facing her, holding up a small golden eagle that seemed to be a paperweight, and then she was on her feet and there was a sudden silence, thunderous in its expectancy.

"Forty years," she began in the high, clear meditative tone that she had rehearsed so many nights at home. Then she cocked her head as if the words were a piece of statuary that she was contemplating from a different angle. "Forty years," she repeated musingly. "To many of you, to most of you perhaps, it is a lifetime. At least it encompasses *your* lifetime. To all of us it embraces what we think of as modern times. For the world, our world, was born with the end of the first war."

As she paused she heard distinctly, from somewhere behind her, a high, plopping sound like a pebble falling into a still pond: a hiccup. There was a sudden startled ripple of laughter from the younger girls, followed by a tense hush.

"But there was a world before our modern world," Mrs. Abercrombie continued, raising her chin to counter the vulgarity and insolence of that interruption. "The thing that most consoles me for growing older is that I was born early enough to have had a peek at that world. It was a quieter, slower, more gracious world . . ."

Hic! Once again the impertinent little sound supplied her with an unsought semicolon. This time the laughter spread to the associates, but Mrs. Abercrombie heard Mr. Tilney's angry "Hush!" Silence was restored except for one girl who, with a hand to her lips to hold in evident hysteria, hurried from the room. As Mrs. Abercrombie resumed her speech she became aware, from the intent eyes and clenched fists of one young man before her, that he was making the same violent effort to repress his laughter.

"A more gracious world," she reaffirmed in a louder, clearer tone. "A world where the telephone was reserved for important communications. Where a letter had to be thought about because it had to say something. Where there were no coffee breaks, no lady smokers, no machines for selling Coca-Cola . . ."

Hic!

And now came pandemonium. The room seemed fairly to explode into an orgiastic roar of laughter. The repressive forces which had been used to maintain the silence hitherto had only swollen the ultimate furor. Juniors, abandoning themselves now to the general mood, heedless of the consequences, and then, almost immediately, jubilantly relieved to see their seniors in the same fix, threw back their heads, clapped their hands and howled. One of the office boys actually rolled on the floor. Mr. Webb, holding his hands over his big stomach, afraid perhaps of tiring his heart, made appalling, gasping sounds. But worst of all was Rutherford Tower. He behaved like a creature demented, hugging himself with his arms and swinging his torso to and fro as he screamed in a high pitched voice: "Oh! Oh! *Oh!*"

Only Mr. Tilney did not laugh or even smile. He continued to gaze at Mrs. Abercrombie with eyes of gentle and inquiring sympathy as if there was no commotion, as if the speaker had simply paused to turn a page of notes, or to take a sip of water, and would resume in a moment. And then Mrs. Abercrombie, gazing back at him, felt a sudden weight in her knees and shoulders, felt the desk behind her as she sagged against it, and knew at last that it was she herself who had hiccuped.

She hesitated only a moment the next morning before pushing open the glass door to the reception room. Yet in that moment she raised her chin and squared her shoulders in the manner of a French noblewoman ascending the steps to the scaffold. The receptionist lowered her eyes and barely whispered her morning greeting; the two office boys, waiting for messages, nudged each other; an associate hurrying by in the corridor hurried a bit faster. It was some consolation, Mrs. Abercrombie reflected grimly, that they were all more embarrassed than she. She walked directly to

Mr. Tilney's office and paused before the busily typing Miss Clinger.

"May I see him, please?"

Miss Clinger looked up with false surprise. "Oh, good morning, Mrs. A. Yes, go right in, why don't you? He's on the phone now, but he shouldn't be long."

Mrs. Abercrombie's eyes softened as she stood before the desk of her telephoning employer. He was listening at the moment, but he raised a hand and smiled broadly in a friendly greeting that made them intimate. Painless to her already was the memory of last night's taxi ride to Brooklyn, when he had taken her to her very door, protesting all the while against the "barbarous" custom of office parties, assuring her that everyone knew that hiccups were caused more by ginger ale than by liquor, apologizing for the rudeness of the younger people and associating himself with her as members of a dwindling minority who still realized that without form, substance was merely clay. He had even warned her, at her door, to tell her husband nothing about the matter and to come to the office the next morning and "face down" the whole sorry crew. And she had done it. He would see that she was not unworthy of his trust and of his generosity.

"Mr. Tilney," she said when he had put down the instrument, "I just stopped in to tell you one thing, and then I'll be off, for I know what a busy man you are. Here it is. I thought when the Surrogate died that the last of our really great gentlemen had gone. I now know I was wrong."

He did not let her down. He did not spoil their moment by words. He sensed that her compliment was one that could only lose by acknowledgement. He simply sat and smiled at her, nodding his head gently, until she turned away to hide her tears and hurry from the room.

She passed Mr. Tower's room and noted that he was peeking at her from behind his *Law Journal*. With stiffly averted head she continued to her own desk where she found her telephone ringing. It was Mrs. Grimshawe.

"Oh, dearie, you *did* come in. I'm so glad."

"Of course I'm in, Lois. What do you want?"

"Mr. Tower called ten minutes ago to say he didn't

think you'd be in, and could he have a girl from the pool?"

"Tell Mr. Tower," Mrs. Abercrombie answered gratingly, "that that will not be necessary. *I* will take care of his work. As usual."

Hanging up, she reached for Tower's unopened mail and dumped it in her "Hold" basket. She then opened the Foundation account book and started making slow, careful entries of elaborately rounded figures. At half past ten his head at last appeared in her doorway.

"Could we do some dictation now, please, Mrs. Abercrombie?"

She looked up and gazed at him in bland astonishment. "Why, I think so, Mr. Tower," she replied cheerfully. "Just as soon as I've finished with the account books. Mr. Tilney told me last night that he wanted everything up to date by the end of the year."

The long head and the sallow face disappeared, and Mrs. Abercrombie reflected, with a deep sigh of satisfaction, that she still had a whole half year to make him pay for those cries of the night before.

THE MAVERICKS

HARRY REILLEY occupied a peculiar status among the associates of Tower, Tilney & Webb. He had not been netted by the hiring committee in its annual Christmas canvas of the editors of the Harvard, Yale and Columbia law reviews. He was thirty-two and clerking for a small firm of real estate lawyers in Brooklyn when Clitus Tilney had decided to bolster Tower, Tilney's small department in that field by hiring a young man, already trained, from the outside. Harry had understood that he was being employed as a specialist with little chance of ultimate partnership, and he had not minded until he had discovered the tight little social hierarchy into which the firm was organized. Then he decided that working in his status was like climbing the stairs in a department store while alongside one an escalator carried the other customers smoothly and rapidly to the landing.

The real estate department of Tower, Tilney had for years been run by an old associate, Llewellyn Buck, a dry, scholarly gentleman who spent most of his time studying Plantaganet law reporters through thick glasses and who was referred to about the office, with a mild and affectionate contempt, as one who had made nothing of a brilliant start.

"Real property, my dear Reilley, was the golden field of the common law," he had told Harry at the beginning. "Everything else grew out of it. That's why everything else is warped, and only the law of conveyances is pure. Stay with purity, my boy. Also, it's a wonderful field in which to study your fellow mortals. There's something about a deed or a lease that brings out the meanest and the pettiest in them. I've seen a man lose a ten million dollar corner property over a difference of opinion about the reading of an oil meter!"

Harry cared little for legal philosophy and less for the opportunity to observe his clients at their less becoming moments, but he liked the salary and stuck to the job. He was used to the small print of deeds and mortgages and was not bothered by detail; his mind, like his body, was tough. He was a big man with big shoulders, and he walked in a stiff, blocky fashion that was yet consistent wtih a fine muscular coordination. He had a large round head and a bull neck, thick blond hair that he wore in a crew cut and small, greyish-blue eyes with a habitual expression of reserve that bordered on suspicion. His nose was straight and wide, his jaw square and the slanting lines of his unexpectedly delicate upper lip were almost parallel to his cheekbones. Harry was handsome with the handsomeness of a hundred and ninety pound Irishman in the prime of life, but the danger of overweight already hung about him.

He would have got on well enough with the other clerks had he been less sensitive about real or imagined condescension. When Bart French, Tilney's son-in-law, the rich young man who worked harder than all the others simply because he was rich, paraded down the corridor to go out to lunch, followed by the little group with which he was working on a corporate indenture, and paused at the door of Harry's office to ask cheerily: "Care to join us—" Harry would wonder if he was not performing an act of charity to the poor slave in real estate. But he would join them and listen, bored, while they discussed in tedious detail the problems of their current indenture until Bart, towards the end of the meal, would turn to him with a perfunctory show of interest and ask in that same maddening, cheery tone: "What's new in the metes and bounds department? Have you caught any covenants running with the land?"

Harry had been a prickly soul since the age of fourteen when his father, a seemingly successful Brooklyn building contractor, had gone to jail for looting his company. Harry, the youngest of seven, had been the one to feel it most keenly and, in the ensuing years of retrenchment and hardship, had been his mother's primary consolation. After his father had been released, and when he had taken to whiskey and self-pity, Harry had been passionately and articulately bitter in his resentment of him. But fathers like Angus Reilley always

win in the end, and his death of cancer in Harry's
freshman year at Fordham had so crushed the latter
with remorse that he had seemed doomed for a time to
the paternal alcoholic course. Indeed, his elder brothers
and sisters, including Joseph, the priest, had gloomily
prognosticated that Harry would go to the dogs, but
Harry seemed to have a stabilizer built into his character which, when he tipped too close to the fatal angle,
suddenly, if with a great deal of churning and throb-
bing, succeeded in righting the lurching vessel. He had
finished Fordham and Fordham law in the first third
of his classes; he had fought as a marine in Korea
and been decorated, and he had supported himself
creditably in the law ever since. It was a disappointment to his mother that he had preferred a room in
Manhattan to the family home and a dissolute bachelor
existence to the safer joys of early matrimony, but when
he came to the Reilleys' Sunday lunch he always looked
hearty and well, and he was charming with all the little
nephews and nieces. The family had to concede that
when Harry wanted to put his best foot forward, he
had a very good foot to offer.

In Tower, Tilney, however, this foot was seen more
by the staff than by the lawyers. Harry blandly ignored
the elaborate etiquette laid down by the late Judge
Tower. He called the stenographers by their first names
and went out to lunch with the men in the accounting department. He maintained an easy, joking, mock-
flirtatious relationship with the older women: Mrs.
Grimshawe, as head of stenographic, Mrs. Lane, the
librarian, and Miss Gibbon, the chief file clerk, as a
result of which he got as good service as Clitus Tilney
himself. In fact, Mrs. Grimshawe, "Lois" as he im-
pudently called her, had been known to leave her desk
on the little dais from which she supervised her department, grab a pencil and pad from one of her girls and
go to Mr. Reilley's office to take dictation herself!

Among the law clerks his only two friends were the
two whom he considered, like himself, to be maver-
icks: Lee Ozite, the managing clerk, who handled the
court calendars and arranged for the service of papers,
and Doris Marsh, the single woman lawyer in the

office. Doris' interest in Harry was immediate and lively, aroused by nothing greater than his merely civil appreciation of herself as a woman. To the other clerks she might as well have been neuter, a tall, pale, tense, awkwardly moving figure of near thirty in a plain brown suit, distastefully associated with taxes, whose black hair was lightly flaked with a premature grey. But Harry did not, like many working men, relegate sex to nonworking hours. A woman to him was always a woman, and, without finding Doris particularly his type, he could perfectly see that her skin, if chalky, was nonetheless smooth and soft, her breasts full and fine and that, without the glasses and the nervous smile, her face might reveal the firm, rounded lines of a Greek statue. Harry could picture Doris sitting on a rock naked, looking out to sea, her hair blown in the wind, and he deplored the fate which had confined her to a city desk.

The first time they lunched together, he discovered that she was a great talker. She drank a martini before her meal and a glass of ale with it and complained at length of the difficulties of being a woman lawyer in Tower, Tilney. She gave instances of discrimination in the tax department: of how she was paid less than associates who had come in after her and not asked to the office outings at the Glenville Beach Club. What just saved her from being a bore was the dry accuracy of her observation and her evident sense of the foolishness of the whole show.

"Now don't ask me why I don't get another job," she concluded, taking off her glasses and gazing at him with a stare of bland seriousness. "It would be very ungentlemanly because I wouldn't have a thing to say. Let's put it that I have a persecution complex."

"I thought perhaps you hoped to marry one of the partners."

"Which?"

"Why not Madison? He's single, isn't he?"

"That he is." She maintained all her air of gravity. "He might be just mean enough to do it to save the pittance he now pays me."

"And think of the income tax deduction you'd bring

him! For a man in his bracket that might even make up for a wife who reads herself to sleep with the Revenue Code."

Doris startled him by throwing back her head and uttering a long, rather wild laugh. But she cut it off with equal abruptness. "I *crave* you, Harry Reilley. You're human. One of the few people in the whole damn shop who is. Do you realize you're the first of the associates who's ever asked me to lunch? The very *first?*" She paused to reflect. "Except Ozey, and they treat him, poor man, like the janitor."

For the rest of lunch they took apart, one by one, the partners of the firm. Doris, of course, had more to say, because she knew them better. At first she showed some slight degree of reticence, but she rapidly lost it as she drank her ale, and by dessert she was speculating freely that Waldron Webb was a sublimated homosexual and that Morris Madison had a neurotic fear of women. It was the most obvious kind of female revenge against a male community: she simply denied that they were men.

"It must be a sorry prospect for a single woman," Harry observed as they walked back to the office. "You should have gone into advertising."

"But things have looked up since they started hiring big Irishmen. I may stick around a bit."

They both laughed and went back to work as easily as if there had been nothing between them but a common employer. Yet Harry was faintly ashamed of his little game of coaxing the woman out from behind the tax computer. It took so little to do it. Doris developed the habit of dropping into his office once a day to smoke a cigarette and "reset her sights," as she put it. She pretended that it was essential, after a certain number of hours of work at Tower, Tilney, to become "rehumanized." Together they laughed at things and people, and he found her office gossip amusing, but basically the world in which he lived began outside the doors of the office while hers ended on the same threshold. The little bites of the legal hierarchy raised small red welts in his sensitivity which he could afford to ignore, or at the most irritably scratch, but in her they seemed to secrete a subtle poison which by dint of the constant application of antitoxins had become a necessity to her nature.

He had had too much to do with women not to be aware that the least advance on his part would be immediately and gratefully misinterpreted, and he was determined that no such advance would be made. She had asked him to two cocktail parties at the apartment which she shared in Greenwich Village with another woman lawyer, and he had declined both. Doris had chosen to accept his lame excuses literally and had had the sense not to betray any disappointment that she might have felt. But when the approach was made by a third person, Harry's plan of action, or inaction, was upset, and so he came to be committed to a weekend with Doris in a cottage in Devon, a small sandy summer settlement on the south shore of Long Island.

It was Lois Grimshawe's cottage, and the invitation came from her. Nobody knew better than Lois the incongruity, under Judge Tower's rules, of such a bid from even a senior staff member to a junior associate, and her sense of the indecorum was pasted all over her round, smiling, pink and yellow countenance when she came into Harry's office.

"You may think it very bold of me, but you have been so very friendly—not at all like the other associates—that I wondered—if you were going to be stuck in town over next weekend—whether you might not like . . ." She paused here, still smiling, and stuck a finger in the high pile of her dyed auburn hair. "Oh, no, but you wouldn't, of course."

"Wouldn't what, Lois?"

"Wouldn't want to spend that weekend with me in my little place in Devon. Oh, it's just a shack, you know. We do all our own cooking and everything, but there's plenty of whiskey and nice neighbors and lots of sun and sea, and if I say so myself we do have fun." Here Lois giggled.

"Of course I'll come. I'd love to."

"Oh, goody!" Lois clapped her hands in excitement. "There'll be just you and me and Doris Marsh and Harry Barnes, an old friend of mine. He's a senior

cashier at Standard Trust. Really a lovely person. And
Marjorie Clinger—you know, Mr. Tilney's secretary—
has the cottage next door, so you'll see some familiar
faces!"

Harry sighed when she had gone and debated how
best to get out of it, but this, he finally decided, was
unworthy. It was insulting to attribute too much design
to Doris and absurdly weak of himself to be afraid of
being able to resist it, if design there was. He had taken
care of himself on the beaches of Korea; he could certainly do so on those of Devon. The way to take life
was as it came.

And, indeed, it seemed to come easily enough. The
cabins of Lois Grimshawe and Miss Clinger, like doz-
ens of others along the dunes of Devon, were small
weatherbeaten shingle structures, like overgrown bath-
houses, each with a back porch facing the sea on which
drinks were constantly mixed. There was a great deal
of laughing and joking on arrival, and much shouting back and forth between cabins and many hilarious
references to last weekend's hangovers, but one could
do, apparently, as one pleased, and Harry, after changing to a pair of red bathing trunks and sitting for a
few minutes with the group on the beach, took off
alone down the dunes at a pace that was no invitation
to any woman to join him. He walked for miles, past
larger cabins, past huge summer palaces, past swimming clubs, and every half hour he would run down
into the water and plunge in the hissing surf. It was
glorious exercise, and he did not return until eight
that night when he found a noisy picnic of some
twenty people going on in front of Lois' cabin. Lois
had already drunk too much to be cross at his dis-
appearance, and when he had changed to a shirt and
blue jeans and joined the group, he felt better than
he had felt all summer and in a mood to drink deeply.

Which he did. Much later in the evening when the
others were singing songs, he was sitting above the
group on a ridge of dune with Doris Marsh. She looked
very well in the moonlight and in the flicker of the
fire below. Her hair blew in the wind, and her figure
was well accentuated by her long velvet pants. Harry

was reminded of his earlier vision of her naked by the sea. Yet Doris seemed absorbed in a melancholy and reflective mood. She, too, was interested in drinking.

"You know, Harry, on a night like this, under all those stars, it just doesn't seem possible that Monday will find me back in that sweatshop writing a memorandum on Miss Johanna Shepard's capital loss carryovers."

"Why go back, then?"

Doris squinted at the moon. "Just a little matter of bread and butter."

"Oh, can it, Doris. You could make more money for half the work. What about Uncle Sam? Ever think of the Collector's Office? As a matter of fact, I've been turning the idea over myself."

"Oh, no, Harry, don't you dare!" Very solemn now, she turned to shake her head at him. "You're not like me, you know. You *could* make the grade."

"What grade?"

"You could be a partner. No, dear boy, don't grunt and throw sand. I know exactly what I'm talking about. And I know all about the real estate department not being the best place to start. Sure, it's a dead end. But you don't have to stay in it. You could go to Mr. Tilney and ask for a transfer. And with your personality, you'd get it. Believe me, Harry!"

"Oh, bosh. They don't want my kind in their paneled offices. Give me that cup and let me get you a drink."

"Here's that cup and by all means get me a drink, but I still know what I'm saying." As he took her empty cup she turned away and hugged her knees, facing the soft breeze. "And I'm a fool to tell you, too."

"Why?"

"Because when you *do* make the grade, you certainly won't come down to spend weekends in Devon with Lois Grimshawe and Doris Marsh."

"Dry up, will you, Doris?"

"I *am* dry," she said without turning. "Why don't you get me my drink?"

When he returned with the full cups he was determined not to let the conversation get back to Harry Reilley, even if it had to become sentimental about

Doris Marsh. "How did you ever get into this racket?" he asked her. "Why aren't you living in the suburbs with a station wagon and three children? With one eye on your husband and one eye on somebody else's?"

"Would you really like to know?" she asked rhetorically. "Would you really like to hear my dreary tale? I went to law school because of a guy. I went into practice because of a guy. I molded my whole life into a particular twisted shape to please one guy, and I didn't even catch him." She turned to give Harry a friendly little push on the shoulder. "It's your fault if I bore you with my love story, old man. You asked for it. You shouldn't be so God-damn sympathetic with your questions."

Harry listened with mild interest, as he sipped his drink and watched the moonlight on the waves, to her tale of "Phil" who was now practicing law, still unmarried, in Hawaii. It seemed that Phil was one of those men who could not live with or without Doris. She had waited for his mother to die, then his father, but these events had brought him no closer. And finally he had left the country.

"It was all I could do not to follow him to Honolulu," she concluded mournfully. "I suppose I might have, had I thought there was really any chance. The trouble with Phil was that he couldn't face up to the fact that he was in love with me."

"You were well out of it," Harry said curtly. "Phil sounds to me like a first-class heel."

"You say that because you didn't know him. You'd have liked Phil."

"The hell I would."

"What about *you,* Harry? What's kept you single this long?"

"I haven't found anyone who would have me."

"Don't look too hard." He knew there had to be a meaningful gleam in her eyes, but he could not make it out in the darkness. "Of course, I was a fool to think you'd tell me anything," she continued with a grunt. "You're a real Irishman. You speak with blarney and raddle out all my sordid little secrets. And what do I get in return? Nothing. What will anybody get? Nothing."

"Maybe there's nothing to get."

Lois Grimshawe came stumbling up the dune to whisper in Doris' ear. Then she hurried off with a "Thanks, dearie" and went to the cabin. It was very late, and the party was breaking up.

"What's on old Lois' mind?"

"She told me to ask you not to notice if Henry Barnes wasn't sleeping in the living room," she replied with a slow and careful articulation. "You can imagine where he *will* be sleeping. Evidently, she's not 'old Lois' to him."

Lois' cabin contained two small bedrooms over the living room. The plan had been that she and Doris would occupy these while the men slept on a sofa and daybed below. "I don't give a damn where Barnes sleeps," Harry retorted. "Except I'm glad it won't be with me. He looks like a snorer."

"You're not hopelessly disgusted at our sordid little ménage?"

"Be your age, Doris!"

They finished their drinks and rose to walk back over the now deserted beach to the cabin which was dark. Doris stumbled in the sand, and he put an arm around her waist, and as she leaned heavily against him, he knew that he was not going to resist any further. He had had many drinks, but he was not drunk, and he saw clearly that what he was going to do he might regret, but he doubted that he would regret it very much. And, anyway, what the hell? There was a touch of fall wind in the air which reminded him that he had been chaste since June.

"Oh, Harry, please come up with me," she whispered as they reached the outside stairway. She clung to him in sudden desperation. "Please, *please!* I'll be so lonely if you don't, I can't stand it."

"I'm coming, don't worry," he said and chuckled. "Go on up, scat!" And he turned her around and gave her a slap on the buttocks to send her stumbling up the stairs.

It was not so much that night that was the mistake

as the following night. Doris and Lois spent all Sunday on the beach, in a hazy mood between the pleasures of remembered satisfaction and the misery of their hangovers, while Mr. Barnes slept and Harry took another of his hikes. When he returned, late again, the others were drinking cocktails, and again he drank too many, and again he slept with Doris. But this time she was soberer and more demanding, and when he rose at five, for he had to drive to a real estate closing in Jamaica, leaving the girls to come in by train, and contemplated the gently snoring figure with the messy greying hair on the bed, he knew that he was never going to share a room with Doris Marsh again.

He did not get to the office until noon, but he had not been at his desk ten minutes reading his mail when he looked up to see her in the doorway, gazing at him with limpid eyes.

"Good morning, Harry," she said softly and then continued her way down the corridor. That she did not even wait for him to return her greeting was all the proof he needed that she regarded him now as her own. Harry sighed and prepared himself for the job that had to be done.

Nor did he have much time. In ten minutes Doris was back in his doorway to ask: "How about lunch?"

"Sorry, Doris, I've got to write up a closing memo. I may just have a sandwich sent in."

"Why don't you order two, then? I'll come in and eat it with you."

"I said I was working."

"My, my, aren't we busy all of a sudden? Are you trying to avoid me?"

Her tone was light and teasing; it was obvious that she did take his truculence seriously. Harry rose. "Step in, Doris, will you, please?" he asked abruptly and closed the door behind her. "Now let's get one thing straight," he continued, looking directly into her startled eyes, "and then everything will be easier. What happened this weekend was great fun, but it was *just* a weekend and *just* fun. Is that clear?"

"You mean you're not coming next weekend? Lois told me to ask you."

He noted how quickly she tried to shift the discussion from the general to the particular. "I'm sorry. I don't believe in repeating these things."

"It's a question of kiss and run?" She laughed with sudden harshness.

"I'm not running, Doris."

She gasped. "Do you think, Harry Reilley, that I'm the kind of girl who behaves that way every weekend?"

"Not every weekend, no."

"Oh!"

"Well, you don't expect me to believe I was the *first*, do you?"

The tears jumped into her eyes as she exclaimed: "What a brute you are! I should have known better than to have had anything to do with you!"

Harry was uncomfortable when she had gone, but he knew that it was better and kinder to put things in their proper setting at the earliest possible moment. Whatever Doris should say about him in the future, she would not be able to bracket him with Phil.

It had required a certain flexing of the muscles to stand up to Doris, but no similar exertion was required with Lois Grimshawe when she came to his office that afternoon.

"May I see you a minute, Mr. Reilley?" she asked from the doorway in her high, sweet, synthetic tone.

"Why, certainly, Mrs. Grimshawe."

She sat in the chair before his desk and darted her head forward so that her chin was over the edge of his blotter. "What's wrong, Harry? Doris says you won't come down next weekend. I thought we all had such a good time. Didn't you enjoy it?"

"I enjoyed it very much."

"Doris Marsh is one of the kindest, sweetest creatures that ever drew breath!"

"Exactly a reason for giving her fair warning. Before she begins to get proprietary ideas."

"You might have thought of that *before*."

"I don't see why. A good time was had by all. Can't we leave it at that?"

"But I'm not just thinking of Doris. I'm thinking of

you, Harry. Isn't it time you settled down? And where in the world would you find a better wife than Doris?"

"Wife!" Harry laughed, but his laugh was not pleasant. "I hardly think your role last weekend, Lois, was one that justifies your playing the outraged father with the shotgun!"

Lois' comprehension was slow, as manifested by the gradual deepening of her color behind a disconcerted stare. "I think that's a very nasty way for you to talk."

"I think you've brought up a very dangerous topic."

"Then you have no morals?"

"I have those of Devon."

At this Lois Grimshawe took her dignified departure, and Harry's popularity with the staff was over once and for all. What vicious tales she spread about him he was never to know, but Miss Gibbon only grunted now when he went to the file room and Mrs. Lane in the library gave him cursory nods in exchange for his cheerful greetings. And, needless to add, the stenographers sent to him from Lois' "pool" were the greenest she could find. Doris never spoke to him now and seemed to want others to observe her coolness. When they passed in the corridor, she averted her face in an unmistakable cut.

Harry's effort to convince himself that he did not care was not altogether successful. He had formed so few friendships in the firm that the loss of his easy bantering relationship with the girls on the staff made the office a cold place. Had he loved his work, it might have made the difference, or had he had any reasonable hope of a transfer to a more interesting department. He decided that if he was going to stay, he would have to re-examine his position, and to do this he determined upon an interview with the senior partner.

As he turned the corner of the corridor on his way to Clitus Tilney's office, he almost collided with the large, broad-shouldered, tweeded figure coming out.

"Hello, Harry." Tilney made a point of addressing each associate by his first name. He was about to walk on when he stopped suddenly. "Oh, Harry."

"Yes, sir?"

"Mrs. Tilney and I have never had the pleasure of

seeing you in our home. I wonder if you'd care to take family supper with us next Sunday. Quite informally. At seven o'clock?"

"Why, I should like to very much. Thank you, sir."

"Good. We'll expect you, then."

Harry had heard of the Tilney suppers and had always assumed that only "disciples" were asked. Now, as he gazed in surprise after that retreating figure he grunted in self-derision at his own fatuousness for remembering what Doris had said about his future in the firm.

He would never have believed that home life in New York could be as attractive as he found it that night at the Tilneys'. The house had a dark cool leathery, masculine comfortableness. One felt that Mrs. Tilney had done it all, but had done it with her husband in mind. It was an ordinary brownstone in size, but the ceilings were higher than average, and the walls were covered with landscape paintings of the Hudson River school and photographs of bar groups and judges. The chairs were low and deep and hard to get out of, and the big low mosaic tables invulnerable to spilt drinks. Clitus Tilney himself turned out to be an excellent host. He moved cheerfully about the room with a big silver cocktail shaker from which he poured very cold dry martinis into chilled silver mugs. He was evidently not a man who confined his perfectionism to the law. Mrs. Tilney was attractive, in a large, serene way, but she let her husband take the lead, which Harry liked.

There were a dozen people in the room, mostly associates and their wives. Harry looked suspiciously about to see with whom Tilney had classed him, half expecting to find Doris Marsh and Lee Ozite. Would it be a pickup for all the oddities in the office hitherto neglected by the great man? But he had immediately to admit that his suspicion was unfair. All the other men were "disciples," and as he was putting this together, Bart French, who had married the oldest Tilney girl, came up to him.

"Good to see you, Harry. You'll find my father-in-law makes a *very* dry martini."

"Is that a warning or a compliment?"

"Both, I guess."

Harry was not sure that he liked being made to feel at home by French, and he looked stiffly at that long oval brown face with the tired eyes that Doris Marsh had once described as charming. French was what Harry called a "boy scout." He was always pretending that, like the other clerks, he had to live on his salary.

"Quite a place your old man's got here."

"Isn't it?" French responded eagerly. "What I think of as a real lawyer's house. I hope some day I'll be able to afford one like it."

"Can't you now?"

"On what they pay us clerks at 65 Wall? Fat chance!"

"But I thought you had a large private income."

"I don't know what you call large," French muttered, and moved away, obviously put out by such bad form.

Harry was delighted to have ruffled him so easily. Besides, there was someone far better to contemplate, as he finished his drink, than Bart French, and that was the youngest Tilney daughter, who had just entered the room. He learned that her name was Fran from the nice old grey woman passing cheese and that she taught English at Miss Irvin's School. She was thin and pale, with soft long auburn hair and small brown eyes that had an odd shine, almost a glitter. Her face was the least bit long and her features were delicate, her nose turned up and her skin, Harry observed as he moved closer, almost translucent. Despite the slightness of her frame and the quick nervous gesticulations of her arms, she conveyed, in the rapid, soft tone that he could just hear across the room, the sense of a brittle, bright intelligence. Taking his refilled drink to a corner by a globe of the world that he could pretend to be turning, he resumed his contemplation of Miss Tilney. Suddenly she turned, as if aware of his gaze, and walked over to him.

"You must be Harry Reilley. I'm Fran Tilney. We're going in to supper now, and you're next to me. Can you bear it?"

Harry would not have thought, as he followed her down the narrow stairway to the dining room, that anything could have spoiled that evening, and yet her very first question at the table did so.

"What do you do in the office? Are you in 'green goods,' too?"

This was a term used downtown, always with a perfunctory snicker, to describe the department which dealt with corporate securities. Every other lawyer at the party was in "green goods."

"No, I'm an untouchable," he said gruffly. "I'm in real estate."

"But that must be interesting, too. Or at least basic."

"As interesting as anything else, I guess."

"That doesn't sound as if you had a very high opinion of the law."

He shrugged. "It's a living. If it was too much fun, people wouldn't pay you to do it."

Miss Tilney looked at him more closely. She was a very serious girl. "But Daddy *loves* his work."

"I daresay. But he's on top of the heap."

"It's not a question of his being on top, Mr. Reilley. It's a question of his caring about his profession."

"I beg your pardon, Miss Tilney. It's a question of his having hired help to take care of the boring details."

"I never heard anything so cynical," she exclaimed, obviously shocked. "In a learned profession none of the details should be boring."

"But they are. Writing up all that small print so the client can get out of a bad bargain." Harry paused, marveling that the urge to be unpleasant at the expense of his superiors could be stronger than the urge to make friends with a beautiful girl. "Your father's a very clever man, you know. He knows he has to idealize the law for the benefit of all those young men who followed him around like faithful hounds. If he didn't make them feel like Jesuit missionaries, they wouldn't be happy, and if they weren't happy, they wouldn't work so well."

It was clear that no such heresy had been talked in the Tilney house before. "You mean Daddy says things he doesn't *mean?*"

"Let's put it that he counts on different interpretations at different levels."

"Of which mine must be the lowest!"

He saw that he was making her really angry and bitterly regretted his course. But it seemed like a one-way street; he had to go to the end to turn around. "You're not a lawyer," he tried to explain. "But your dad certainly knows that the greater part of securities work is jamming as many ads into a prospectus as one can slip under the nose of the Securities Exchange Commission."

"I think you'll find the facts to be otherwise if you take the trouble to look into them," she said in a chilling tone. "My father cares passionately that only the exact truth be stated in his prospectuses."

"What is truth? Pilate asked."

"I really can't understand, if you feel that way, why you work for Tower, Tilney at all."

"I told you, it's a living."

"Surely there must be an easier one."

"Let me know if you hear of it."

She turned away abruptly to the man on her other side, and Harry was graced with her back for the rest of the meal. After dinner, too, she avoided him, and it was only when he was leaving and had the excuse to bid her goodnight that there was an opportunity for further interchange.

"I guess you only talk to green goods. The poor 'basic' real estate man has hardly had a word with you all evening."

"It's not that at all, Mr. Reilley. I haven't talked to you because it seemed to me you had such a poor opinion of us all."

"Of you all? Not of you, surely."

"Oh, I don't pretend to set myself apart."

Something tore now in his heart at the stupidity of it. Particularly when he sensed, in the very tensity of her anger, that she, too, was aware of something in the atmosphere between them. "Look, Miss Tilney. No, let me call you Fran. I've been an awful ass tonight, saying a lot of things I didn't mean at all. Playing the cheap cynic. The only thing I really wanted to tell you was what a beautiful, bright girl I think you are. Give me another chance, will you? Let me take you out to dinner some night. Any night you say. I'd like to show you I'm not a complete hick." They were standing alone, by the door to the living room, and she was staring at him with intent, startled eyes. "How about it? Tuesday night?" she still said nothing. "Are you too mad at me? Or are you engaged to be married, or something like that?"

"No, nothing like that," she said at last and laughed flatly. "I'll be glad to go out with you on Tuesday, Mr. Reilley. Harry, I mean."

He had to walk home that night to work off his excitement. What he marveled at most, as he looked back over the evening, was the miracle of his own apology at the last moment. If she had gone to bed early, if she had slipped out of the house for a later engagement, or if she had even been standing with her father when he came up to bid her goodnight, all would have been lost. She would have gone out of his life forever. It would have been simply another closed chapter in the long wasteful history of his truculence. Never before could he remember having experienced so sudden an attraction. He had not even dared to shake her hand in leaving. And she had been glad he hadn't, too. Oh, yes. She had felt some of the same pull. It was a pity that she should be quite so identified with her father's firm, but that was something he could not help. The whole evening, for that matter, was showing signs of developing into something that he could not help. And where, after all, had helping things got him?

She was waiting in the front hall when he called on Tuesday night. Not for her was the pose at the piano, the startled look at the clock, the "Good heavens, is it seven already?" She tucked her arm under his as they went down the steep stoop and suggested an Italian restaurant on Third Avenue.

"I see you have my pocketbook in mind," he said as they got into a taxi.

"Well, I hate to see a lot of money spent on ravioli. And ravioli is what I've been looking forward to all day."

Harry reflected that to some men her abruptness in taking the lead might have been slightly offensive. But he felt no need to assert himself in the matter of the choice of restaurants. As he watched her, he saw her shoulders twitch, in a sudden involuntary spasm. Was she afraid of what she was doing, afraid of going out with him? Because he wasn't the right type of young man? He wondered if she had told her father.

At the restaurant he ordered a cocktail and she a glass of Dubonnet. She ordered it with the promptness of a habitual nondrinker who knows that a man likes her to have something in her hand. He guessed that she would not finish it, which turned out to be correct. He guessed later that she would drink one glass of red wine with her ravioli, and this, too, turned out to be right.

"I behaved very badly at your family's the other night," he apologized again. "When I'm faced with people whom I basically admire, or even envy, like your father, I have a tendency to revert to the nasty little boy I once was. I try to tear them down. My father went to jail when I was fourteen, and I suppose a psychiatrist would say that I can't admit that anyone else's could be any better."

He watched her carefully as he said this to see if she would set her face in the mask of the young lady determined to show that she can't be shocked. But she was quite natural. "Your father went to jail! How perfectly horrible for you."

"It wasn't fun."

"What had he done? Or what did they say he'd done? Or would you rather not talk about it?"

"No, I was the one who brought it up. Of course I'll talk about it. My dad was guilty of the dullest of crimes. He was caught with his hand in the company till. And it wasn't to get money for his wife and kiddies, either. It was for more exotic pleasures."

"Poor man, I hope he enjoyed them."

"Don't feel too sorry for him. He felt sorry enough for himself. In fact, he died of self-pity. Not to mention the unkind cracks of his youngest born."

"Was that you? You mustn't mind. We always exaggerate our meanness to the dead."

"Not I," Harry retorted with a bitter laugh. "I won't horrify you by giving particulars."

She was too wise to insist. "When I hear about other people's hard lives, I realize how easy my own has been," she said ruefully. "I've been very spoiled. Or blessed, as they call it."

"My life hasn't really been hard. But I was banking on your thinking it was. I figured, if I shot off my mouth about my old man, you'd forgive me for being such a crumb the other night."

"You don't mean you made it all up?"

"Oh, no, it's true enough," he reassured her, smiling at her instant spurt of indignation. "God knows, it's true enough. My father was always sentimental about ideals. That's what made me distrust them."

"Daddy's not unlike you, you know. He has his black moods, too. The days when he describes Tower, Tilney & Webb as 'Shyster, Beagle and Shyster.' "

"As *what?*"

"It was the name of the law firm in an old Marx Brothers comedy. Mother can always tell Daddy's mood by the sound of his step in the hall. If she looks up from her needlepoint when he comes in and asks: 'How's Shyster, Beagle and Shyster?' then I know it's one of *those* days."

"You make your old man sound almost human."

"Oh, Daddy's the most human person in the world! You'd love him, Harry, if you got to know him."

Harry smiled at the incongruity of such a verb to describe any potential relationship between himself and the senior partner. "Of course, he asked me to dinner," he allowed. "I owe him a lot for that, no matter how snooty his green goods boys are."

"Are you snooty?"

"Well, I think they are," Harry said with a shrug. "But maybe it's just because I'm not one of them. Does your father know you're out with me tonight?"

She looked away. "I didn't tell him."

"Why not?"

"Because I don't tell Daddy everything I'm doing," she retorted with an edge of irritation. "Why should I?"

"Not because he'd hate to have his daughter going out with a mick?"

"Oh, *Harry!*"

"I'm serious. Do you know that I have a brother who's a priest? And two first cousins who are nuns? How would that sit in his Presbyterian soul?"

"My father is above religious prejudice," Fran said with dignity. "Besides, he'd never have asked you to the house if he'd objected to our being friends."

"Oh, so that's it. You wouldn't have gone out with me if I hadn't been asked to the house?"

"Really, you're too ridiculous. I wouldn't have known you if you hadn't been asked to the house. But if you can't get that log off your shoulder, I'm going to take myself straight home."

"No, no, Fran, please don't do that. I promise to be good." He took her hand calmly and folded it in both of his, but, although obviously surprised, she made no motion to pull it away. "Don't worry about the church. I haven't been to mass in a year. Only you probably mind that even more. All right, I'll go. Next Sunday. Or with you to your church."

"I don't know where you got the notion that either I or Daddy are such bugs on religion. Honestly, I don't care if you're a Moslem."

"Be careful now or I'll be shocked. That's the way with bad Catholics. We want all you Protestants to be good as gold."

It was now apparent that they were going to be the best of friends. There had been talk in the taxi of a movie, but they went instead to a bar where they sat in a booth and she drank ginger ale while he drank beer. He talked an outrageous amount about himself, even working in the Korean war and the wound in his leg. She listened perfectly, but she talked, too. For the Korea war he had to hear about the girls in her Shakespeare class at Miss Irvin's. It was all very fair. In the taxi afterwards, as they drew up at her door, he kissed her. It was a very light and gentle kiss, and like the Dubonnet there was only one of them, but he did not press her for a second. He had made enough botches for one lifetime. Something had intervened in his destiny, and he was learning to be wise enough to give it a free hand.

2

LEE OZITE, "Ozey," as he was known to all, received a tense, minute-to-minute satisfaction, during the working hours of the day, in his merited reputation for efficiency. "Have you asked Ozey about that," or "Has anyone put Ozey on the job?" was the first question a partner would ask when brought to a halt by any kind of procedural snag. As managing clerk it was his duty to see that the court calendars were answered, the papers served on time and the litigators notified of their dates for oral argument, but his jurisdiction, spurred by his own eagerness, had spread to cover traffic tickets, tips to court clerks, detectives in morals cases, any field, in fact, where the right word to the right person could solve the difficulties of the individual in conflict with the minor officers of organized society. To assist him he had three night law students who worked a six-hour day running his errands over the city and calling in every hour when he would give them a further task or else cry: "Head in!" in the bark of an operations officer sitting over a map. It made for a busy and satisfying day, but sometimes during the long evenings in Queens, where he lived in an apartment with his old mother and aunt, he would suffer doubts about his position in the office. Were the jocular compliments of the partners sincerely meant? Or was he just poor old Ozey with his panting law students and his ringing telephones? Like a mouse on a treadwheel?

At such moments he would become absolutely still except for his almond eyes which moved furtively from side to side. His aunt would glance up from her detective story and comment that he was looking like a Buddha again. And Miss Ozite was right; there was something synthetically Oriental about her nephew, something of Charlie Chan, something grinning and hand rubbing and faintly sinister. Fortunately, at just the right moment, somebody always laughed, and Ozey laughed with them.

"But some day I won't," he would tell himself grimly. "Some day I'll have the last laugh."

His fear of being laughed at had a natural counterpart in his fear of being unattractive to women. He realized, intellectually, that this fear was a foolish one. Ozey was bald on the top of his head and inclined to be fleshy, but his round head and face and firm, well-formed features went well with baldness, and his extra weight was evenly distributed over a short but muscular body. He liked to think of himself as the bald sexually potent Siamese monarch in *The King and I*. But he could never get over the apprehension that women, particularly "ladies," would find him somehow unpalatable, perhaps, dreadful thought, even "greasy," and his sexual experiences—up to his present and thirty-sixth year —had all been purchased.

But Ozey had one great hope, and that was marriage. He knew that women were more interested in marriage than in anything else and that they gave even unlikely proposals their most serious consideration. Ozey felt that allied to a handsome, good-tempered woman of size—he always pictured her as larger than himself—he would be surer of the respect of the world that he had to face. He had another vision of Lee Ozite, again as the Siamese potentate but this time drawn in fiercer lines, a touch of Tamburlaine added, leading a large white naked Christian slave girl by a slender cord about her neck. Of course he would be nice to her, very nice to her. And the more he entertained this vision, the more he saw Doris Marsh in the role of the docile captive.

In real life, however, and as a tax associate, she ranked the managing clerk, and he would never forget her cool, justified reproach when one of his boys had filed a tax return at the wrong bureau. Yet on all other occasions she had been perfectly friendly, perfectly democratic. Unlike some of the associates she gave herself no airs and would linger in his office after checking the calendar for a few minutes of chat and jokes. When she leaned over his desk to read the law journel that was always spread out there, the proximity of her breasts and the sound of her breathing excited him uncomfortably. She was just the height of his Christian slave and had the same white soft skin. He would have preferred blond hair to black and grey, but, after all, the real world could never match fantasy. Was she aware of her effect upon him? Was she tantalizing him? When he had asked her once to lunch, she had agreed readily enough, and they had had a pleasant hour of shop talk, but when he had tried to push away the money that she handed him for the check, she had simply laughed and said: "Come now, Ozey. This isn't a date."

Did she mean she wouldn't have had one with him? Ozey brooded furiously all that afternoon. But when he left the office, she happened to be going down in the same elevator and told him: "I enjoyed our lunch, Ozey. Do you realize not one of the other lawyers has ever asked me? You might think I was some kind of pariah." Ozey was too thrilled to sit, in the subway, and all the way home he hung on a strap in a half-empty car, calculating the wisdom of a sudden proposal. She would be startled, to be sure. It might be fun to see just how startled she would be. There would be something titillating about marching into her office and suggesting the most intimate of relationships without a single preliminary. Right there and then, before the set of Prentice-Hall tax services and before she had had time to take off her glasses. Could she *afford* to turn him down? Shrewdly, rather meanly, he assessed her. She was near thirty; she would never be a partner; she was an orphan of obscure origin. Yet as Mrs. Ozite all these liabilities would immediately become assets. She would not be too much younger than her husband or too much more successful a lawyer, and she would bring no tiresome in-laws. Besides, since she was a professional woman, his mother and aunt were bound to dislike her, which would make the inevitable break with his own family a cleaner, neater thing.

If Ozey, however, was precipitate in his thinking, he was cautious in his actions, and it was a good two months from the day of their lunch to the day of his decision to ask her for a date. But as he stood in the doorway of her office with a sheepish smile, the question fluttering about his lips, she anticipated him.

"Ozey! I was just coming to see *you*."

"Well, that's nice."

"Can you lunch with me? Or rather *on* me. I want to take you out and buy you a cocktail and pick your brains. It's a personal matter."

He grinned broadly. "You mean a date?"

"Would it were anything so pleasant." She frowned and shook her head. "The fact of the matter, Ozey, is that I'm in a bit of trouble, and I need your advice."

"What are we waiting for? Let's go!"

In the restaurant Doris drank a martini rapidly and then, to his surprise, ordered another. She seemed very agitated, as if she were finding it cruelly difficult to bring out whatever was on her mind. He watched her closely.

"You'd just better spit it out, Doris. Try to pretend I'm not here."

She turned to him with a sudden defiance as if he had merged with his whole sex into a single enemy. "Very well, I'm pregnant," she declared. "I'm having a baby, and I've got to get rid of it. It's very early, so it shouldn't be too hard." She seemed to sense now from his gaping face that he, at least, was without responsibility for her plight. "I've come to you, Ozey," she continued in a humbler tone, the tears starting to her eyes, "because I don't know where else to turn. They all say you can do anything. I thought you might be able to get me a decent doctor."

Pregnant! Ozey was transfixed. For a few moments he could not swallow, so thick was his throat, so wild and overwhelming his mental pictures. So *that* was what this tall, cool tax girl had been up to while he was blushing for the fantasies of what he had wanted to do with her! At first this new idea of her moral abandonment made her even more desirable, and he felt himself swooped up by the dizzy thought that he could have been the father of her child. But then the truth and jealousy, like a team of plow horses, came crashing into the fragile barn of his illusions.

"Who is the man? Do I know him?"

Ozey's aggressive tone took her by surprise. "What does that matter?"

"A lot. If he's in the office, I don't want the risk of speaking to him. Much less of shaking his filthy paw!"

"But, Ozey, he doesn't even know!"

"Then he *is* in the office?"

Doris seemed helpless before this new complication. "All right, he is. But what good will a quarrel between you and him do me? Please, Ozey, can't you help me?"

"Of course I can help you. I can get you the best doctor in the business this afternoon. It won't be cheap, but what's that when your life might be at stake? And if you can't raise the money, I'll lend it to you."

"Oh, Ozey." Her tears fell freely now. "What a friend you are. What a kind, true friend. What a man. What a real man."

"You needn't worry," he said with a swelling heart. "I shan't make a scene with your friend. I shall go to him quietly and firmly and see that he pays your doctor, if nothing else."

Doris looked at him with murky eyes. "I'm in your hands, Ozey. I must do as you say. I must trust to your discretion. It was Harry Reilley."

"Harry Reilley!"

Reilley was the associate whom Ozey most admired in the office. He was not only large and blond and easily sure of himself, qualities notably lacking in Ozey, but he was somehow above, or at least aside from, the petty rivalries of the hierarchy. There was absolutely no difference in the way Reilley spoke to Ozey and in the way he spoke to Clitus Tilney. Ozey had been pleased, rather than soured, but the current office rumor that Reilley was taking out the senior partner's daughter. But now!

"I thought he was after the Tilney girl," he said in a flat voice.

"No doubt he is," Doris said bitterly. "Dear Harry makes a brave show of being one of the people when all he really wants is to marry the boss's daughter. I was just a rung in his ladder. And a fool not to have known it."

Ozey wondered from what level to what Doris' "rung" had conducted her ruthless lover, but she was obviously in no mood for analytic inquiry. Besides, the maddening idea that Harry's open, candid front had all along been only the mask of a mercenary ambition made him want to believe her. What did Reilley really think of Ozey? As a poor sap, grateful for a smile and a clap on the shoulder, who would still be managing clerk (if he was lucky) when the firm was known as Tower, Tilney & Reilley?

"I guess we've both been rungs in Mr. Reilley's ladder," he said bitterly. "But Mr. Reilley hasn't reached the top of that ladder yet. And rungs can break, you know. And send him toppling down."

"He's a cheap, lying Irishman! And if that's what Miss Tilney wants, with all *her* advantages, all I can say is that I congratulate her on a splendid match!"

For the rest of their lunch they tore Harry to pieces, but over the coffee they turned to the matter in hand. It was agreed that Doris, who had still a week of vacation due her, would take it starting the following Monday and that Ozey would get hold of his doctor that afternoon.

Everything proceeded as smoothly as matters ordinarily did in Ozey's department. It took him only two discreet teelphone calls to secure the doctor, and on Monday the abortion was successfully performed. Ozey had visited the doctor on Sunday and paid him a thousand dollars in cash. It had contributed not a little to his excitement that he had obviously been regarded as the father. When he called on Doris at her apartment on his way home from work, three days after the operation, he found her in a dressing gown, a bit pale and teary, but very grateful and glad to see him. She threw her arms around him and gave him a hug.

"Oh, Ozey, you old darling, how good of you to come. Do you know I haven't even told Madge?" Madge was the girl with whom she shared the apartment. "She thinks I've just got some woman's trouble.

Which God knows I have! But what a friend *you've* been, Ozey. Sometimes I think my only friend!"

She insisted on moving about the room to mix him a drink, to get him an ash tray, although he begged her to sit still, and when they were settled at last, she kept staring at him with eyes of poignant humility. Ozey was pleased with the change from the easy, assured professional woman, and it somehow seemed, because he had produced the money and the doctor, because he was sitting there in the full armor of a business suit while she was vulnerably attired in an old blue dressing gown and a pair of soiled pink slippers, that it was he and not Reilley who had brought her to this sorry pass. He shuddered with excitement at the idea that one good tug at that dressing gown could transform her into his Christian slave.

"I *want* to be your friend, Doris," he muttered. "You can't imagine how much I've always wanted to be your friend."

The next morning, at half past nine, Ozey went to Harry Reilley's office and demanded in a barking tone the price of the abortion. Harry's face hardened as he listened.

"Assuming that all you say is true and that I was responsible, why should I deal with you?"

"Because I'm acting for Doris. And because I paid the money."

"Why don't you get it from her, then?"

"Do you mean to tell me, Reilley, that you'd put all the expense on her?" Ozey's voice became high and shrill. "Is that the kind of guy you are?"

"Now wait a minute, wait a minute," Harry said angrily, "before we start the name-calling. Since you seem to know so much about it, you may as well get it all straight. Doris and I spent a weekend together. She was just as keen on the idea as I was. But a girl her age who's been smart enough to be admitted to the bar ought to be smart enough to take precautions. I don't see why I should be stuck with the whole cost of that weekend—always assuming, of course, that it *was* that weekend . . ."

"You cad!" Ozey cried, jumping to his feet.

Harry was on his feet at the same moment, and with a heavy hand on Ozey's shoulder, he pushed him roughly back into his chair. "Now let's take it easy, shall we? Let's not get ourselves hurt. I don't know why you're involved in this, and I'm not going to ask. But in return for my tact, I insist that you appreciate my position. I do *not* know that I'm the guy who knocked Doris up. But I admit I might be. And considering all the factors in the situation—and a few that you don't know about—I think I'm doing a hell of a lot more than most men would do in offering you five hundred bucks."

Ozey debated the beautiful gesture of spurning this, but when he left Harry's office he had the check in his billfold, post-dated to give Harry time to raise the money. As he passed Mr. Tilney's office on his way back to his own, he felt that the dragging weight of his hatred for Reilley was what brought him to a halt. He took a quick step past Miss Clinger's desk and pushed his head boldly in the open doorway.

"May I see you a minute, Mr. Tilney?"

Tilney looked up in surprise. His dealings with the managing clerk were infrequent and usually handled through Miss Clinger. "What can I do for you, Mr. Ozite?"

Even with his present preoccuption, Ozey had a sour moment to reflect that Tilney made a point of calling the other associates by their first names. "It's a personal matter, sir. May I close the door?"

Tilney stared. "Oh, I hardly think that will be necessary."

"I mean personal to you, sir," Ozey explained. "It's about your daughter."

Tilney's eyes flashed forbiddingly, but he rose, walked quickly to close his door and then turned to face Ozey with his full height and presence. "Now, Mr. Ozite," he said softly, "will you be good enough to tell me what's on your mind?"

"It's about Mr. Reilley, sir. Harry Reilley."

"You said it was about my daughter."

"I mean that it concerns your daughter, sir. I doubt

if you will wish her to have any more dates with Mr. Reilley when you hear what I have to say."

"Hearing about my daughter is one thing," Tilney said irately. "Hearing tales by one associate about another is a different matter. You may go, Mr. Ozite."

Ozey, dazed with anger and humiliation, almost ran to the door. To his surprise, Tilney continued to bar the way.

"Pray excuse me, sir."

But Tilney remained there, motionless. Then he suddenly rubbed a hand over his broad brow. "I'm sorry, Mr. Ozite," he said, blinking. He walked slowly back to his desk. "I spoke too rapidly. Please be good enough to forgive me and tell me what you know about Mr. Reilley."

He resumed his seat and bent his shaggy grey head over his desk as Ozey, standing in the middle of the room, told him in a high, clear, excited tone of the iniquities of Harry Reilley.

"I see," Tilney said gravely when he had finished. "Thank you very much. Of course, we don't know what degree of enticement Miss Marsh may have exercised."

"Miss Marsh is a lady, sir!" Ozey exclaimed. "As much of a lady as any member of your own family."

Tilney looked up and regarded Ozey with a quizzical expression. "Did she behave as ladies behave?"

"When they're seduced, sir, yes!"

Tilney looked back down at his desk, and Ozey had the uneasy suspicion that he might be hiding a smile. "If you have Miss Marsh's interests so much at heart, Mr. Ozite, it occurs to me that you might have considered the damage to her position in the firm of such a revelation to me."

"I *have* considered it, sir!" Ozey exclaimed in triumph. "Miss Marsh will no longer have a position in the firm. She is planning to resign at the end of the year."

Tilney glanced up again quickly. "Oh, see here, I don't say anything like that is going to be necessary."

"It's not for the reason you think, sir."

"Oh? Has she been offered a better job?"

"Yes. As Mrs. Lee Ozite!"

As Tilney, after a rather blank stare, smiled and rose to congratulate him, Ozey felt with pride that the senior partner was for once overwhelmed. He, Ozey, had taken the lead in their short interview and had held it to the end. It was only much later that it occurred to him that Mr. Tilney's predominant reaction might have been simple embarrassment.

3

CLITUS TILNEY was sick at heart. He was sure that he would never again be able to think of Harry Reilley except in reference to the shabby tale told him by his smirking managing clerk. Harry's assets and liabilities had barely balanced before this splashing entry had dyed his statement in irredeemable red. Tilney had liked the young man well enough and had admired his forthright manner and seeming straightness, but when Fran had taken him up, in her own determined way, he had reflected ruefully on the Irish Catholic background and the criminal parent which, for all his sincere efforts to overcome his upstate, smalltown prejudices, seemed still to have a natural connection. And now Miss Marsh! To have seduced a bespectacled, pathetic old-maid tax lawyer! For Tilney irritably brushed aside the memory for flitting moments, passing her in the corridor and greeted by her low, pleasant "Good morning, sir," when he had thought of her as something else. And, for Reilley to have come from the sweaty pleasures of Miss Marsh's couch to flirt with his own daughter at the dinner table! And then to chisel on the cost of the abortion and send poor Miss Marsh to the arms of such a one as Ozite. No, the man was obviously a lecher of the coarsest sort who was after Fran for whatever promotion he could get out of her father.

How far had things gone with Fran? Alas, Tilney was almost sure that she was in love with him. He knew that she had been out with him half a dozen times at least, and she was perfectly frank now about her interest in him. Only that morning at breakfast she had begged him to try Harry in "green goods," and her face had been radiant when he had said he would consider it. Of course Reilley had put her up to it. And then Ada, too, had been all for Reilley, and had lectured him roundly when he had muttered his doubts about the Reilley background. Ada, whose instinct about people he had always considered so flawless! He groaned aloud as he thought of his Fran, his youngest and favorite child, as pure and fine and good as God had ever made a woman, with a power of sympathy and love to raise a man to greatness, wasted on such a cynical wretch. And a Catholic to boot. Even if she woke up to what he was, he would probably refuse her a divorce!

After a miserable hour of these considerations he summoned Harry to his office and, turning his chair away to the window, he dryly reported the facts that he had learned from Ozite, ending with the terse question: "I suppose it's all so?"

"Yes, sir. It's so."

Tilney whirled around in his chair to face the stiff, truculent young man whose hands, he at once noticed, were clenched. "If you have anything to add to that statement," he snapped, "I'd be glad to hear it."

"I have nothing to add."

"In these matters I like to think I'm not a complete Victorian," Tilney grumbled, but in a more reasonable tone. "I realize a young man can be inveigled into situations."

"I'm not that young a man, sir."

Tilney surveyed him critically. He liked the fact that Harry sought no excuses. "What pains me most about the whole wretched business is how recent it was."

"I'll say only this, sir. It was all over *before* I met your daughter."

"Yet it can't have been more than a matter of days." Harry was silent. "Well, Fran's not a child," Tilney continued with a sigh. "She can make up her own mind about it. You realize, of course, I'll have to tell her?"

Some of the obstinacy faded from Harry's eyes. "Would you have to tell her if I didn't see her any more?"

"No, I don't suppose I would," Tilney said slowly,

surprised. "Of course, I don't know how things are between you. Or how much of a shock it would be to
her."

"That's not for me to say, sir. But I'm sure it's not
anything she won't get over. There's been no engagement between us." Harry flushed as he added: "Or anything else you need worry about."

"Thank you, Harry," Tilney responded in a kinder
tone than he had ever expected to use again to the
young man. "Well, suppose we try it that way? And see
what happens?"

"As you wish, sir."

Tilney felt worse when Reilley had left than before
he had come. He tried to interpret Reilley's willingness
to give up Fran first as indifference and then as simple
sullenness, but he was not successful. He had an uncomfortable suspicion that the young man's feelings for
his daughter were of a very different variety than those
(if any) that he had entertained for Miss Marsh. And
the very fact that the latter had so rapidly consoled
herself with such a man as Ozite was evidence that
she had not been too deeply involved with Reilley. But
where Tilney remained adamant was in his conviction
that he would still be acting in his daughter's best interests to get Reilley out of her life.

He did not dare tell Ada, for he was afraid that she
would disagree, and he wondered how he was to bear
alone Fran's silent unhappiness—for he knew it would
be silent—in the terrible breakfasts that were bound to
follow. The next morning and the one after were without incident, but on the third Fran asked him: "Daddy,
tell me. Did you ever move Harry to 'green goods'?"

"Not yet, dear. But I have it in mind."

"Do you happen to know if he's working particularly
hard at the moment?"

"Well, most of the boys *are* pretty busy. I don't happen to know about him. Why?"

"Oh, nothing. I just thought he might have called me
about something. It doesn't matter."

When she had left for school, Ada turned to him.

"You don't suppose Harry's lost interest, do you?"

"I haven't the faintest idea," Tilney retorted irritably.

"And I'm not at all sure I care if he has. Fran can do a lot better than Harry Reilley."

"But she *cares,* Clitus. I'm warning you. She cares!"

"I'll be seeing him tonight at the firm dinner. *If* he comes," he added, remembering Harry's truculent face. "I'll find out if he's been working nights."

"Why don't you bring him home for a drink afterwards?"

"Because I shall be tired and want to go to bed," he said snappishly, and raised his paper between them to run his eye down the obituary column.

The firm had a semi-annual men's dinner at the University Club where it was customary for certain of the partners to speak on the highlights of the season's practice. Tilney sat in the middle of the principal table, between Chambers Todd and Waldron Webb, and was grateful that he did not have to speak that night, for he could think only of Fran. The image of her pale face and of the glimmer of pain in her eyes had ejected every other from his mind. He noticed Harry Reilley at a far table and heard the sound of his loud laugh. It was too loud, that laugh, too defiant. Tilney wondered if he was drinking too much and regretted the custom of having bottles of whiskey on the table.

Chambers Todd was the last speaker and discussed a committee of the City Bar Association of which he was chairman and whose other members he was trying to persuade to recommend to the State Legislature the abolition of an excise tax that was particularly onerous to a trucking client. There was nothing in the subject to distract Tilney from his speculations on the effect of Harry's defection. Would it kill Fran, as sometimes happened in Victorian novels? Would she droop and pine away? Or would she master her sorrow and never show it, but remain for the rest of her days a bright, brittle, useful, dryly smiling old maid, a sacrifice to her father's prejudice? Tilney suddenly leaned forward and put both hands over his face, and Waldron Webb whispered in his ear: "Are you all right, Clitus?"

"Oh, yes, yes."

The speeches were over, and he rose to indicate that the meeting was adjourned. As he lingered to light a cigar and to let the firm file out of the door-way, he saw Harry Reilley walk over to Todd. What followed he could not help but overhear as both men had carrying voices.

"May I ask you a question, Mr. Todd?"

"Go right ahead, my dear fellow." Todd was mellow with the evening's whiskey and the sense of a success-ful address.

"In your speech tonight you spoke of using your position on a bar association committee in favor of a client. Isn't it the duty of committee members to render unbiased opinions on behalf of the association?"

Todd's heavy features congealed as he took in the unexpected attack. "You speak like a first-year law student," he said curtly. "If you ever have the good fortune to secure a big company as a client, you will learn that the word 'unbiased' has no further meaning for you. A good lawyer doesn't forget his clients when he closes his shop. A good lawyer eats, lives and breathes for his clients. A good lawyer represents his clients even in his sleep!"

Harry laughed unpleasantly. "I had been wondering what the difference was between your kind of lawyer and a lobbyist. Now I see there's none!"

Tilney stepped forward to touch the young man on the arm. "I want to talk to you, Harry." He turned abruptly and walked to a corner to get away from the now livid Todd. "I can't let you commit suicide like that," he continued. "Come back to my house and have a drink with me."

"Won't Fran be there?"

"I don't know. It doesn't matter."

Harry stared. "You mean the ban's off?"

"Must you tie me down? I mean *I* won't fight you any more."

The glitter in the young man's eyes went far to con-vince Tilney that he had done the right thing. "She'll be sore as hell I haven't called her."

"Tell her you were out of town. Invent a business trip. I'll back you up. That's easy. The guy who has the really tough job is the guy who's going to have to save your neck from Chambers Todd. And that guy is me!"

In the taxi Tilney tried to reduce some of the constraint between them by reverting to Harry's interchange with Todd. "Actually, I agree with what you said. I wish we could return to the old days of greater integrity. When a lawyer could argue one interpretation of a statute in the morning and its opposite in the afternoon. Before we were captured by the corporations. Before we became simple mouthpieces."

"It doesn't worry me as much as I made it appear," Harry replied with a candid laugh. "I'm used to politicians in my family. My old man knew so many. What I can't stand is sanctimoniousness. And your partner, Mr. Todd, is sanctimonious."

Tilney wondered if he shouldn't object to such familiarity. "You don't like Mr. Todd?"

"I don't like any of them, to tell the truth, Mr. Tilney. Except yourself. I've just about decided that your firm is not the place for me."

"Well, don't let's make the decision tonight," Tilney said hastily. "If you and I get along, it's always possible to work something out. The partner's aren't all Chambers Todds. Wait till you know them better."

"It's up to you, sir. If you say stay, I'll stay." He laughed again. "I guess it's pretty clear that I want to see Fran."

Tilney had figured out that Ada would wait up for him on the chance that he might have learned something about Harry, and he was correct. Yet with her usual control she did not manifest the least surprise at seeing his companion. When Fran came in from the library where she had been correcting homework, she was equally impassive.

"Good evening, Mr. Reilley."

Harry got up and took her by the hands. "I'm sorry, Fran. I was sent up to Boston on a rush closing. I haven't had a minute."

"Not even to telephone?"

"You know how those things are. Ask your father."

Fran looked around at her father and then shook her head dubiously. "You both look so foxy. What have you been up to? Sometimes I think I hate lawyers."

"Perhaps you should get them a drink, Fran," her mother suggested.

"I think it's the last thing either of them needs."

But when she turned to go to the dining room, Tilney knew that the damage had already been repaired. It was only the tiniest shadow on the sky of his relief that Harry should have lied so convincingly. There were things about that young man that he was obviously never going to understand. But, as Ada would have said, *he* was not going to marry him. There had to be a point where he stopped playing senior partner at home.

4

IN THE large square room decorated with light blue wallpaper and French travel posters showing the châteaux of the Loire Valley, Fran stood by a window, gazing down at the East River, while her class of tenth graders wrote their ten-minute theme on *Cymbeline*. In her mind she was writing a theme of her own, for she had to do something to keep within bounds the agitation of her happiness. Her theme was about the heroines of the romantic comedies, Imogen, Helena, Portia, Rosalind, those noble, radiant, resourceful women, so finely intelligent, so pure and yet so gay, so graceful in men's clothing and yet so innately feminine, who come to us somehow embellished even by the fulsome encomiums of Victorian admirers, somehow in the images of tall, golden-toned actresses on old postcards. She was too happy to be in the least ashamed of her own exuberant conceit in likening herself to them.

"Miss Tilney?"

"Yes, Gretchen." Gretchen Kay was always the first to ask a question after the theme. She was the serious girl of the class, nervous, dark and disliked by the others.

"Wasn't it very bad of Posthumus to make a wager on Imogen's virtue? And then to let her be tested?"

"Very bad."

"And to want to kill her afterwards?"

"No, I don't think that was as bad," Fran answered, turning from the window. "After all, he thought her faithless."

"Yes, but even if she had been, was that a reason for *killing* her?"

"Perhaps." Frank shrugged lightly. "In those days. People were more violent then."

"Would it have been all right for her to kill him if *he'd* been faithless?"

"Oh, no." Fran was very sure about this. "That would have been altogether different. None of the comedy heroines have men who are worthy of them. Except perhaps Rosalind. Bassanio was after Portia's money, and Bertram had to be trapped into loving Helena. And Posthumus—well, we've seen how *he* behaved. But I sometimes think the goodness of the heroines depends on their having to put up with such things. If the men were as good as the women, wouldn't the women seem a bit dull?"

"Do you think that's true in real life, Miss Tilney? Is it better for a girl to go with a boy who's mercenary or faithless or unkind?"

The other girls laughed mockingly, but Fran did not join them. "It may be, Gretchen," she said gravely. "It may indeed."

She was troubled for the rest of the morning, as well as surprised, by her own ready acceptance of what had seemed at first the idlest of speculations. She was afraid that she had been disloyal to Harry. While none of the girls in her class knew that she was engaged, they would find out in two weeks' time when it was announced. And then would they speculate that he was a Posthumus or a Bertram or a Bassanio? It made matters worse that Harry in the three months following the night of the office dinner had been the gentlest, the most considerate of lovers. Lovers, she noted mentally, as if one of the girls might read her thoughts, in the Shakespearean sense. Why then did she want to represent him as someone hard or callous? Was it part of his appeal that he had seemed so on the night of their first meeting? Was she so debased that she wanted a man who, as Gretchen might have put it, would "kick her around"? Of would she all her life be a schoolgirl who wanted to play Imogen, or rather who wanted to play Ellen Terry playing Imogen?

Her mood darkened as the day progressed, and by the time school was out, she was deeply depressed. She had dreaded to face the real origin of her trouble, but at home in her room, looking at her own startled eyes in the mirror, she made herself do so. Had not Harry, in a single quarter of a year, become rather too much what her father had set out to make him? He worked in "green goods" now, along with Jake Platt and Bart French and the other "disciples," and he seemed to be thoroughly content. Certainly, her father did not share her misgivings—if "misgivings" was not too strong a word. He was even demonstrative in his pleasure at how Harry had "taken hold" and hinted to Fran that he might still—despite the unhappy scene with Todd—have a future in the firm. Was it all too early? Did she respect less the more conservative Harry, in darker suits with darker ties, in white shirts only now, who tried to get on with Bart and laughed so roundly at her father's jokes? How contemptible of her!

That evening her father telephoned to say he was bringing Bart and Harry and Jake Platt home for supper and that they were going to work in the library afterwards. It was a primary rule in the household that he could always do this. Ada would be ready, at an hour's notice, to supply hot soup and beans and cold cuts, salad and beer to any number of young men from the office. It was the only way, at times, that she could get her husband home. She always invited the wives, too, if they could leave their children, and the ladies would play cards or knit and chat during the long evening.

They had a buffet supper that night, and Fran sat in a corner of the dining room with her brother-in-law, Bart, watching Harry, who was talking to her sister across the room. She could see that he was trying to make a good impression by the rather dainty way that he held his fork in scooping up the last of his beans. She despised herself for noticing this. After all, he didn't really hold his fork any more daintily than the others. It was simply that he held it more daintily than he had used to. Daintily! The very word was a dye strong enough to discolor the image of any man. She had to watch herself.

"Harry fits right into the groove now, doesn't he?"

There was no mistaking the antagonism in Bart's tone, and Fran turned to him in surprise. Bart was so rarely antagonistic. "What groove?"

"That of the smooth young associate of Tower, Tilney."

"The Bart French?" she asked crisply.

"If you will." He shrugged. "It doesn't seem so very long ago that he was telling off partners at firm dinners and wearing silver ties with green bubbles on them."

Fran found that she was trembling all over and knew that it was less because Bart had remembered that tie than because she remembered it herself. "You don't like him, do you?" she asked softly.

"No," he answered with a strained little smile that did not in the least disguise his awareness that they were having a very important discussion. "And I guess it's about the last chance I'll have to tell you so. I should have done it earlier, but you've moved so fast."

"That's all right, Bart. Tell me why you don't like Harry."

"I hate people who say somebody's not their type. Okay, I hate myself. Harry's not my type. Or yours either."

"I guess I'm the best judge of that."

He shook his head. "The worst. A girl in love is the very worst. But anyone in Tower, Tilney can tell you about Harry. He's the guy who was the great rebel until he found it was worth his while to make sheep's eyes at the senior partner's daughter."

Fran closed her eyes for a moment. "Thank you, Bart," she half whispered. "I know it wasn't easy for you to say that."

"It wasn't. And the ridiculous thing is I'm not even sure that I want to influence you." Bart's long face was strangely alive with his perplexity. "I just thought you ought to know."

"I think I ought. And I assure you that it will *not* influence me." She even managed to smile now at her brother-in-law. "But go and talk to someone else for a bit, Bart. One may appreciate candor, but it's impossible not to resent the candid. For a day or so, at least. Don't worry. It won't last forever."

Fran went to her room after supper, on the excuse of correcting school papers, and sat alone in the dark to hug her misery. What an absurdly fragile thing happiness was! When she thought of how she had felt only that morning! Yet as small a thing as the memory of an ugly tie—no, more than that, a *vulgar* tie— was enough to blow away all the shining cobwebs of her good humor and leave her alone in as drab a mental chamber as was ever occupied by Bart French. It might have been a judgment for the hubris of likening herself to Imogen and Helena. It was not easy to imagine *them* being distressed by a lover's way of holding a fork or by a silly tie. They were not petty snobs. Middle-class snobs. There was at least the expiation of knowing that she could make up for a part of her meanness by being a good wife to Harry. But happiness, where was happiness?

When she answered the knock at her door and saw Harry, she suddenly threw her arms around his neck. "Oh, darling, how wonderful! Are you through already?"

"The boss broke up school early tonight. Come on, I'm taking you out for a drink."

At the Third Avenue bar where they had gone on their first evening together he stared a moment into his beer and then looked up at her with an embarrassed smile. "I have something to tell you. Something about myself. Unless your father's already told you."

"Daddy knows? It can't be so bad, then."

She listened in fascinated silence as he told her, in brief, bleak sentences, without embellishment or apology, the story of his affair with Doris Marsh. At first she found herself thinking of Imogen again and the hero whose defects threw into greater relief the virtues of the heroine. Then she found herself thinking that Bart French could never have done such a thing. That at least he would have paid the doctor's full bill. And all the while from a wonderful shivering within, she knew that the full glow of her morning ecstasy had been restored.

"Has she really married Mr. Ozite?" she asked when he had finished.

"Oh, yes. Weeks ago."

"Perhaps you should give her the other five hundred as a wedding present."

He saw in her eyes that his cause was undamaged, perhaps even curiously enhanced, and he laughed. "Is that all you have to say? I sometimes think women have no morals."

"Not where other women are concerned, anyway." She cleared her throat with a little cough. "And now I have something to tell *you*. Something much worse." When she saw the hard, bright instant gleam of alarm in his eyes, she added quickly: "Oh, not what you're thinking. It's not about another man. It's about you. I was criticizing you in my mind tonight. For seeming too much like Bart and Jake."

He looked confused. "But how?"

"By being too much the smooth young Tower, Tilney associate."

"You mean a toady?"

"Oh, no. It was just that you seemed less like Harry Reilley."

"And now I'm old Harry again? Because I'm the hero of a dirty story?"

She laughed at the absurdity of it. "I guess so. That's the kind of illogical thing a woman is."

But Harry was not in the least amused. He was suddenly very angry, and two bright red spots appeared just under his cheekbones. "It gave you a thrill that I wasn't a gentleman, is that it? You only cared about the mick? You don't want me in the same dancing class with Bart French—I look too pathetic in those silk tights and black pumps? Is that it?"

"Oh, *Harry*," she whispered appalled.

"Do you think I give a God-damn about those precious little disciples of your father? Do you you think I give a God-damn about his sacred firm? Do you know that I was going to resign the day he asked me for dinner? Every case I've worked on since then, every shirt and tie I've bought, every drink I've passed up, every snotty partner I haven't told off, has been because of you. And what a sweet ass that makes me! When all you wanted was a tough mick to give you a black eye!"

In the suffocation of her shame Fran felt a sudden terror that he would leave the bar and walk out of her life before she had found her voice. "Oh, my darling," she gasped, "forgive me!"

His anger faded to exasperation as he looked into her desperately pleading eyes. "Well, you needn't make a soap opera of it."

"I love you, darling!" she reached across the table to seize his hand. "Does anything else matter?"

"For Pete's sake, Fran!"

"No, listen to me, Harry. *Please*. It's only fair to give me a chance to explain. You see, I've always had a fetish about the office. Because it was Daddy's world, that shining man's world that I could never get into. And then when you came along, and without even caring about it, without in the least admiring it, made it yours, I began to wonder if it could have been so great a world, after all. And because that idea was painful to me, I had to accuse you of conquering it unfairly!"

"I haven't conquered it yet. By a long shot."

"But you will! I know you will. And all the while I should have been telling myself that it's not because Daddy's world was weak but because you were strong!"

"Tower, Tilney doesn't mean that much to me," he grumbled, and she saw that she had said enough. More than enough.

"Of course it doesn't, darling! Why should it? And in the future it's only going to mean to me what it means to you. Is that a bargain?"

When she saw him smile at last, if reluctantly, she could only pray that the crisis had been averted and swear an inward vow that she would never play Imogen again.

THE POWER
OF APPOINTMENT

SYLVESTER BROOKS had reached the age of seventy without making the professional blunder, the dread of which had darkened his life. The apprehension had started in law school where he had learned to identify himself with those bungling practitioners whom his professors, in the meanness of their detachment, were never tired of excoriating: "Of course, this case wouldn't have come up if the testator had hired someone better than a monkey to draw his will," or: "This company wouldn't have lost its charter if it had spent a few more bucks on its brand of counsel." Young Brooks, laughing with the others—and he always laughed with the others—nonetheless immediately saw himself as that monkey or as the author of that defective bylaw. Yet he managed through law school and, indeed, for the first twenty-five years of his professional life, both as an associate and later as a partner of his magnificent older cousin Reginald Tower, to keep his anxiety within reasonable bounds. Hidden away from a large office in his small, closed garden of accountings—accountings of trustees, of guardians, of executors, accountings of anybody accounting for anything—he was immune from the terrible decisions of the courtroom or the corporate board meeting. It was not until he was fifty and collided with a litigious widow who wanted to surcharge the Standard Trust Company for half a million dollars that he lost his nerve and persuaded the client to a bad settlement. It was young Waldron Webb, his assistant, who alerted the senior partner, with the result that the case was promptly taken out of Brooks' hands, the settlement quashed and the widow roundly defeated. The dreaded blunder had not been made; it had been averted. But Sylvester Brooks, who was never to recover his lost nerve, suffered a breakdown which kept him out of the office for a year.

When he returned, he was still in no condition to be in charge even of accountings, and he would have been lost but for the kindness and tact of his cousin. Tower, a huge, grumbling, waspish, exhibitionistic lawyer, who concealed a genius under the splashing flow of his platitudes, had a sense of responsibility, amounting almost to an obsession, for his family. Brooks was his mother's nephew, and Brooks had to be looked out for. He conceived the plan of justifying Brooks to the other partners in the role of a business getter, or at least of a business holder, and he made him the firm's personal representative, placing him on charitable boards and committees of lawyers' associations, sending him to legal banquets and bar conferences and delegating to him the entertainment of clients. And Brooks, responding with the deepest gratitude, adopted as best he could, as the years in this new niche sped comfortably by, the appearance of what his cousin presented him as being, that of the perfectly charming and worldly-wise old gentleman. His figure was slim and dapper; his soft thick hair cut into his high forehead in a fine grey triangle, and his long, brown intelligent handsome face bore spots but no wrinkles. What was best of all was that his friendly twinkling sky-blue eyes and his fine aquiline nose gave the impression of a domesticated eagle who remembered the days of his soaring above pine forests and rocky crags. When Brooks told the young clerks stories of old lawsuits and distant triumphs, in his pleasant, crackling, beautifully modulated voice, with a gesture here and there that seemed the replica of one made in oral arguments before Holmes or Cardoza, they believed him. They believed him implicitly until they were disillusioned—which, alas, was only too soon the case—by their seniors of a few months.

"Mr. Brooks? A splendid old fraud. Something out of Dickens. The partners put up with him because of the boss. When old Tower kicks the bucket, they'll send Brooks to the glue factory."

And, indeed, when the surrogate died, and the scramble for his clients began, poor Brooks could not even get his nose in the pot. The Standard Trust Company, prize of the collection, went, of course, to Tower's successor, Clitus Tilney, and the corporations to the other corporation partners. Even the individual clients passed Brooks by. Old Miss Johanna Shepard, with all her city real estate, went to Waldron Webb, and the Baxter family to Morris Madison. But the bitterest blow of all was when Mildred Tower, the widow, told the new senior partner that she would prefer to have her husband's estate handled by his nephew than by his cousin. And who was this nephew but the bungling Rutherford whose gaffes in will drafting had been more than once covered up by Brooks before they could be spotted by the stern avuncular eye? Where was there even a bush in his jackal-infested desert?

Clitus Tilney called Brooks in for a conference. He was as kind as he could be, as kind as old Tower himself, but he was not a relation. Had Brooks thought of retiring? He, Tilney, personally wouldn't have believed it had he not checked the records, but facts were facts, and Brooks *was* sixty-nine, four years over the mandatory retirement age in all the big banks. A pension of sorts could be arranged, perhaps half of Brooks' current drawing account. What about it?

"Oh, it's not the money, Clitus," Brooks said grandly, knowing full well that Tilney was aware that he could barely get by on his present percentage which was smaller than the most junior partner's. "With taxes what they are, a little more or less income won't make all that difference. But what happens to an old war horse when he's turned out to pasture? Othello's occupation and all that? What would I do?"

It was indeed a question. Brooks had no life outside the firm, except for Mrs. Brooks and their polio-crippled daughter, Angelina, and the function of those two pale-browed, serene and uncommunicative women, besides keeping up the Gothic shingle house in Staten Island, was to provide, in long evenings of needlepoint, the appearance of an audience for his saga of the day's battles. The firm was his club, his fishing lodge, his cottage on the seashore; it was the source both of his gossip and of his intellectual satisfaction, the fountain of his friends, his brothers and now of his sons.

"I thought perhaps that in the evening of life, as they put it," Tilney pursued gently, "you might like to be free of the cares and troubles of practice."

Brooks, looking into those large encompassing grey eyes, understood that Tilney pitied and sympathized. "But what is life without cares and troubles?" he riposted, maintaining the pose of the old soldier obliged to seek the assistance of the younger general, an assistance, however, that would be amply repaid by the old soldier's experience in days of yore. He knew that Tilney saw through it, but at the same time that he was grateful for it. It preserved the dignity of each. "Is the game worth the candle otherwise? Can a man really love if he doesn't know jealousy? My biggest kicks have come out of the things that have given me my biggest worries. And I hope it'll go on that way for a bit. Not too long, Clitus, but just for a bit. I'd like to die at my desk like my cousin, Reginald."

Tilney coughed and looked down for a few moments at a memorandum. When he spoke, it was in the harder tone that he used for definite propositions. Tilney never allowed the discussion to be general for long. "I've always had a theory, Sylvester, that the office should have a final court of appeal to review the wills and trusts. One partner who should read them before they're executed to check for violations of the rule against perpetuities and so forth. He would put his initials in the margin of a special copy with the date of his approval, and that would be the green light to go ahead with the signing. Never before. To let a client execute a trust before those initials appeared on the copy would become a capital offense. How would such a job appeal to you?"

Brooks smiled warily. The idea had instant appeal, but he caught a whiff of danger, and he knew that now or never was the time to treat with Tilney. "I could review the instruments for any mistakes under the law of wills and trusts, of course," he answered and then cleared his throat cautiously. "That is, if I don't flatter myself. But I don't think I could be responsible for all the tax aspects. Tax law has gotten so complicated that it really needs a specialist. We old-timers can't be expected to keep up with every last wrinkle of regulation that the Commissioner dreams up."

Tilney moved swiftly to tie up his bargain. "I guess

we can leave taxes out of it. But you will be the last word on everything else." Tilney frowned and shook his head ruefully. "Including typographical errors. Our girls get sloppier and sloppier. The new system will start on Monday. Oh, and Sylvester." Tilney always put his visitor in the position of being about to rush off and having to be detained. "I want you to take a ten percent cut next year. The young men keep crowding in on us, you know. Age must make way gracefully. A couple more years, and I'll start hacking myself." He rose to walk with Brooks to the door. "Remind me if I don't, Sylvester. Remind me if I become piggy. We all have to remember that the young men are the future of the office."

Brooks, however, was too elated to do more than make a mental note that he would have no further traveling or entertaining to do, he could save money on clothes. The new project was announced at the partners' Monday lunch. He had hoped that Chambers Todd would not be present, but this hope proved vain. Todd was the partner of whom he was most afraid, Tilney's blunt, direct "executive officer," who made no secret of his conviction that everyone and everything in the firm that did not promptly pay should be ruthlessly eliminated. And the worst thing about him was that he was a total success himself, not only in the practice of corporation law, but even in the field of Brooks' own supposed priority, that of business getting. Todd's methods made Brooks'—the easy chats on the golf course, the tactful charm at the dinner party, the conviviality of the fishing trip—seem fruitless and out of date. Todd at any social gathering would go straight to the most important man in the room, flatter him in the crudest possible fashion and, more often than seemed decent, add him to the roster of Tower, Tilney clients. When Tilney had finished his brief statement, Todd promptly raised the point that Brooks had known he would not miss.

"What will be the extent of Sylvester's responsibility?" he demanded. "In wills, for example, will he pass on the accuracy of a marital deduction formula?"

Brooks was too old a hand at concealing his panic

to betray any of it in the apparently casual glance that he directed at the senior partner. He seemed to be merely yielding the floor to one who had the easy and obvious answer. But the marital deduction! He would have been hard pressed to explain what it was.

"No, we thought that would have been a bit too much for one man," Tilney replied. "I think the partner whose client it is must assume responsibility that the tax problems have been met."

"But, for Pete's sake, what does that leave Sylvester?" Todd persisted in his crude way. "Seeing that the measuring lives of a trust are all in being? Checking that the executors are exempted from bond? Any kid right out of law school who can't do those things should get the axe. Let's face it, Clitus, we live in a tax era. Everything's taxes. Whether a client wants to make a trust, or form a corporation, or get a divorce, or even go into bankruptcy, what's the first thing he asks? What are the tax consequences?" He looked around the table and gave a short, contemptuous snort. "I sometimes wonder what the hell lawyers did before the big taxes. Fuss around with the commerce clause, I guess, and try to break wills."

"Oh, come, Chambers, you're going too far," Tilney protested. "I think this emphasis on taxes today can be overdone. The old problems, like the poor, are always with us."

"*Are* the poor always with us?" Todd asked. "Where are they? I pay my cleaning woman more than old Tower paid me my first year in the office."

In the laughter that followed Brooks knew that the discussion would be lost, and relief overflowed his heart and seemed to bubble into every part of his being that his new job was safe.

That had been a year ago, and now, at seventy, he still had not made the dreaded error. The new job had started beautifully, with a memorandum issued by Tilney to all hands which described Brooks as the "supreme arbiter" of trusts and testaments. The young men called respectfully at his small office around the corner from the file room, with its neat, clean desk and spotless blotter and its white walls chaste except for a charcoal sketch of Judge Tower, and would nod, with deferential smiles, as they asked: "May I bother the 'arbiter' with a small matter?" Happily, the first month had contained a number of routine wills and trusts, with such simple provisions as: "to my wife for life, remainder to my issue," or: "all my residue to my widow, but if she shall die before me, to Saint Andrew's Hospital." Brooks began to gain confidence as he read them, and as he completed his study of each, he would call the draftsman on the telephone and say, after a preliminary throat clearing, "Oh, Tomkins, is that you? Brooks. I've finished this Catlin will. Could you drop in and discuss it with me a minute?" Of course, he could have placed his initials, in large, blue, sweeping arcs, in the lower left margin of the document and tossed it in his "out" basket with the name of the draftsman clipped to the top. But this procedure would have been offensive to Brooks. He did not like the idea of confidential documents being carried through the corridors by messenger boys. It was more consistent with the dignity of an estate and trust practice and, obviously, with his own function as supreme arbiter, to have the lawyer seeking the approving "S.B." call upon him in person. It was the least, too, that Brooks' age and seniority should command.

"Have a seat," he would say, when Tomkins appeared, leaning back in his own chair and packing the tobacco into his pipe. "I don't know that there's terribly much to say about your matter, but we'll see." He would then go through the form of fumbling through a drawer. There was no point in letting Tomkins know that his whole morning had been occupied by that will. "Ah, here it is. I see I've initialed it. Let me just recall it to mind." He would put on his glasses and scan the familiar first page. "Ah, yes. A good, sound, simple testamentary scheme. In my humble opinion there's too much unnecessary complication these days. Trying to beat the government out of the last red cent and forgetting the more basic things, like what a family really needs. We lawyers can be too smart for our own good sometimes. Do you know how long C. V. Babcock's will was? A document that disposed of a hundred million dollars?"

"No, sir."

"Three lines." Brooks smiled amiably at the young man and then slapped the table. "Three little lines. Let me recite them to you, because I regard them as a classic in the history of estate planning. Oh, I know, they wouldn't fit every situation, of course, but it's a good idea to remember that they might fit more than you think." Here Brooks would clear his throat again, eye the young man with a steady, smiling stare and then recite in a low, dulcet tone: " 'I devise and bequeath all of my estate, real and personal, to my wife, Mary A. Babcock, and name her executor thereof, to serve without bond.' " He struck the table again, but this time it was only a tap. "Pretty good, you must admit.

"I suppose in those days, sir, things were simpler."

"But the fundamentals were the same!"

Brooks prided himself on being nobody's fool. He knew that the young men were anxious to get back to their work and begrudged the time taken out of a busy day to listen to his reminiscences. But he still thought it was good for them. Where else in the office could they catch the flavor of the past, and without a touch of that flavor did the law not become a mere jumble of tax regulations, to be practiced with a slide rule? He had always had a secret hope that survival would be his own method of triumph. He had loved to visualize himself, in daring moments, as the charming, discursive, admired old gentleman of Tower, Tilney & Webb, the partner whose common sense and broad experience were to prove, in the end, more valuable to the firm than the mere technical expertise of others, the man who was able to unite the generations, to explain Waldron Webb and Chambers Todd to the young and the young to them. He even had a fantasy in which he saved the firm from a schism by raising his arms for peace over a sordid quarrel as to whose name should go first on the door and reuniting the warring factions with the skill of his diplomacy. Even Todd would have to recognize that Brooks' love of the firm transcended all petty ambition.

"Well, thanks, Mr. Brooks," Tomkins would be saying as he got up from his chair. "And now, if I may take the will, I needn't intrude on your time any further."

"My time is your time, my boy. Any time an old man can be of help."

It did seem to be working out. Even the file clerks recognized that Mr. Brooks had a new importance in the office. Miss Gibson had to see that no signed will was placed in the vault until a copy with Mr. Brooks' initials had been affixed to the record file, and she enforced the rule with her usual rigidity. Sometimes at partner's lunches he told stories now, to the general amusement, of typographical errors and curious clauses, and occasionally a group of two or three clerks, passing his door on the way to lunch, would ask him to join them. At home Mrs. Brooks and Angelina listened with a new attention as he described the personalities of the young men. Brooks began to wonder, like Rabbi Ben Ezra, if the best was not yet to be. But the concept of "best" instantly suggested its opposite, and didn't his present situation provide just the atmosphere to materialize the ancient specter of his still unmade blunder? Perhaps it had waited all these years to make its grim visit to Brooks, the arbiter.

His craft had soon glided over the shallow waters of the initial documents to the murky depths of those succeeding. He was staggered by the "marital deduction" wills with their elaborate mathematical formulae and found himself covering scratch paper with numerators and denominators and running to his old friends, the accountants, for help. Even if not responsible for taxes, he had to be able to read the instrument. And then came a collection of interlocking trusts, created by a rich Hungarian refugee family. Brooks would never have believed that laymen could have imagined such a medley of contingencies, each one to be met with a different scheme. And on top of these came a will whose residuary clause divided the estate into two hundred parts, some in trust, some outright gifts, some gifts to charity, some to charitable trusts. He began to realize that the first two months of his apprenticeship must have been a period of unprecedented lull in the manufacture of the more usual type of Tower, Tilney documents.

He tried to conceal his fear of complexity behind a philosophy of simplicity. "It's one thing to write these wills," he would tell the young men who came to his office. "It's another thing to administer them. Have you thought of that? All right, suppose you *do* save a few thousand bucks in taxes. Aren't you adding it right back to the costs of administration?" But the young men did not seem to think so. They listened politely enough, but they would always insist that what the client wanted the client should get. Brooks had the uneasy feeling that they knew he found it difficult to keep up with them and knew, too, that they had only to appeal to the partner in charge if he refused to sign. And so, grumbling, he signed.

Once, however, he made a stand. It was over the will of an old maid who wanted to divide her estate among her nephews and nieces in such a way as to make them, taking into account the private resources of each at the time of her death, of equal wealth. The will was a prodigy of ingenuity, but repulsively difficult to read. It bristled with rules and equations. How much, for example, did one debit a nephew who had a trust fund, as opposed to one who was a partner in a law firm, or who ran a small business? Brooks took the will home to Staten Island over the weekend and puzzled in vain over its tortured language while the women of his family worked on their needlepoint. On Monday morning he gathered up the bits and pieces of his atrophied courage and flung them in the face of the frowning young associate who had prepared the instrument.

"I'm afraid I can't put my initials on your masterpiece," he said, with what he hoped was his nicest smile. "Perhaps you deserve an honorary degree from Harvard for creative imagination. It's a fantastic job you've done here, and I give you full marks. But I can't get away from the fact that it's an invitation to a lawsuit. I'll bet this will would have to be construed a dozen times!"

"But I maintain it's entirely clear, sir."

"*You* do, of course. But what about the nephews and nieces?"

The associate shrugged and left, and Brooks next heard of the matter when he was summoned to the senior partner's office. Tilney had the disputed will before him and a pad on which he had jotted some figures. He smiled as he looked up at Brooks.

"This will of Miss Shepard's is something, isn't it? I've been checking it out, though, and it seems to work. Did you think it wouldn't?"

"I don't say it isn't accurately drawn," Brooks answered quietly, hoping with soft speech and firm manner to convey the impression that he, too, had been able to check it out. "But when you've played around with wills as long as I have, Clitus, you know that complexity spells trouble."

"I thought just the opposite was the case," Tilney insisted unexpectedly. "I thought it was the simple, homedrawn will that ended up in court. There's nothing wrong with complexity if the draftsman knows what he's doing. And I suggest that this draftsman does. In fact, I intend to keep an eye on this young man. Now the wisdom of the will is another matter. But we can't control that. If Miss Shepard wants to do this kind of thing with her property, that's Miss Shepard's privilege. And why should we complain? She pays us. If every client wanted an all-to-my-widow will, they'd soon start using stationery store forms."

"But even so, Clitus, it seems to me there are limits."

"Everything has limits," Tilney said in the sharper tone that he used when a subordinate failed to take the proferred "easy out." "But I fail to see that they have been reached here. It takes time and effort to understand a document like this, but I think you will find that if you take that time and make that effort, it will become clear."

Brooks rose quickly and took his pen from his upper vest pocket. "I *have* taken that time, Clitus, and I have made that effort. My objections were all in principle, but as you're the final judge of that, I withdraw them." He smiled down at the senior partner as if they were adjusting a minor matter. "Let me put my John Henry on that document here and now."

As he leaned over to scratch his initials in the margin, he knew by Tilney's grunt that all was well again. Well between them, perhaps, but with a stifled sigh, he knew that all would never be well again inside himself. For he had placed the approving "S.B." at last on a paper that he did not begin to understand. It could only be a matter of time now before Nemesis struck.

He was never sure whether the change in his office status that followed this episode was real or imagined. Had the word got about among the clerks that old Brooks had been peremptorily overruled by Mr. Tilney and that henceforth one had only to cough significantly if he withheld his initials? Or was it merely his own abashment at realizing that he had been caught out in laziness and timidity and had ignorantly approved a will that might as well have been written in Chinese? Were the associates frankly bored now when he stopped in their offices to chat or was he simply more conscious of those drumming fingers, that eye on the clock? Surely, it was a fact that the documents for his approval were more often sent to his desk now than personally delivered. And surely it was another fact that if he was in a clerk's office and the telephone rang, the clerk no longer told his caller: "I'll ring you back." *Was* he more boring, more contemptible? Or was it rather that terrible thing about old age, that everyone expected one to be boring and hence one was? Just as they expected one to forget everything or to be deaf. Brooks, whose hearing was unusually acute, suffered increasingly from a world that shouted at him. But his only answer to the real or imagined sneers, the true or fictive yawns was to redouble his efforts to be agreeable, to smile more broadly at the clerks, to laugh more loudly at the jokes at the partners' lunches, to put an occasional flower on the desks of the senior ladies of the staff. He began to be as jaunty and twinkly as an old vaudeville actor.

The outward expression, however, was not the sign of any inward truth. Behind the rumbling laugh, the oft

cleared throat, the anecdote of the glorious past, lay
the old dread, intensified, close to panic, relieved only
by periods of damp, dull resignation. The mistake
would happen soon enough; the law of chances alone
decreed it. A good third of the instruments that he now
meekly initialed contained clauses that he no longer
even pretended to himself that he understood. When
he asked a draftsman to explain, he would concentrate
so hard on his own expression of intelligent listening
that he would forget to listen, and when he asked
questions, he was apt to be silenced by the answer:
"But, Mr. Brooks, aren't *you* meant to be expert on
that?"

At night he often lay awake and tried to visualize
the different ways in which disaster might strike. It
would be a will in which the percentage shares of the
residuary estate were found to total more than a
hundred. It would be a trust where the remainder vested
in a dead person. There would be angry voices and
pointing fingers, and the initials "S.B." on the guilty
copy in the files would be the death warrant from
which there was no appeal. Ah, well, he sometimes
thought, as he wiped the cold drops from his forehead,
it might even be a relief to have it over.

When it came at last, it came with an awesome
simplicity. Old Titus Baxter died, and in his will he exercised a power of appointment, conferred upon him
by his long deceased mother's will, to prolong a trust
for the lifetime of his daughter. It was not one of the
complex wills that Brooks had so feared; it was, on the
contrary, one of the simple ones that he had applauded.
The trouble was that the daughter had been born *after*
her grandmother's death. This small basic fact, known
to all—apparent, indeed, by the very recitals in Titus'
will—had, incredibly enough, been overlooked by the
drafting clerk, the senior associate, the partner in
charge, and, in the end, by Sylvester Brooks. The exercise of the power had necessarily failed, and a quarter
of a million dollars now tumbled, "in default of a valid
appointment," into the lap of old Mrs. Baxter's unsus-
pecting but grateful pet charity, the Institute for the Re-

lief of Indigent Descendants of American Revolutionary Officers. It was a mistake that any law student, working in the office for a summer salary would have been expected to pick up. It was indeed a grave question whether Miss Baxter did not have a suit against the firm for malpractice. Only the large bequests to her in other articles of the will might incline her to mercy.

Brooks first learned about it on Monday morning from Morris Madison, the partner in charge of the Baxter estate. The invalidity had been pointed out late Friday by the executor, Standard Trust Company, and Madison had spent the weekend in the office with a team of associates, frantically digging out the law to see if anything could be done to save Miss Baxter's trust. Nothing could. Madison seemed tired, but resigned.

"I thought you'd better hear about it from me before the partner's lunch," he told Brooks. "Of course, we're all to blame, but the major blame is mine. Some harsh things will undoubtedly be said, and I suggest we sit together, and you let me answer the questions. I don't know how you feel about this sort of thing, but, frankly, I'm not inclined to be too apologetic. It's the kind of ridiculous blunder that might have happened to anybody. It's like an act of God. There's no point calling it careless. I don't happen to be a careless lawyer. Unless I'm to be judged by this and this alone."

Brooks had always regarded Madison as an aloof, superior person, too exalted on his peak of tax brilliance even to scorn such fumbling practitioners as himself. Madison rarely addressed more than a perfunctory greeting to him, except once when he had examined him in astonishing detail about the genealogy of the Tower family. Madison was known in the office for his way of suddenly turning in a corridor to stop people whom he had hardly ever spoken to and asking them rather personal questions. But now Brooks decided that Morris Madison was the first gentleman of the office, and the phoenix that rose from the ashes of his career was a vision of the drama of facing the partners with so gallant an ally. The long heralded crisis had come, but it found him ready. He had felt it as a man for a lifetime; he could dispute it like a man for a day. When he walked into the dining room after Madison, he was even able to smile at the sullen face of Chambers Todd.

Yet Todd was as bad as anyone could have feared. The man had so identified his personal ambition with Tower, Tilney that his agony at the Baxter debacle was as acute as if he had made the error himself. Despite Clitus Tilney's coughs and hints, he kept returning to the subject, long after the others had accepted Madison's brief, dignified statement.

"You say it was Jonas McClintock who prepared the original draft?" he demanded of Madison. "Then it was McClintock who made the error of using Miss Baxter as a measuring life?"

"I've already told you, Chambers, the responsibility is mine."

"Never mind this I'm-the-captain-of-my-ship attitude," Todd snapped with a rudeness that shocked the table. "This isn't a court-martial, and I don't give a damn for fancy concepts of responsibility. The point is that we can't afford to have juniors who make such gaffes. McClintock must go."

"He's a good man, Chambers."

"Oh, rats. He *was* a good man."

"You think an associate should not be allowed even one mistake?"

"When it's a mistake like that, I certainly do! If each of them pulled that kind of bull, we'd be out of business in a year's time."

"I think we've said about all that can be profitably said on the subject," Clitus Tilney intervened from the head of the table. "The committee on associates will consider McClintock's case. No doubt they will give Mr. Todd's suggestion the weight that it is due. Now may we pass on to other matters?"

Sylvester Brooks, however, was not going to be deprived of his minute in Morris Madison's finest hour.

"May I say one thing, Mr. Tilney," he began and then paused to clear his throat impressively. "If there's any firing to be done, I don't think it should be confined to associates. My initials are on the office copy of the Baxter will. Chambers Todd may not care about responsibility, but I do. I'm responsible for every clause in that document."

"We don't fire partners," Todd retorted roughly. "That would be firing ourselves. But if we can't read wills properly, we have to hire young men who can. And might I suggest one thing, Sylvester? If you'd spend less time telling the associates tales of the great past, they might have more time for work and make less mistakes."

There was a gasp around the table, and Tilney exclaimed sharply: "That will do, Chambers! You're going too far." He nodded apologetically down the table at Brooks. "I hope you realize, Sylvester, that the rest of us do not go along with that last remark. I shall now ask Bayard Kip to report on his very interesting conference with Commissioner Caplin on the elimination of tax deductions for business entertaining."

Brooks uttered no word for the rest of the meal, but kept his eyes fixed, with a concentrated expression of sympathetic interest, on the gravely articulate Mr. Kip. But he was only reflecting that the furies had claws as sharp but no sharper than he had dreaded. The cruelty of Todd had been very terrible, but very anticipatable. Now it was over, and Brooks hoped that he had played his part in the fifth act as becomingly as any of them. There was only one more thing to do before the final curtain, and he did it, immediately after lunch, in Clitus Tilney's office, standing solemnly before the senior partner's desk.

"But, my dear fellow, I shan't *permit* you to resign," Tilney said immediately, waving his right hand in expansive protest. "No, no, no. At least not under these circumstances. This thing will blow over, don't worry. If, when it has and you still wish to retire—as you're entitled to at your age—that's another matter. But I won't have you quitting under fire after forty-five years in this office. Forget about Chambers. His bite may be worse than his bark, but I know how to muzzle him."

Brooks stared at him with the bewilderment of a supporting actor who finds the star suddenly extemporizing. "But if I stay on, what will I do? How can you use me?"

"Use you?" Tilney demanded in surprise. "Why exactly the way we've been using you all along, as our esteemed arbiter of wills!"

"You mean you'd *trust* me?" Brooks demanded, almost in indignation. "You'd trust me again after this Baxter mess?"

"Of course I'd trust you. I'd trust you with anything, old boy. Now get out of here and go back to work and don't let me hear another word of this nonsense!"

As Brooks walked down the long corridor from Clitus Tilney's large office to his own small one, he wondered in a daze whether the final curtain would ever fall between himself and the audience of his own panic. There were no lines now, no play, no scenery even; he was speechless on a deserted stage. He stopped in his doorway as he noticed something in the middle of the clean white blotter on his desk. It was the carbon copy of a will, placed there for his inspection and initialing, placed there fastidiously, so that its sides were parallel with the sides of the blotter, placed there as if to mock him with its neatness and hidden dangers. And somehow hovering over it, unseen but sneering, vaguely fetid, somehow ridiculous, he sensed at last the presence of his ancient specter and understood what it was.

"I've been made a fool of," he whispered with a groan, half in awe at his own discovery. "I've been made a perfect fool."

For the dreaded mistake had come and gone, and nobody cared that he had made it. He had been forgiven because there was nothing to forgive. His job was a form, an ingenious face saver, conceived by a benevolent senior partner to keep an old body occupied. Those initials in the margin were like revenue stamps on a recorded deed. They did not speak for the validity of the document, but for the power of the taxing state. Brooks, however, was not a man to draw out his crisis. He had his cue again. He walked briskly to his chair, put on his glasses and pulled the will towards him. For a moment he examined it without reading a word, then nodded, took off his glasses, reached for his pen and traced with his customary slow care the high blue wavering letters in the margin. If initials were required, initials would be supplied, right up to the last day of his partnership. His recompense to Tilney for what Tilney had tried to do for him would be to conceal his own discovery of the stratagem. If the show had to go on, at least he had found his lines, and with lines an old actor could get through anything.

FROM BED AND BOARD

WALDRON P. WEBB had always been proud of the fact, so much deplored by that arch-organizer, Clitus Tilney, that the litigation department of Tower, Tilney & Webb was a firm within a firm. A great trial lawyer, Webb maintained, like a great diva, had to be supported by a large, well-trained cast, and the last interference with any of his law clerks, or even of his stenographers, made the smooth pink cheeks of the senior litigator, so evocative, with his cotton-white hair and round belly, of a jovial Santa, turn to a mottled red and the silky voice to a stertorous clatter. Webb gave his people different hours of work and different salary raises from the rest of the office, and the discord which he thus created, far from being harmful, in his opinion, to the spirit of a law firm, was conducive, he boasted, to the development of the litigious genius. "Can you imagine a Clarence Darrow," he would demand sarcastically of Tilney, "emerging from that dull grey military academy which you call the corporate department?"

Litigation, indeed, was more than Webb's profession; it was his catharsis. He was one of those unhappy men who always wake up angry. He was angered by the sparrows outside his bedroom window in Bronxville, by the migraines of his long-suffering wife, by the socialism in the newspaper, the slowness of the subway, the wait for the elevator, the too casual greeting of the receptionist. It was only the great morning pile on his desk of motions, attachments and injunctions that restored his calm. Sitting back in his red plush armchair under the dark lithograph of an orating Daniel Webster, facing his secretary and two chief law clerks, he would open the day with a rattling dictation of letters and memoranda. Gradually, as he talked and telephoned, as he stamped again and again on the hydra-headed serpent of presumption that daily struck anew at his clients with the forked tongues of legal subterfuge, as he defeated motion with countermotion, question with accusation, commitment with revocation, the earlier irritations of the morning subsided, the Santa Claus began to predominate over the Scrooge, and Waldron P. Webb assumed his midday look of benevolent, if rather formidable cheer.

There was one type of case, however, that, instead of calming his nerves, aroused the same fury evoked by the morning sparrows and newspapers, and that was divorce. Webb claimed, like most lawyers in the financial world, that he handled divorces only for old and valued clients, paying the conventional lip service to the downtown tradition that matrimonial matters were not merely unpleasant and sticky, but bad pay. Yet the fact remained that he handled a considerable number of such cases, and, in some instances, for total strangers. Clitus Tilney had deeply angered him once, at a firm lunch, by commenting with a snorting laugh, in relation to a much publicized decree which Webb had obtained depriving a young wife of custody of her children, on the "sex antagonism" latent in the divorce bar. It was simply not true. At least it was not true of Waldron Webb. When he represented a wife he pursued the husband with exactly the same angry passion. All he had to do was to see a spouse on the other side of an issue, and his heart began to swell with the indignation of one who at the helm of a storm-tossed ship hears that a careless sailor has left open a porthole. Waldron Webb had been a faithful husband to an ailing wife for thirty years. He felt that he was no hypocrite in exacting high standards of others.

The bitterest of these cases began on a bitter winter morning when the subway had been particularly slow, the receptionist more than usually offhand and the morning pile of mail disappointingly small. There was really no excuse to keep his first appointed caller waiting for more than half an hour, and at eleven o'clock he received a slim, handsome, agile man of thirty-odd, with thick curly hair, already grey, a light, almost a child's, skin and troubled eyes, who had been referred to him by the president of the Standard Trust Company. Peyton Hobart was a name associated in Webb's mind with Cholly Knickerbocker, polo and Westbury,

but the antagonism so initially aroused was soon sub-
dued by his visitor's air of deference and by the fact
that in downtown territory and dressed in a business
suit (Hobart worked, apparently, in his family's insurance business) he had the look of a schoolboy on Sunday, yearning for green fields, but obliged for morning
chapel to encase his neck in a white collar and his body
in blue serge.

"I've always thought Georgette and I had a perfect
marriage," he was saying. "You could have knocked me
down with a feather when she told me she was in
love with Tommy Gwinnett. We've been married thirteen years. You may laugh, Mr. Webb, but that's a long
time in our crowd. Maybe it's our bad luck year." He
shook his head with a charming, if despondent smile.
"Or maybe we're not as different from the others as
I've always liked to think."

"What did you tell Mrs. Hobart?"

"What was there to tell? *She* did all the telling. She
told me she wanted a divorce."

"And you agreed?"

Hobart looked up in surprise. "Well, how can I hold
on to a woman who doesn't want to stay? And would
I want to if I could?"

Webb, with a little grunt, proceeded to elicit the vital
statistics. He did this in the offhand fashion of a doctor, who, concealing his own awareness of his patient's
natural embarrassment, asks him to strip. Peyton
Hobart had two children, a boy and a girl. He had
securities worth three quarters of a million and expected much more on his mother's death. Georgette,
aside from considerable jewelry, had nothing. It was
always astonishing, Webb reflected, how relatively poor
society people were. He himself had a larger income
than Hobart, and could he have dreamt of polo ponies?

He turned to more personal matters. Had Mr. Hobart
ever misbehaved himself? No, he did not mean drinking
or flirting; he meant only one thing. No? Mr. Hobart
was quite sure? He would be safe, in the event of a New
York divorce proceeding? What about Mrs. Hobart?

"Really, Mr. Webb, I don't want to hurt Georgette.
She's been a perfectly good wife, up until now. It's not

her fault that she's fallen for this guy. Most of her
friends have."

"Then you propose to let her go?"

"I suppose I must."

"And to make her a settlement?"

"Well, doesn't a wife always get something? I want
to do the right thing."

"And the children? She's to have the children, too,
I assume?"

"If it's customary."

"Customary?" Webb's voice rose shrilly. "I don't
know the word! You don't come to a lawyer like Waldron P. Webb if all you want is to be the docile American husband who hands his fortune and children over
to the man who's seduced his wife!"

A faint pink, of irritation and surprise, appeared in
the upper sections of Hobart's long, narrow cheeks.
"See here, Mr. Webb, we don't have to go that far.
Tommy Gwinnett's not exactly an adventurer, you
know. We were both in the Fly Club, and he's a good
deal richer than I am."

"I don't 'know' anything about Mr. Gwinnett. Except
that he'll certainly be richer than you are when he has
your money. Why, if he's so well off, does Mrs. Hobart
need anything from you? Why can't he take care of
her?"

This at last seemed to strike Hobart, for he frowned
and nodded. "There's something in that, isn't there?"
he exclaimed, with naïve surprise. "This whole thing
was Gwinnett's idea. Let Gwinnett pay for it!"

"Let him indeed," Webb agreed promptly, sighing
inwardly at such evidence of a flightiness that augured
ill for the success of prolonged negotiations. "And now
to the question of the children. Have you stopped to
consider that if your wife has custody, Mr. Gwinnett
will be their real father? Oh, I know, you'll see them
on Saturday afternoons." Webb's shrug and raised hand
anticipated Hobart's argument. "*If* it's convenient.
And you'll take them to the circus. And you'll be allowed, perhaps, to sit in the second pew when they're
married." Webb half closed his eyes as he sat back to
deliver, with mocking softness, his customary lecture.

"You'll be the man with the perpetual lollypop, trying to amuse the unamusable. Intruding a woebegone, unwanted face into a tightly knit family group. Too alien to be confided in. Too pathetic to be disliked. And no matter how successful in business you may be, to them you'll always be the man Mummy left." Here he paused ominously, "All that, of course, is the *best* you can hope for. The worst is that she'll shut you out altogether and change their name to Gwinnett."

"Oh, she wouldn't do that!"

"Wouldn't she? What makes you so sure?"

Webb's client brooded over this. "It's true she's never liked being called 'Hobart'—she says it sounds like a dentist."

"And didn't a Gwinnett sign the Declaration of Independence?"

"Damn it, that's right!" Hobart was now sufficiently aroused to slap a hand on Webb's desk. "It's probably just what they would do. Tommy doesn't have a son. Just girls. Well, let him have my girl but not my boy. Damn it all, Webb, they can't have my boy!"

"My dear fellow, why should they have either?"

Webb felt that he had reason to be satisfied with the strengthened attitude of his client at his first interview with Mrs. Hobart's counsel. Mr. Clarence Cup was small and grey and very neat; he walked with a jerky confidence to the chair before Webb's desk and sat with his two little round white hands on top of a bulging briefcase, as if it were full of missiles too deadly, or too explosive, to be entrusted to the floor or any table.

"I suppose you hate these domestic matters as much as I do, Mr. Webb," he began. "I wish there was some way we could figure out to duck them."

It was the time-honored downtown opening, but it irked Webb that a regular divorce hack like Cup should presume to use it to him.

"It's all in the day's work," he said dryly. "We lawyers can't pick and choose."

"Quite so." Cup paused to glance about the room as though trying to find a clue for a new approach. His gaze lingered on the silver framed photograph of Mrs. Webb, in a dull brown evening dress snapped at the Waldorf as she was being introduced to Tom Dewey, and on another of Waldron Jr., looking very large in football clothes against a small gymnasium. "What a fine young man. Your son, of course? May I see him closer?" Cup rose and leaned over the picture. "I'm sure you feel as badly about this business as I do," he continued, his back to Webb. "It's a tragedy, that's what it is. Two young persons with everything to live for. I make it a point never to open negotiations until I've been convinced that every last step has been taken towards a reconciliation."

"I'm afraid that's up to your client."

"There's never been a situation in my experience where it was all up to *one* side. We're dealing with human beings, Mr. Webb. Human beings who are confused and unhappy. Human beings who need help. Your help and mine."

Webb winced. If there was anything in the world more nauseating than hypocrisy, it was sentimentality. "Of course I can't speak for your client, Mr. Cup. But I know that mine engaged me as a lawyer and not a marriage counselor. I'm afraid I must limit my advice to the scope of my retainer."

Cup's round cheeks slowly filled with pink. "I'm sorry to hear you take that attitude. Very sorry."

"It's not *my* attitude, Mr. Cup. It's my client's. Shall we proceed to business? It shouldn't keep us long. There's no question, I take it, of alimony?"

Cup's voice now sank to a mild, incredulous whisper. "May I ask why?"

"Surely the divorce is all of Mrs. Hobart's seeking?"

"The divorce may be of her seeking, Mr. Webb. But only in the sense that a woman in desperate agony who blindly takes an overdose of drugs may be called a suicide."

"Desperate agony? From what?"

"From neglect, Mr. Webb." Here Cup, who was not a man to fear the dramatic, struck his hands together. "From financial stinginess, Mr. Webb. From attentions to other women, Mr. Webb!"

"I know of no other women."

"Not even Mrs. Marsden? I should have thought that the most casual reader of the evening papers would have learned of Mr. Hobart and Mrs. Marsden."

"I don't read gossip sheets," Webb retorted angrily, "and I don't choose to have them quoted at me by those who do. Mrs. Hobart has asked for her freedom to be able to contract another alliance. Very well. Let her renounce all interest in Mr. Hobart's property. Let her release him from all further obligations for her support. Let her . . . "

"Mr. Webb!"

"Let me finish, please, Mr. Cupp. Let her give him custody of the children, subject to rights of reasonable visitation. And *then* she may have her divorce."

There was a pause, and Mr. Cup rose. "Obviously, our positions are too wide apart to make further discussion fruitful."

It was now Webb's turn to be taken aback. "You don't wish to state your position?"

"What would be the use?"

"It might interest my client. Who knows? He may be more accommodating than I. I can't decide for him."

"You can't?" Cup sat slowly down again and opened his briefcase a crack, as if to let out only the top item of its bursting contents. "First off, I should insist that your client settle on his wife the sum of two hundred and fifty thousand dollars."

"Outright?"

"Outright. Plus a third of his gross income before taxes, until such time as Mrs. Hobart dies or remarries. And, of course, I should insist upon absolute custody of the children. A mother's prerogative. With reasonable rights of visitation to Mr. Hobart, so long as he behaves himself."

"Anything else?"

"Oh, yes," Cup continued, as if the inquiry had not been sarcastic. "Mrs. Hobart is worried about the influence of a future wife, or wives, on Mr. Hobart. We would ask him to place half his property in trust to ensure that it would go to his *present* children on his death. And that, I think, is all. Except, of course, for my fee, which I should expect him to pay."

"You were quite right, Mr. Cup." Here Webb rose and stretched out a hand of farewell across the desk. "We *are* too far apart for fruitful discussion. Our clients must learn to bear their chains of wedlock."

At India House, where Webb took his client for lunch, amid prints of clipper ships and the patient smiles of Buddhas, he explained the interview as best he could. Peyton Hobart was obviously distressed.

"So what do we do now?"

"We sit tight. We sit tight and sit it out."

"And how long does that take?" Hobart demanded fretfully.

"You should be able to answer that better than I. How long can Mrs. Hobart wait to marry Mr. Gwinnett? Or, more important, how long will *he* wait? Bear in mind, she'll have to behave herself, for, of course, we'll have her watched. One misstep, and you'll get your divorce right here in the empire state!"

"What about *my* missteps?"

Webb became very grim. "There'd better not be any."

Hobart, who normally looked ten years less than his age, now looked twenty. The frank boyish petulance of his expression was not agreeable to behold. "See here, Webb, I came to you for a divorce, not a waiting marathon. I told Mrs. Marsden I'd be free to marry her in a month's time. What am I to tell her now?"

But if Peyton's petulance was that of a schoolboy, Webb's frown was that of a schoolmaster. He reflected with ire how quickly the spoiled polo player betrayed his innate contempt for the professional man. No doubt this very whippersnapper across the table from him, who could not have graduated from college, much less from law school, referred to Waldron P. Webb as "my little man downtown."

"You never told me about Mrs. Marsden," he said sternly.

"What was the point? I told you Georgette had asked

me for a divorce, and she *had*. Did you expect me to remain a monk for the rest of my days?"

"Hardly." Webb smiled with faint sarcasm at the vision of such abstinence. "But I expected you at least to tell me that your hands were tied before I sent you into the boxing ring."

"I didn't know I was going to have to fight! Can't you help me, please, Mr. Webb? I was told you could do *anything*."

The sudden, unhappy note of appeal went far to make up for Webb's vision of that "little man downtown." "I'll do what I can, of course," he said in a milder tone. "But we'll have to bargain. And if we bargain, we'll have to give. Have I your authority?"

"Without a string!"

The first conference between the lawyers had been at Tower, Tilney & Webb; etiquette required that the second should be at Cup's. Yet Webb was not, when he called, after the diplomatic lapse of a week, kept waiting, as he had expected to be. Cup was evidently too clever a tactician for such crudeness. He came out himself to the reception room to lead Webb back to an office whose walls were covered with Victorian prints of legal scenes: "The Reading of the Will," "First Day in Court," "The Judge's Nap."

"It's a great pity, indeed, Mr. Webb," he said, when the latter had made his opening statement, "that this offer to negotiate comes so late. Unhappily, it was my duty to communicate your prior position to my client. She felt—and not without warrant, I'm afraid—that it impugned her character. As a consequence, she has withdrawn my authority to bargain. I'm afraid that the terms which I offered you are final."

"You mean you won't even *discuss* anything else?"

Cup shrugged in assumed helplessness. "How can I? It's beyond the scope of my retainer."

It was always said in Tower, Tilney & Webb that Waldron Webb knew when to lose and when to find his temper. But there was nothing planned about the explosion that followed Cup's exasperating use of his own earlier phrase. "Don't give me that kind of talk, Cup. We both know you put her up to it."

Cup rose promptly and stretched out his hand. "My dear Mr. Webb, you forget yourself. It's not like a litigator of your reputation. Let us conclude this conference before more painful things are said."

An hour later Webb was still furious as he paced up and down his office, relating to Peyton Hobart the case of his wife's obduracy.

"There's only one thing to do now." He paused and wheeled suddenly on his staring and fascinated client. "Hobart, do you really want to marry Mrs. Marsden?"

"Of course!"

"And does she really want to marry you?"

"I hope."

"Enough to give up New York?"

"Gee, I guess so. Would we have to?"

"Listen." Webb's speech became conspiratorial and rapid, punctuated by sharp taps on the furniture with the silver paper cutter that he grasped like a weapon. "If your wife had been reasonable, you could have had a 'quickie' divorce in Alabama or Mexico. But if one side refuses, they're out. What we have to get you is a *valid* divorce in a 'quickie' jurisdiction. To do this you'll have to go to Idaho and establish a *real* residence. Not just six weeks, but a real one."

"You mean I'll have to stay there forever?"

"Forever's a long time. But you'll have to stay until this thing is worked out. Are you willing?"

"I'll do anything you say, Mr. Webb. I'm in your hands."

"Good. Now here's what you do. Ship all your securities out of New York. Today or tomorrow at the latest. Don't tell anyone where they are. Perhaps you know brokers in San Francisco. I say no more. Next, I want you to resign from the family insurance business. And, finally, I want you to pack bag and baggage—secretly—and take yourself off to Boise. I'll have a lawyer meet you who will take care of everything. All you have to do is *get* there!"

Hobart's eyes had the excitement and wonder of a young soldier who has been ordered for the first time to the front. "And Olive? Can she go with me?"

"She can follow. But be discreet! Be discreet, and you'll be married to her in three months' time!"

When Cup discovered that his client's husband had left the state with all the certificates of his participation in American industry, he called up Webb and, in a voice that was almost a scream, threatened to report him to the Grievance Committee of the City Bar Association. Webb simply chuckled and settled back to watch the ineffective fury of his opponent as expressed in a series of lawsuits which dashed as harmlessly as seething surf over the wet black rock of his own maneuver. Cup sued to enjoin Hobart from getting an out-of-state divorce and secured an order, but how could he enforce it? He proceeded to attach everything of Hobart's that he could find in the state, but he could find nothing but half of the Westbury house already occupied by Georgette and a remote interest in a couple of old family trusts. He dared not appear in Idaho, for fear of thus validating the very divorce that he was contesting, but he paid a visit to the district attorney and warned Webb that if his client ever appeared in New York married to Mrs. Marsden, he would find himself jailed for bigamy.

On the other hand, the news from Idaho was exhilarating. Mrs. Marsden loved it, and she and Peyton Hobart skied daily at Sun Valley and danced all night. Webb read his client's letters with a sentimental eye. The more he found out about Hobart, the worse he decided Georgette must have behaved. He had none but the softest feelings now for the handsome young man with the prematurely grey hair and unhappy eyes who was finding contentment at last after the embittering experience of marriage to a faithless wife. Webb could be very severe indeed about "society" people (not that they were any more *real* society than the descendant of six generations of Webbs from Utica), but he was quick to appreciate the charm of their spontaneity and ease once they had made it clear that they were not looking down their noses at the senior trial partner of Tower, Tilney & Webb. And not only did "Peyton" (as he now called him) write daily to Webb, but "Olive"

added the sweetest postscripts about the beautiful job
he had done. On the day they were married, a case of
Moët et Chandon was delivered to Webb at his home
with the telegraphed message: "All our love and gratitude to Waldron, our lawyer, judge and friend, whose
heart is as big as his brain."

But it seemed, as in classic tragedies, that this trio
of new friends had reached only the illusory peak of
third-act success, and that the fourth and fifth were to
contain the required nemesis. Olive had not been married two weeks before she began to tire of Idaho. She
belonged to that exotic class of New York women who,
like certain wines, did not travel. Spring had driven
away the snow and her friends, and she pined for a
glimpse of Manhattan before a seaside summer. Webb,
against his better judgment, finally allowed them to
move to California where Peyton was promptly met
with a summons and suit for maintenance. San Francisco counsel defended on the grounds that Georgette
had abandoned her husband, and Georgette struck back
by removing the children from private school, even
though funds for their tuition had been offered by Peyton's mother. The latter came down to call on Webb,
and they took an instant liking to each other. Mrs. Hobart, Sr., was a thin, freckled, dark-skinned, husky-
voiced, blue-haired lady of seventy, dressed like a
debutante, who hated Georgette with a depth of emo-
tion that seemed out of all proportion to her mild
affection for her son.

"I wouldn't suggest this to everybody," Webb told
her, "but I have a feeling that you could see it through.
My theory is that Georgette is coming to the end of
her rope. She can't marry Gwinnett so long as she won't
recognize the divorce, and if she waits much longer, she
may lose him. She dare not risk that. What we need
now is a bit more pressure in the right place to crack
her. I suggest that you bring suit in Nassau County
asking custody of your grandchildren on the grounds
that her relations with Gwinnett make her an unfit
mother."

Mrs. Hobart remained still and expressionless, but

her eyes showed a faint reptilian glimmer. "Could we prove it?"

"We could give them a run for their money. You never can tell what we may turn up in a trial, with evidence of all-night drinking parties and things like that."

"There've been plenty of those," Mrs. Hobart said grimly. "And you can count on me all the way."

Which, indeed, he found he could. The custody suit moved the Hobart divorce from the gossip columns onto the front page, and the public began to take sides. Letters flowed into Webb's office, some hysterically accusing him of persecuting an innocent woman, others lauding him for upholding, in a decadent era, the remnants of a moral code. The photographs of the senior Mrs. Hobart reflected the opinions of the editors. In some she appeared like a savage old witch, who must have wanted the children only to put them in her oven; in others she looked noble and sad, as if forced out of a well-earned retirement to face bravely the mud of a lawsuit to save her posterity. Georgette, in similar fashion, was shown either at El Morocco in a paper hat blowing a whistle, or hiding her face with a handbag as, weeping, she hurried into the courthouse in Mineola for a pretrial examination. Peyton telephoned daily from California, worried about what "Ma" was going through, and if Webb had not feared that Cup might be tapping the wire, he would have replied that she was having the time of her life.

It was a war in which victory was bound to go to the side that could hold out for the last fifteen minutes, which made it the greater torture for Webb when Hobart, despite all his lawyer's passionate telephone invocations and encouraging epistles, collapsed. Olive could not abide California; she had to return to New York, and Peyton, driven to desperation and not daring to express his surrender orally or by letter, sent a peremptory telegram, demanding a settlement with Georgette. Webb, disgusted and wrathful, sat in his office in silent gloom for half an hour before he finally asked his secretary to call Cup.

"But he's here, Mr. Webb," she told him. "He's

been waiting in the reception room for fifteen minutes. You said you would see nobody."

"Send him in, for the love of Mike!"

The moment Cup appeared in the doorway, Webb knew that he had won. He was too old a hand in the art of appearances not to recognize that defiant, sulking half-grin and the furtive glitter of those eyes. As he rose to usher his opponent to a seat, his heart went out to a fighter betrayed as he himself had been.

"Mr. Webb," Cup began in a wistful, reflective tone, "I've come to make one last effort to see if you and I can't straighten out this sorry mess. I think the time has come for us to rise above partisanship and to consider the real victims of this tragedy: two small, helpless children, who are going to be scarred for life by what has happened already."

Webb nodded gravely and admiringly. It was exactly the opening which he had planned for his own appeal. "You're right, Mr. Cup. I was telling my client only last week that the children were the greatest sufferers. I think we should each be prepared to give a little for their sakes."

"I'm very happy to hear you say that, Mr. Webb. In fact, anticipating that you might take the larger view, I have come armed with a few propositions."

And then, in half an hour, they proceeded to settle a dispute that had lasted for a year and entailed no less than six separate lawsuits. Webb conceded the custody of the children which Peyton had never really wanted, and Cup reduced his demands for money which the future Mrs. Gwinnett was never going to need. A new divorce action would be entered, and the senior Mrs. Hobart leashed. There remained only the question of fees, and for this discussion Webb and Cup lit cigars and settled back to view each other with now friendly eyes. It was immediately agreed that Peyton would pay both lawyers. The husband, in such cases, always did.

"I've been over my time sheets," Cup said with a sigh, "and even cutting the wretched business to cost, I don't see how I can do it for less than thirty-five."

Webb took a long puff of his cigar and closed one

eye as he stared at his crystal inkwell. Thirty-five thousand was what he had decided to charge Peyton, exclusive of out-of-state counsel costs, but it was preferable to be able to show him that he was charging less than Georgette's lawyer. "I presume that doesn't include the custody suit."

Cup's expression betrayed surprise only in that it betrayed nothing. "Oh, of course, not," he said promptly. "I shall want another seventy-five hundred for that."

Webb put down his cigar carefully and slowly rose to his feet. "Mr. Cup," he said as he extended his hand across the desk, "I think we have a deal."

As they shook hands warmly, they might have been two old veteran soldiers, emerging from opposing trenches, having fought each other long and well, to embrace on the morning of an armistice brought about by politicians behind the lines, an armistice that was, in the bitter opinion of each, a disgrace to both their nations.

A year and a half later Waldron Webb made one of his rare excursions into the countryside to attend the firm outing which was held annually, under the auspices of Clitus Tilney, at the Glenville Beach Club on Long Island's north shore. Webb always dreaded these outings, as he had never played golf or tennis, hated the water and did not wish to become identified with the small, repulsive, story-swapping group that spent the afternoon in the bar. He was the kind of lawyer who was happy only in his home, in his office or in court, and it was not pleasant to be protected and entertained by an expansive and condescending Tilney, perspiring after eighteen holes on the golf course, who seemed to find the rewards of a successful professional life, as manifested in the gleaming yellow pavilion and red umbrellas of his club, as exhilarating as the work itself. Yes, Tilney, taking his arm for a stroll down the terrace, Tilney, pointing out his eminent fellow members lying about on the sand, Tilney laughing loudly at remarks of Webb that he hadn't quite heard, might be treating him as a co-consul of the little empire of Tower, Tilney & Webb, but wasn't it the treatment that the aging and muscular, the still romantic Mark Antony, had meted out to a stout and puffing Lepidus?

"Now there's a sight that ought to interest you, Waldron," Tilney said, pausing and waving an arm towards a group of children playing in the sand by what appeared to be two pairs of parents. Under the umbrellas, all in bathing suits, with pails and shovels for the children and cocktails for the adults, they made up a gay and colorful group. On the porch nearby two large grey, black-hooded baby carriages with shining spoked wheels were being rocked by two nurses in white. "Don't you recognize your old client?"

Webb stared into the group until he made out the familiar boyish features, under the dark suntan and over the unfamiliar brown bare lissome torso, of Peyton Hobart.

"Is that his new wife with him?"

"His new wife?" Tilney tilted his head back and let out his high, mocking laugh. "Bless you, my friend, it's *both* his wives. Let me read you the dramatis personae, starting from left to right. It's a lesson in Long Island mores!" Tilney cleared his throat and proceeded to point boldly from one figure to the next. "Over here, we have two infants, tended by two expensive white-robed presences. They are little Olive Hobart, child of your client and his second spouse, and little Button Gwinnett, named for the ancestral singer, child of Georgette and Tommy. Playing near the carriages are Tommy Gwinnett's three daughters by his first wife, the two Marsden boys, and the Hobart boy and girl over whose custody you raised such a rumpus. Turning now to the adults, you will observe how peace and concord have returned at last to the shores of Long Island Sound. The four individuals drinking gin in the bright sunlight and laughing the laughter of youth, are, besides your client, the following: his present wife, Olive, his former wife, Georgette, and her present husband, Tommy Gwinnett."

Webb stared in fascination at that beautiful, promiscuous, near-naked quartet, with their host of beautiful, near-naked children. Who would have believed that a scant eighteen months before they had been engaged in no less than six bitter lawsuits? And now, with children tumbling over each other and over them (children who hardly knew, perhaps, which adult was a parent and which a stepparent), laughing and sipping gin, making jokes, perhaps, of their old days of discord, making jokes—oh, agony to think of!—of their "little men downtown" who had taken their squabbles with such amusing, passionate seriousness, they might have been the foreground in an advertisement of an exotic foreign car, so congenial, so gay, so pearly-toothed, did they all appear.

"Rabbits," he muttered angrily to his partner as they turned back to the club house. "They're nothing but rabbits. People like that don't deserve the time the courts waste over them. They should do their breeding without the sanction of law!"

THE DEDUCTIBLE YACHT

THE KIPS always boasted that their blood was the finest in New York. They had managed to restrict it, since the eighteenth century, to the small group of families that had then been considered Manhattan society. The temptation to wade out, as the sand dried, into the endless waves of new fortunes that lapped the city had been sternly resisted. A Kip lady had been denied to a nephew of Mayor Hone in the 1830's and a Kip gentleman to a Gould heiress a half century later. Even Standard Oil would not do for the Kips, even the House of Morgan. There had been a now legendary Miss Kip, not blessed in looks or fortune, who seated alone at a ball had rejected the proffered introductions of her hostess, saying: "Thank you so much, but I'm perfectly happy sitting here and thinking what everyone in this room would give for one drop of my old Kip blood!" The Kips wanted to be left alone, and their wish had been gratified.

Inevitably, they became too numerous to be supported forever by the bit of old farmland in downtown Manhattan on which a famous office building squatted. Long before the disaster of 1929 "Kip Keep," the turreted shingle castle of the Beekman Kips in Newport had been razed, and the tall gabled matching Dutch houses on Madison Avenue of the Tyler Kip sons converted to stores. By the middle of our century the male Kips were mostly at work, as lawyers or brokers or insurance salesmen. They still managed to send their children to private schools and to get out of town in the summer, but where were the marks to set them aside from the crowd? Where were the distinguishing features?

These were the questions that disturbed Bayard Kip, who as a tax expert and, at thirty-four, an about-to-be partner in Tower, Tilney & Webb was considered the prodigy of the family. But what was a Bayard Kip who had to help his wife with the dishes and take his children to the park on Sundays? What was a Bayard Kip who had to hire a sitter when he went out in the evening and whose apartment rang with television phrases? Were there not thousands such? Was not this fatal competence in adaptation more extinguishing to a family than any other quality? Bayard might polish and repolish his London shoes and wear waistcoats throughout the hottest summer; he might roll his umbrella until it was as thin as a cane and wear the darkest suits and the darkest ties—it was all no use. The face that looked back at him in the morning from his grandfather's mahogany-framed shaving mirror had none of the high-cheekboned, hooknosed superciliousness of a colonial governor, none of what Bayard's grandmother, pronouncing it in French, had called *race*. It was a mild, soft-eyed, square-jawed, straight-nosed blemishless American face. It might have been looking at him from across a soda fountain.

The government agents and auditors with whom he had to work seemed equally unaware that he had any particular claim to distinction. They found him reserved, impassive, even "stuffy," but his patience with every demand, his quiet reasonableness in argument and his clear, exact mind for figures made him a popular lawyer to deal with. One of the agents, a hard-fisted, cynical Irishman, Tommy Reardon, became almost a friend. Reardon was intrigued by Bayard's economic philosophy which he liked to describe as somewhat to the right of Louis XIV.

"Does it never occur to you," he asked Bayard at lunch after they had completed auditing a great building contractor's return, "that there's something wrong with a country whose best brains are spent in attacking and defending the shenanigans of an old trickster like Inka Dahduh?"

"You will understand that I must disassociate myself from any such description of a client," Bayard replied in a cool but unindignant tone.

"You know what Dahduh is! Far better than I. A man who never went to school, much less college. A man whose highest ideal is to give nothing for something! Yet here we are, two well-educated, thinking

men with consciences and ideals, utterly absorbed in his
shifty little deals. You trying to sweep them under the
rug and I to sweep them out!"

"I have swept nothing of Mr. Dahduh's under the
rug," Bayard insisted.

"All right, leave him out of it. Let's just say a
client. Surely you won't maintain that *all* your clients
are angels?"

"Let me put it this way," Bayard said, after a moment of judicious reflection. "I believe that all the returns which I have prepared—or which have been prepared under my supervision—represent an honest dis-
closure of the pertinent facts."

"Oh, for Pete's sake, Kip!" Reardon exclaimed impatiently. "Isn't it bad enough for you to have to work
for these new tycoons without justifying them? All this
easy money, these phony deductions, these blown-up
expense accounts, these crazy corporate shells—all this
slick financing to give the public a shoddy product—
why must *you* defend it? What do you get out of it
but a wretched salary, fully taxable, at that? Where
are your deductions? You remind me of those ladies'
maids in the French Revolution who followed their
mistresses to the scaffold because they were too blind
to see that the Jacobins were their real friends!"

"Is that what you plan for us, Tommy? The
scaffold?"

"Well, if we could have *your* head, my friend, Uncle
Sam would collect a lot more taxes!"

They laughed and parted, as usual, friends, but
Reardon's comparison to the ladies' maids rankled
deeply in Bayard's heart. For Inka Dahduh, the son
of an Armenian rug peddler who now owned buildings
in every part of the city, was to Bayard the incarna-
tion of the destroying spirit that had laid low the poor
old shabby, genteel past. Whole blocks of beautiful
sober red-faced Federal houses had fallen before his
bulldozers; churches and shrines had been sacrificed to
make way for his thinly built, highly priced, spare
grey cubes. And Inka himself looked like a conquering
Tartar, a scimitar-swinging Tamburlaine, smiling at the
discomfort of his victims. He was a tall, wide-shoul-

dered, big-stomached, formidable man, with a blue complexion, a hawk nose, glittering black eyes and long thick oiled black hair, who spoke with a rumble and laughed in the sudden, explosive way of one whose temper, however massive, is always at the service of his shrewdness. He lived on top of one of his many buildings in a penthouse constructed of glass and bamboo, in the great bare reception halls of which, painted red and yellow and gold, hung his Pollocks and De Koonings and Klees, and through which sauntered the endlessly eclectic assembly of his guests.

Dahduh, on the other hand, regarded Bayard with the greatest admiration, It gave him especial pleasure to watch this cool young man, cool on the hottest day in the hottest conference, the only person not in shirt-sleeves, work out the most tangled problems with the aid of a slide rule and a single sheet of paper in one corner of which his sharp pencil jotted the minimum of figures. "It's old New York," Dahduh would announce triumphantly to the partners of his venture. "My little Kip here is a bit of ancient Yankee stock. He can even teach the old Armenian tricks!" Bayard at such moments felt like a captive Athenian scholar in the court of a Macedonian king.

But the most burdensome part of his duties for the builder were social. Dahduh had an old yacht on which he liked to take a motley group of helpless guests for weekend outings in Long Island Sound, and on the Sunday afternoon following the day of his lunch with Reardon, Bayard and his wife were included in one of these. Peggy Kip was a bright-eyed, tense little woman, with a habit of always pursing her lips, and although she did not share her husband's umbrage at the present obscurity of the Kips, being quite contented with the mild distinction in her little set conveyed by such heirlooms as the Duncan Phyfe horsehair sofa and the Eastman Johnson conversation piece, she had to the fullest the Kip sense that anybody, be he Pope or President, who was in any way "different" was "funny." And Inka Dahduh was the funniest of all. She made no effort to mix with the other guests, but sat at the long table in the main saloon, turning the pages of the visitors' log with half-suppressed giggles.

"I suppose I'm being awful," she whispered to Bayard with perfunctory remorse. "I suppose I should be more respectful."

It was true, of course, that she was behaving badly and that the wife of any other clerk in Tower, Tilney & Webb would have been up on deck with the host uttering little squeals of admiration over the boat and its fixtures. But Bayard had never asked Peggy to be a good office wife; he would have scorned to do so. He did, however, observe, over the slowly widening gulf between her domestic preoccupations and his long downtown hours, that it never seemed to occur to her that she owed him more.

"If you find the visitors' log amusing, why shouldn't you express your amusement?" he asked.

"Doesn't it amuse *you?*"

"Ought it to?"

"It's so vulgar, Bayard! All those passée movie actresses with their florid messages. It's like an old copy of *Movie Mirror!*"

"I sometimes think there's nothing so vulgar as poor gentility," he said with a small sigh. "But let me look at it. This yacht is supposed to be used for business entertainment."

"Is that what you call business?" Peggy demanded with a snort, pointing to where Inka was standing on the fantail, the arm of a blonde tucked under his. "If I amused Mr. Dahduh, would you let him deduct me?"

Bayard's gaze followed her impertinent finger and rested for a long moment on his host. Then he turned with a new interest to the log. In fact, in the ensuing half hour he examined every one of its pages. Although he was not familiar with the names of stage and screen, the exclamatory messages beside the signatures, the poems and limericks in the margin, the caricatures drawn all over, the dirty pictures, made it entirely clear that he was not dealing with an assemblage of brokers or contractors. As he was closing the book he felt a friendly grip on his shoulder, and the rumbly voice from above his head demanded:

"Quite a varied group of friends, isn't it Bayard?"

"That's what I was trying to determine. *Is* it?"

Inka, however, seemed unconscious of any special meaning in his lawyer's tone. "You should mingle with the others, you and your pretty wife," he continued. "You should meet my guests and not just read about them. They may not be in the Social Register, but they can teach you a thing or three. That's why I keep this yacht. It's like a desert island, on which we're stranded. We're cut off from our roots and all the little props that we depend on. For one afternoon we have to be on our own. We have to rely on our wits and our tongues. We have to amuse. Yes, my dear Bayard, you can learn a lot from a day at sea. It's an experiment with democracy!"

As their host moved off, waving his big cigar in the air, Bayard followed his broad retreating back with narrowed eyes. Peggy, who never seemed to listen to a thing he said, had a way of noticing his smallest change of expression. "Now, Bayard, you're not going to get in one of your moods, are you? What do we care what he uses his silly yacht for?"

"I happen to care very much."

"Oh, dear," she said apprehensively. "Why couldn't I keep my mouth shut? What are going to do now?"

"Do?" Bayard's tone was detached again. "I'm going to do what our host suggests. I'm going to take a little stroll on deck and meet my fellow passengers. I'm going to rely on my wits and my tongue. I'm going to find out exactly what each and every one of them does for a living! And *why* they're here."

Lying awake early the next Monday morning and gazing from the faded shepherdesses of their bedroom wallpaper to the flaking paint of the ceiling, Bayard prepared in his mind, with a grim, tense satisfaction, the things that he would do when he got to the office. He would take the Dahduh income tax returns to Mr. Madison and lay them on his desk with a slight respectful bow. "If *you* wish to sign these, here they are, sir. I'm afraid I can no longer be responsible for defrauding the Collector." He smiled a thin smile as he imagined the habitual look of preoccupation on the long grey face of the senior tax partner as it would dissolve into astonishment. "What's that? What?" And then anger. Anger and recrimination. Bayard rose quietly so as not to disturb Peggy and went to the window with a suddenly quickening heartbeat to stare down at the back yard of the apartment house with its garbage pails and two bare trees. Would it cost him his partnership? Did he care?

At breakfast with the children he gave a lecture on the use of "Good morning" instead of "Hi." In the subway he read the market news and a tax periodical. And all the while his curious exhilaration persisted. He remembered the French duchess in the revolution that his friend Reardon loved to cite, who, on the verge of denying her correspondence with the enemy, suddenly shrugged and said: "No, no, life isn't worth a lie." That was it. No boasting of moral superiority, no vulgar dramatic oratory, no affectation of heroism—simply a shrug and a life tossed away. If one was a Kip, there was, after all, a gesture still to be made, a gesture that for all its quietness was a repudiation of rottenness, a repudiation, indeed, of the whole wretched age in which he had to live. Had not the first Bayard Kip been ruined for resisting the Astors? Had not his own great-grandfather lost a fortune by disdaining the bribes of Jim Fisk? They had consciences as simple as the brownstone behind which they had lived, consciences that stemmed from the quaint old days of eighteenth century finance, consciences that antedated the venality of steam and oil. Bayard was grateful to the son of an Armenian rug peddler for providing him with the opportunity to show that the Kips still stood apart.

Mr. Madison did not disappoint him. His bewilderment and irritation were all that Bayard had hoped.

"But why do *you* have to be the judge of what's a business deduction?" he demanded fretfully. "Why do you have to go snooping into what he uses the yacht for? The client *tells* you it's for business. All right, put it in the return that way."

"I have. But I won't sign it."

"But Dahduh will blow up—" Madison stopped when he saw Bayard's shrug. "Look, Bayard, I'm not asking

you to do anything dishonest. I simply want you to recognize that if we do make you a partner, it will be
largely to work on Dahduh's matters. He *depends* on
you!"

"I know he does," Bayard said grimly. "He depends
on my signature. If he's ever prosecuted, he can always
make the defense that his lawyer signed the return."

"But damn it all, you can't *know* all the uses he puts
that yacht to!"

"That's just it. I can."

"Well, *I* can't!" Madison exclaimed angrily, picking
up the return. "And *I* can sign it!"

"As you wish," Bayard said quietly and withdrew.

He did not see Madison again that day, but the real
scene occurred that evening when he told Peggy.

"I think it's the meanest thing I ever heard!" she
wailed. "You're going to blast your career at the office
because *I* sneered at Mr. Dahduh."

"You were right to sneer at him."

"But I never thought you'd *do* anything about it.
All I meant was that I didn't want to see him *socially*."

"You think it's all right to make your living off a
man like that provided you don't see him socially?"

"Well, *naturally*. Hasn't that always been the rule?"

"It has never been mine," Bayard said sternly. "Nor
has it ever been that of my family. It may interest you
to know that my great-grandfather Kip lost a . . ."

"It may *not* interest me to know it!" she exclaimed
fiercely. "It may interest me to know that you care more
about your silly family pride that you do about your
wife and children! I believe you're actually *happy* about
this thing. I bet you did it to spite me!"

Bayard, however, was little touched by her hysteria.
After all, the children were not going to starve. Only
promotion was at stake, and it was clear that Peggy, a
creature of her age, was not willing to sacrifice the
smallest part of it for integrity, that she expected him to
succumb to the modern sentimentality of basing moral
decisions on the material needs of his family. But things
were right or wrong, and life was only worth living if
one acted with some consistency in the face of this
simple premise. Peggy's charge that he was motivated

by a desire to hurt her was quite irrelevant. Motives mattered only if one asked for credit, and he was asking for none.

It was an anticlimax, therefore, the next day, when he was summoned to Madison's office, to be ushered into the big smiling presence of Inka himself.

"Bayard, my boy," he said, putting a thick arm over the younger man's slim shoulders, "I want you to come straight to Daddy Dahduh when you have doubts about his virtue. Don't leave the job to poor old Madison here. When I walked into his office this morning I caught him in the act of signing my returns. 'Hey, there,' I said, 'isn't that Bayard's job?' Well, he started to explain, and you should have heard him stammer! The great Morris Madison, the glibbest advocate before the Tax Court! But I gradually made out that you think your friend Inka's a fraud and a phony. All right, so he's a fraud and a phony! But don't you think you owed it to me to come and tell me so yourself?"

"It wasn't my place as an associate," Bayard explained in his gravest manner, "to make that kind of communication to a client of Mr. Madison's."

"Oh, I *see*," Inka said, nodding emphatically. "Well, then, let us hope that you may not be an associate forever. But to the question of my poor old yacht. Of course we'll knock the deduction out of the return. I would have done so myself had I only thought of it. She was originally used for business, but in the past months—you're quite right—she's been more of a personal plaything. As a matter of fact, I wonder if the time hasn't come to get rid of her. Do you know any yacht brokers, Bayard, my friend?"

They were both grinning at him, Madison and Inka, but Bayard did not grin back. He was disturbed to recognize the sudden little weight in his heart as disappointment, and he remembered what Peggy had said.

Promotion, when it came, came as it so often does, fast. In two months' time Bayard was a junior partner with an office overlooking the East River, a full-time secretary and his lunch club dues paid. Peggy was able to redecorate the apartment and have the family pictures cleaned and the silver lacquered. For the little family party at which they celebrated this advancement a butler was hired, and Bayard, sipping his sherry under the now gleaming Rembrandt Peale of General Kip and glimpsing through the freshly painted, open doors of the dining room and glitter of the old candelabra, began to feel that the Kips were coming back to life. It was a bit startling to have life turn out to be as simple as his own principles, to have the ashes of martyrdom so promptly converted into the downy pillows of success, but mightn't it be the ultimate justification of his lifelong adherence to the creed that a family, with faith and tenacity, *could* stay on top?

When he next lunched with his friend Reardon, the latter was in ribald mood.

"So you've decided to be a lady's maid no longer," he commented. "You've decided to be a marquise."

"I figure the knife of your guillotine won't feel any sharper."

"Oh, that knife. It's dulled with disuse. As dull as your conscience, man."

Bayard examined those laughing eyes which so ill concealed their resentment. "I know you think that one pays with a bit of soul for each step up in the great world outside of government," he retorted. "Yet in my own case I have found just the opposite to be true. I have found that clients appreciate honest advice, even when it proves expensive to them."

"What kind of honest advice?"

"I was thinking particularly of the propriety or impropriety of certain business deductions."

"Oh, that yacht of Dahduh's," Reardon said with a snort. "I know all about that. The whole main shaft was split. He stung the Better Brands Company for it, and they're charging it off as a bad loss this year."

Bayard's unflinching stare reflected nothing. "You suggest that he was going to get rid of the yacht anyway?"

"I suggest that he was killing two birds with one stone. He got rid of a leaky old tub that might have taken him to the bottom of the sea and acquired in-

stead the lifetime devotion of a brilliant young tax lawyer of unimpeachable respectability. I should say he
had a bargain."

Bayard opened his lips in a faint smile. "So I've been
bought, is that it?"

"Not bought, no. Men like Dahduh don't buy. They
acquire. He needs your advice and the name of your
firm, and he's willing to pay high for it. But what he *does*
with that advice, you'll never quite know. He has his
accountants. And *other* tax lawyers. On a lower level.
And one thing you can be sure of, old man. He's tipped
his hand once to you, and he's learned not to do it
again. All the plays that you'll see from now on will
be straight as arrows."

"Can a lawyer ask more?" Bayard queried coolly
and turned his attention to the menu.

Nobody watching Bayard walk back down Wall
Street after lunch, carrying his tightly rolled umbrella
despite the spring sunshine, would have suspected that
he had received the bitterest shock of his life. He nodded with the same quiet gravity to the receptionist as
he entered the office and with his usual brief smile to
his secretary. But once in his own room, behind a
closed door and seated at his desk, he raised his finger-
tips gently to his temples and closed his weary eyes.
Life, he admitted, was too much for his simple philosophy. One tried to do right and one's wife accused
one of spite. One tried to fight wrong, and the enemy
turned up after the bout in even richer ermine. Perhaps the lesson of it all was that the *appearances* to
which he had so clung, the old family appearances of
honor and scrupulousness, of dignity and aristocratic
distinction, were, after all, the only things that could
be preserved.

He opened his top drawer and drew from it a
photograph of a small, high-gabled, gingerbread villa in
Newport which had just been left to him by his uncle,
Maturin Kip, of whose estate it had been one of the few
assets. It was a bit crazy looking and in poor repair,
but it had been designed by Richard Upjohn in 1853,
and it was unique. Bayard and Peggy had been carefully over their accounts and had reluctantly decided

that they were not yet in a position to afford a summer place. But now he decided that they would risk it. They would be Mr. and Mrs. Bayard Kip, of New York and Newport. They would be listed in the summer, as well as the winter, Social Register. And the old house, with a new coat of paint and a well-kept lawn, would be a credit again to Bellevue Avenue.

THE "TRUE STORY"
OF LAVINIA TODD

LAVINIA and Chambers Todd had been married for twenty-five years. Almost all of these had been spent in Plandome, Long Island, in two houses, first in a small yellow cube in a development and later in a more pretentious Tudor dwelling in the fashionable residential area. They had been happy, busy years, she taken up with her children and home and he with the demands of his law practice. Life had been too full for them to become too critical of each other. She had taken for granted that behind the dark, stocky figure of her irritable but preoccupied husband there still lurked the boy she had deemed so romantic in their common childhood in Hartford, that with more freedom from the clutching demands of Tower, Tilney & Webb he would have shown the interest in his wife and children of the ideal suburbanite. And he had seemed contented with her neat, chintzy house, her circle of girl friends with whose husbands he sometimes played golf and the decisions (all taken by her) as to the education and social life of the children. Leisure had come, at least to her, as the latter had grown up, but she had managed to use it, in her slow, occasionally clumsy but always determined fashion, in the cultivation of the arts: a French class, a painting class, even a class in current events. Until it had all come abruptly to an end.

For the children, a boy and a girl, had married early and well, and Chambers, who had now risen to the position immediately under the senior partner, announced to Lavinia that they were moving to the city to take a more active part in the social life necessitated by an expanding practice. They rented an apartment on Park Avenue, had it furnished expensively by a decorator, and Lavinia, when they were not giving dinner parties for visiting executives or being entertained themselves at restaurants, found that she had nothing to do. For Chambers this new life seemed the

end to which all of their old had been simply the
means. For her the means had been enough.

It was not that Chambers expected her to do nothing.
Far from it. He expected her to improve her bridge
game, to develop a circle of friends from the ranks of
the Social Register, to become a member of the Colony
Club, in brief, to carry the banner of his law firm into
places where men could not penetrate. But it was not
merely a question of her own disinclination to do these
things; it was one of her actual incapacity. She had
been pretty enough and bright enough when she had
married Chambers; she had been a Smith graduate, after
all, and an English major. But somehow with the
years her native enthusiasm had degenerated almost
to gushiness, her love of home to a habit of talking too
much about her children and her nervous intensity, her
most attractive gift, to a near shrillness. The freckled
sophomore with the winning smile and scattered blond
hair was now a matron of large hips and shoulders
(she dieted so desperately that, half starved, she would
go on eating benders fatal to her purpose), of hair
too often waved and too tightly matted to the scalp,
of pale skin and firm, square jaw, of dresses with too
many colors and hats with too many flowers, and of
the big, blue, frightened eyes of a stubborn child. It
was inevitable that, confronted with easy, graceful,
harshly laughing Manhattan ladies, her diffidence should
be intensified to sullenness.

Chambers was blunt in his criticisms and suggestions.
"Stick close to Ada Tilney. She may not seem to have
much style, but people respect her, and I'm sure her
word at the Colony Club would go a long way. Then
there's Peggy Kip. She may be a bit snooty, but she
knows everything and everyone in old New York."

"But I don't care about old New York!" Lavinia protested. "I care about people for what they are, not
who they are. Really, Chambers, you're talking like
the most awful snob!"

"It has nothing to do with snobbishness," he retorted
testily. "It has to do with the good of the firm."

"Not just the good of Chambers Todd?"

"Well, I'm a member of the firm, aren't I? Your

trouble is that you take everything too hard. That's why you don't get on better at dinner parties. The other night, at the Gages' I saw the men on both sides of you talking the other way."

"What was I expected to do? Pull them by the ear?"

"If necessary. But I bet you'd bored them to death talking about the children."

"Well, what's wrong with talking about my children?" Lavinia demanded indignantly. "I'm proud of my children!"

"Yes, but you can't expect other people to be."

"That fancy Mrs. Newbold you admire so much talks about *her* children. She held forth all night about how unfair it was that her boy was kicked out of St. Mark's!"

"When you occupy a position like Florence Newbold's," Chambers replied crushingly, "you can talk about anything you want."

What she could never understand was why *he* got on as well as he did in the world that she found so difficult. He had emerged from a quarter of a century of downtown labor totally ignorant, so far as she could see, of all fields but law and finance. And even in law, she observed, he had confined himself to the special tools of his corporate practice. She had once read a layman's history of English jurisprudence in the hope of being able to stimulate him to further conversation in their evenings at home, but he had never heard of the Statute of *Quia Emptores* or the Rule in Shelley's case, which the author had seemed to regard as basic. In the arts he lacked even a superficial smattering. Lavinia was convinced that he had never read a play of Shakespeare, unless part of *Julius Caesar* in high school and that he would not have blinked an eye had she told him that *Parsifal* was a symphony by Brahms. Yet he did not hesitate now at parties to wade with big feet into discussions of modern art or poetry and to dilute the thin clear streams of intellect with the dirty water of generality until they were full enough for multitudes to splash about in. "What do you suppose a man thinks about when he paints a picture like that?" Lavinia would hear him across the room standing before their hostess' Picasso. The heaviness of his approaches was not lightened, either, by his new habit of drinking three cocktails in rapid succession before dinner. After these he tended to become sentimental, his eyes moistened, and he would sometimes place his hand on top of a pretty dinner partner's as he told her of his long hard climb to the altitude where he was privileged to meet such as her. Ugh!

"My goodness, what a handsome husband you have!" women would say to her. "One would never dream he was over fifty." There would be no comment, of course, about her own appearance giving rise to any such incredulity. "Such dark, ruthless looks. One feels Mr. Todd would be a very just judge but a very stern one. That must be why he understands instinctively so many things he couldn't possibly have had time to study!"

Well, Lavinia could hardly blame them for being taken in by Chambers' looks. She had been herself. There had never been room in her heart for any image but that of the clear-skinned, square-jawed, stiffly muscular high school boy who had supported his mother by working in a bakery at night and who had nearly killed poor Hank Porter for asking for a date with Lavinia Frink. But she doubted that he would have won her so easily had he courted her with the eyes that now beamed at Mrs. Newbold, the eyes of a small boy preparing to blow out a birthday candle.

"He sees through us," Florence Newbold told Lavinia one night when she had been unable to avoid the boredom of two minutes' talk with her. "He sees through us all!"

In a way it was true. Chambers was shrewd about people. But what was unfathomable to Lavinia was how anyone, having once seen through Mrs. Newbold's set, could want any part of it. All during the Plandome years Chambers had shown a lack of interest in his neighbors and in their trifling advancements, in whether they had one car or two and how soon they could afford a summer cabin in the White Mountains, which she had interpreted as the lofty disregard of the dedicated professional man for the outward indicia of success, a disregard, too, which had seemed to her totally consistent with the unflinching stare of that high school boy's unimpressed eyes. And now it seemed that all the while his scorn of the different gradations of Plandome success had been merely the snobbishness of one who had no intention of remaining there, or, worse, the cautiousness of one who wished to avoid too many Plandome ties that might be troublesome when he had moved to the greater world of East Side Manhattan. And the moist eye, the gesticulating hand, the oddly high, post-cocktail laugh were like those wedding presents that had been considered too grand for the young couple and been put away for twenty-five years to be brought out now, out of date but usable, to adorn the long fancy table whose image, unbeknownst to her, had been fixed in his mind as the goal of a lifetime that she had believed consecrated to more serious things.

She got little enough sympathy from her children. Judith, married in Plandome, was a small, pretty, cool blond version of her father, and she and Chambers liked to play at what sometimes struck Lavinia as a rather cynical pantomime of the close, excluding, American father-daughter relationship.

"You mustn't be jealous of people liking Daddy," Judith warned her, "or of his wanting to go out more. He's entitled to branch out a bit now. Lord knows, he's worked hard enough for it."

"But I'm not jealous," Lavinia protested. "I'm envious. I only wish people liked *me*. How do you suppose he does it?"

"By being big and healthy and outgiving. By being so obviously a man who knows what he's after and gets it."

"You mean they want to touch him for good luck?"

"You must fight your habit of sarcasm, Mummy," Judith reproached her. It was amazing, Lavinia reflected, how quickly Judith's bright little box of domestic happiness had isolated her from human sympathy. "If you're bored, you should develop a hobby. Something with your hands is always best. What about those flower paintings you used to do?"

"Oh Judith, they were terrible!"

"What about pottery, then? Charles has an invalid aunt who can make the most beautiful ash trays you ever saw!"

Fritz showed more feeling for his mother, having inherited some of her intensity, but he was a melancholy young man who worried about his advertising firm and a cross, plain wife who had taken it firmly into her head that Lavinia's sole purpose in life was to recapture and redominate her son. He hardly dared to see his mother except in his wife's presence, and Lavinia did not find the atmosphere receptive to any discussion of her own problems. Nor could she very well complain to the abandoned friends of Plandome or to the wives of Chambers' partners. She was truly alone.

Her need for communication came to a burst at Ada Tilney's annual tea for the office wives. Lavinia had always found these gatherings difficult since her junior days when she had been afraid of the older women, and now she hated to think that she struck the younger wives in the same way. That day she felt particularly low, having had a terrible row with Chambers at breakfast. He had criticized her for contributing nothing to a conversation at Mrs. Newbold's about a Samuel Beckett play.

"You're always telling me those people discuss things you don't know anything about," he had observed. "But you'd been to that show, hadn't you? Couldn't you have said *something?*"

"I could have if Mrs. Newbold had been serious. But she admitted she hadn't seen the play."

"What of it? She had everybody roaring at her take-off of those two men in barrels."

"And being funny is all that counts, isn't it?"

"What else, at parties?"

"Chambers," she had protested desperately, "I tried to tell you about that play, and you wouldn't listen. You'd rather hear Mrs. Newbold talk about something she hasn't seen than your wife about something she has!"

"There you go, making a drama out of it. Lord knows, that's one kind of theatre I get enough of. Why can't you make just a *little* effort to be the kind of wife a successful man needs? Is it a sin to be attractive and gay? Is it a sin to be popular? Is it a sin to make your husband proud of you when he goes out?"

"You should have married a woman like Mrs. Newbold!"

"I wasn't in a position to. *Then.*"

His brutal adverb dazed her, and at Ada Tilney's she found that she was still in a state resembling shock. Yet for the first time, as she sat at the end of the dining room table, taking her turn serving tea, murmuring inquiries and greetings as she handed out cups, it struck her that there might be something in common between her plight and that of the other older women. Mrs. Waldron Webb, for example. Not even the shyest clerk's wife could have found anything formidable about her. She looked at every woman who approached her as if she expected to be slapped in the face. And even Ada Tilney, for all her seeming serenity, gave the appearance of one faintly surprised to find herself dispensing hospitality. Had either of them ever really expected to end up where she now was?

A little group of younger wives gathered cautiously about Lavinia, and she heard herself asking the questions that she had been asked two decades before. "Do you think your husband will be able to get off this summer? No? Isn't it terrible? What slaves we women are. Perhaps we should all stand together and strike for better hours." It was the standard partner's wife's comment, to pretend to the juniors that they shared a prison. Some of the inmates, to be sure, had better cells than others, but cells were still cells. The Tilneys were the wardens, to be criticized only with a smile that meant one was making conversation. One could be anything, even a Communist, for the sake of keeping up the conversation at an office party.

"You must be sure always to keep that figure of yours, my dear," Lavinia was surprised to hear herself say to a young woman with bright brown eyes and soft brown hair and the whitest skin of the party. The group of wives had moved away, and Lavinia found herself alone with this obviously intelligent, lively creature whom she could not remember having seen before. "No,

I mean it," she continued, reaching to take a macaroon from her hand. "Don't ever lose that figure. You'll *never* get it back."

The girl laughed, a pleasant rough laugh. "But why should I worry about my figure, Mrs. Todd? Isn't it better to lose it once and for all and get it over with? And then relax in a heaven of macaroons?"

"What about your husband? Won't he object?"

"I don't have one yet."

"Oh?" Lavinia felt even more confused. "Are you one of the lawyers, then?"

"Not even that. I'm Fran Tilney. I just came in to help Mother out. As you see, by eating her macaroons."

"Oh, how silly of me. Of course I know you. But then, as Chambers says, I'm hopeless about names. As a matter of fact, I'm hopeless about everything."

And then it happened. Lavinia had never done such a thing in public before, and what surprised her most was how little she cared. She simply sat there, perfectly erect in her chair at the end of the long table, tears running down her cheeks, and emitting a series of gasping sobs. Nobody but Miss Tilney seemed to notice her, and Miss Tilney was magnificent.

"Let's go upstairs, Mrs. Tood," she said as easily as if it were a question of adjusting a slip. "Let's get away from all these people. Of course, you're not feeling well. It was very good of you to make the effort to come at all."

She took Lavinia by the arm as firmly and quietly as if she had been a nurse and, after helping her to her feet, led her slowly from the room. When Ada Tilney moved swiftly to the door to meet them, her daughter nodded her away with an abrupt litle headshake. Lavinia, grateful and ashamed, half expected to find a clean, turned down bed in the little den on the third floor to which she was taken. Miss Tilney made her sit on the sofa and got her some whiskey.

"Would you like me to sit with you?" she asked. "Or would you prefer to be alone for a bit?"

"Oh, no, please stay, dear. You're such a nice girl, and I feel quite at ease already. In spite of that ghastly scene. I've been tired." She sighed as she gazed into the younger woman's bright, sympathetic countenance and wondered what she could do in return for such kindness. "Don't marry a lawyer, my dear. Not if you can help it."

"But I can't." Miss Tilney's laugh was easy and gay. "I'm engaged to one."

"Well, maybe it's all right if he's not in a big firm."

"But he is. He's in Tower, Tilney."

"Oh, my dear," Lavinia groaned. "You look to me as if you were made for better things."

"You think I should get out of it?"

Lavinia could see by her smile that it was all a joke to her. A joke at which she would have laughed aloud had she not wanted to be nice to a pathetic old woman. "All I can do is tell you what happened to me," she said dolefully. "Perhaps you would come and see me some afternoon."

"Why not tell me now?"

Lavinia, looking deeply again into those kind brown eyes, suddenly felt that she could. "You should go down to the others," she murmured doubtfully.

"I'd much rather sit here with you."

Lavinia finished her small glass of whiskey and then proceeded, in sentences that seemed to spring from her lips fully formed, as if prepared for a year, sentences whose structure astonished her, to tell this charming girl the story that she had never told to anyone before. Miss Tilney said nothing; she did not even nod. She simply sat, absolutely quiet and absolutely serious, until Lavinia had finished. Then, after a pause, she said gravely: "You should write that down, Mrs. Todd. Just as you've told it to me. Every word of it. And more. Much more."

"What would I do with it?"

"That doesn't matter. You would have expressed your problem. I'm a teacher, and I can tell you how rare that is. Perhaps in simply expressing it, you would solve it."

"You don't mean I should *show* it to people?"

"If you wanted to, why not? But, as I say, it wouldn't matter. You would have had your moment of truth, and that doesn't happen to one in a million."

"What a funny girl you are," Lavinia mused. "You have no other comment than that?"

Miss Tilney shook her head emphatically. "How could I presume to offer *you* advice? How could I, who am not even married yet, tell you what to do? Besides, most people's problems don't have practical solutions. I only hope you may have helped yourself by helping me."

"How could I possibly have helped you?"

"By warning me. Of what *can* happen."

Lavinia clasped her hands in dismay. "Oh, my dear, I hope I haven't made any trouble between you and your young man!"

"No." Miss Tilney's smile was radiant. "You couldn't do that."

What Lavinia would have done without the extraordinary lift that Fran Tilney had given to her spirits when she came home that night to find that her dreariest apprehension had at last been realized was something that she was often to ponder in the months that followed. For she was met at her door by the maid who told her that Mr. Todd had departed with two bags and left her a note. This was nothing in itself, as Chambers frequently left home on business trips without notice, but the moment she felt the envelope that he had left, she knew that he had written her at least four pages, and this had not happened since their marriage. She had the presence of mind, however, born of her talk to Miss Tilney, to betray nothing to the maid, but went to her room to open and read the document that she was now convinced would change her life.

The first shock was to find that it was typewritten. Chambers had not thought it worth his valuable time to spare her the humiliation of being arraigned before his secretary. As Lavinia, with reddening cheeks and coldly staring eyes, read through those terrible pages, she was conscious at all times of Mrs. Peters, so small and poised and competent, so superior to every weakness and divagation, so perfectly adapted to be the amanuensis of Chambers Todd who never had the time to smile at a subordinate, much less joke with one. She thought of Chambers, striding up and down his office as if he were dictating just another memorandum to just another difficult client, rolling out the dry words that were supposed to put the mother of his children out of his life forever.

He began by calling to her attention that they had never been really congenial, never shared the same tastes or interests, never even agreed on the simplest ways of enjoying themselves. He suggested that all real feeling had been dead between them for a decade and that nothing but good manners and a respect for the welfare of the children had prevented them from openly recognizing the fact. He pointed out that the children were now independent and that there was no reason that they should not go their separate ways. He admitted that he would like to consider an early second marriage to a more congenial spouse and hoped that she would do the same. He generously went on to state that what had happened was the fault of neither, that there was enough money for both and that they each needed a new opportunity in life. He ended the first section of his memorandum with the avowal of his determination not to allow the success for which he had worked so long to be gutted by domestic bickering.

So far she was not entirely without sympathy for him, except for the bitter fact of the dictation. She was perfectly modest about her own accomplishments as a wife and willing to recognize that if their new life had been hard on her, this very fact had made it hard on him. No man wanted to go to a party with a wet blanket. But what now followed in the memorandum was a blunt demand for her surrender. Chambers had never shown his arrogance more repulsively. He offered her an income for life of twenty-five thousand a year in return for a Mexican divorce. He warned her flatly that his terms were final and that if she went to a lawyer she would only make things harder for herself.

"He won't get away with it!" A terrible shaking fit of anger descended upon her, and she tore the memorandum into tiny pieces. The attitude of her family seemed to be that now that her function as a wife and mother was over, why was it necessary for her to embarrass them with her continued presence on the stage?

Had the curtain not risen on the glittering third act of Daddy's success? Well, they would see that she still had a function! They would see that her function might precisely be to keep them from becoming the barbarians that they wanted to be!

She knew of no divorce lawyers but one whom she had heard her husband and Waldron Webb call a "shyster," and she assumed that this meant that he had once worsted them, or at least held them at bay. She went to the Manhattan directory and sought out the number of Clarence Cup.

He was a small, quiet, reassuring man who sat at his desk with his plump little white hands folded before him while she told her story. Then he read through the memorandum which she had stitched together with Scotch tape.

"Obviously, your husband is anxious to remarry," he said, pursing his lips. "I can promise you, his divorce will cost him a great deal more than he estimates."

"But I don't want to give him a divorce at any price!" Lavinia protested indignantly. "What can I do about it?"

"Do? My dear lady, you do nothing. Nothing at all." Cup raised his clasped hands a few inches from the desk in token of the beautiful simplicity of it. "Go home and go on with your life."

"And if he comes home?"

"Let him. Isn't that where you want him?"

"And if he won't pay my bills?"

"Then telephone me." There was a little flash in Cup's dull eyes, and Lavinia sensed for the first time how such a man could stand up to Waldron Webb. "Then we will bring suit for support. But don't worry. He will pay your bills. He's only bluffing."

Lavinia felt better than she had felt since the move from Plandome as she rode home in a taxi along the glittering blue of the East River. For what had happened, sordid as it all might seem, was that she was living again. She was again in relation with her fellow beings, even if it was a bad relation. It was better to be fighting Chambers than to be resenting him.

Mr. Cup proved to be quite right. Chambers was bluffing. In two days' time, having heard nothing from his wife, he sent Judith to her as an unaccredited ambassador.

"I want you to know right off that I think Daddy's behaving outrageously," she began to her mother in a tone too cool to carry the least conviction. "I've told him so myself. I've said: 'Daddy, you know perfectly well that you've taken the best years of Mummy's life and that she's been a wonderful wife to you.' He didn't even attempt to deny it. As a matter of fact, that's what convinced me that he's absolutely determined to go through with this thing. He's so cold about it all. If there was any feeling left that I could work on . . ."

"Never mind about his feeling, Judith. Let's simply consider his duty."

"But, darling, I'm thinking of *you*." Lavinia shuddered at the term of endearment. Judith had never used it in addressing her before, and it fairly bristled with the superiority of the happily married for the abandoned woman. "I'm thinking of the position you put yourself in. How can you want to hang on to a man who—let's face it—doesn't want to stay? What does it do to your dignity?"

"Only a very young woman would think of her dignity at a time like this."

"Well, of course, Mummy, if you don't *want* my advice."

"I don't dear," Lavinia said softly. "I don't."

She had to do something to fight off the fit of loneliness that struck when Judith departed, and she decided to put her story to paper, as Miss Tilney had suggested. The idea of doing so had never been far from her mind since the day of Ada's tea party. She went to the reference room at her lending library and consulted the little shelf of books on creative writing. They mostly dealt in obvious kinds of generality, but towards the end of her afternoon she happened upon a suggestion that struck her as worth trying. The author counseled the student to write four biographical sketches

of himself in the following order: first, to appear in
Who's Who; second, to appear in the *Encyclopedia
Britannica;* third, to be used as an application for a
confidential government post and finally, to be a *New
Yorker* profile. That night, Lavinia started her homework. The *Who's Who* notice was the most depressing;
it took only three lines to give the date of her birth,
her college graduation, her marriage and the names and
birthdays of her children, · all items that seemed to
point forward—to nothing. For the *Britannica* she listed
her activities in Plandome and gave a brief summation
of Chambers' legal career. The next day she began to
warm to her task and in her government application
she tried to present her knowledge of the suburban
housewife as an asset to any agent who had to deal
with the complexities of Communist propaganda and
sabotage. And, finally, for the *New Yorker* profile she
began a study of her resentments: how many were unfair and how many were justified and how many were
the simple, unavoidable products of the role in life in
which she had found herself cast. But this last she never
finished. For in the middle of it she suddenly saw her
story as she wanted to write it—objectively, coolly, de-
void of self-pity—and she started the next morning and
worked for two days without interruption. She knew
that it was a mood that might never recur.

In the first part she told of Chambers' youth, his
poverty and patience, his kindness to his mother and
of her own easier circumstances and the terrible entrapment of their high school engagement. She empha-
sized that it did not occur to either one of them that
they were not in love until years later. What they had
was love, by their then definition. She went on to describe the extraordinary, immediate fulfillment of her
own private dreams: the first little yellow house in
Plandome, the healthy children, the women's activities,
the damp, rough cheek of her husband to kiss as he
descended from a late train on hot summer evenings.
And then, in a single paragraph, she attempted to convey her own blurred sense of the quick passage of il-
lusively happy years, culminating in the beautiful wed-
dings of son and daughter and the tears and toasts and

champagne. And then death. Quick death, after all that had seemed abundant life.

What she saw now as having happened and what she tried to explain was that overnight all her chief assets had become liabilities. Her love for her children had suddenly become possessiveness and intrusion; her yearning for the deserted house in Plandome, sentimental nostalgia; her unworldliness, a lack of imagination or simple fear. On the other hand all of Chambers' defects had by like token been turned into virtues. His indifference to the children had become a respect for their independence; his habit of buying their affection, a welcome generosity to in-laws, and his unbridled ambition a wonderful vigor in a man of his years. Yes, in a year's time she and Chambers had changed places, and in a world where any demonstrative feeling could properly exist only between newlyweds or parents and small children, Lavinia's love for her family was like a slip that showed. The new world was a world where each member of the family but herself seemed to have a happy and assured place.

The second part of her manuscript dealt with her life in New York and her sorry experiences at parties. It was a bit catty, but some of it was funny, and she enjoyed herself writing it. It had less truth in it, for she was more self-consciously shaping a social satire. When she realized that her story was changing from a memoir to a novel, she stopped abruptly. Rereading the first part she felt that she had produced something valid and good. As Miss Tilney had suggested, it was her brief rendezvous with truth, and she would not be such a fool as to tamper with it. She turned to the last page and added a final paragraph describing Chambers' demand for a divorce. After a few minutes' reflection she decided to quote his memorandum in full. It seemed fitting that her story should be told by two voices and that the last should be his.

It was typed by a public stenographer, and when she called for it, she was startled to hear the stout white-haired woman of the fast fingers and heavy breathing describe it as "riveting."

"You really liked it?"

"I haven't read anything so good in months. Plenty of people will tell you it's a natural for the *Post,* but if I were you, I'd try the *New Yorker."*

"You mean—I should *publish* it?"

"Well, honey, what else are you having it typed for?"

'Oh, just for my own amusement. And maybe a friend or so."

"Suit yourself. But I'm glad *I* read it, anyway. If you'll pardon the expression, Mrs. Todd, what a heel your husband must be. I had one rather like him myself."

"Really?"

Lavinia hurried away in horror, her cheeks ablaze to have heard her husband so described by a stranger, but by the time she had reached her apartment, the copies of her manuscript tightly clutched beneath her coat to keep them from the old doorman's eye, she was feeling so much better that her state bordered on exhilaration. Alone in her living room, she threw back her head and laughed. A heel? Wasn't it exactly what he was? And "riveting"! The nectar of that praise made up already for her apprehension of Judith's disapproving stare.

She knew nothing about the magazine world, but with the help of the kindly public stenographer she made a list of addresses and mailed the first copy to *Metropolitan.* It came back two weeks later with a nice note asking if she would consider fictionalizing the story and whether or not she would like suggestions for a collaborator. She then sent it to *Country Home* which returned it in ten days with the opinion that too many articles had already appeared on the plight of the middle-aged suburban wife. It was next mailed to *The Women's Review,* and a month later Lavinia received a telephone call from the editor himself. When she heard that he wanted to buy her article for fifteen hundred dollars, she dropped silently to her knees on the carpet and pressed her lips to the mouthpiece.

Four months later the article appeared, with two pages of illustrations. On the left-hand side was a large colored drawing of a woman with crisply set, too blond

hair and dark circles under her eyes, sitting alone on a
sofa and staring at a telephone. On the facing page was
another drawing of a dark-haired handsome man in
evening clothes talking to a group of three very ele-
gant ladies under a crystal chandelier. The title, in
huge print, read: *"Does* Life Begin at Forty?" and was
followed by the legend, in smaller type: "A successful
attorney's wife wonders." Lavinia had undergone ago-
nies of apprehension in the months preceding publication. Whenever she had seen a familiar face in the
street she had imagined it changing into an expression
of oblong disapproval. She had fancied the bitter letters
from the old friends in Plandome. She had pictured a
lonely old age, deserted by children and grandchildren.
But now, holding her advance copy open before her, she
felt only a mild disappointment as she thought of the
thousands of magazines and millions of words of print
that appeared every month. Would anyone she knew
even *see* the article?

For a while her misgivings seemed justified. Two
weeks after the March number of *The Women's Review* was placed on the stands, hardly anything had
happened to change the life of Lavinia Todd. She had
received two surprisingly sympathetic cards from
friends in Plandome, a beautiful letter from Miss Tilney and a horrified, bitter telegram from Judith. She
lunched with her editor, drank two cocktails, talked
too much and bored him. She was congratulated orally
by her hairdresser and by her dentist's nurse. But that
seemed to be all, until she heard from the back elevator
man that her article was the scheduled subject of a television debate. And, sitting alone that night in her living room before the screen, she felt, with a mixture of
awe and pain, that her life was changing at last.

The debate was between Virgilia Peterson and
Marya Manners. The first was sympathetic with the
plight of the neglected wife and surplus mother, while
the latter was inclined to be acid about self-pitying
suburbanite women who had failed to prepare themselves for anything but "togetherness." John Crosby de-
voted his next day's column to the discussion and con-
trasted the earlier end of a woman's useful life with her

superior longevity, suggesting that this imbalance between the sexes was a serious failure of modern society.
This attracted enough attention to bring about a re-
showing of the debate on a wider network, and letters
began to appear in newspapers, for and against the
husband and for and against the wife. *Life* gave three
pages to the topic, with pictures of Lavinia and of her
old house in Plandome and with quotations from her
former neighbors. She was asked to appear on Mike
Wallace's program, which she declined in terror, and
was taken out to a delightful lunch by Roger Stevens
who wanted to explore the potentialities of her article
as the basis for a play or musical. When she found two
invitations to dinner from Florence Newbold in her
swollen morning mail, she wondered dazedly why she
had ever been afraid of anything.

But the greatest evidence of her new fame was when
Chambers telephoned and asked her out to dinner.
They went to a French restaurant where he ordered
a bottle of champagne to celebrate her success, and
she recognized the moist look in his eyes as the one
that he had used in talking to important ladies. He
told her about his life during their separation, his business trips and what had happened in the firm. He even
discussed the children for several minutes. But never
once did he refer to the proposed divorce, and she was
the one finally to bring it up.

"Have you talked to Mr. Cup?"

"Cup? Why the hell should I talk to that shyster?
Incidentally, Vinnie, I was surprised and hurt that you'd
go to a man like that."

"A woman who's threatened with divorce has to
have a lawyer."

"Who's being threatened with any divorce?"

Lavinia stared coolly at those suddenly moister eyes.
"I thought I was."

He shrugged and grinned in what struck her unpleasantly as an attempt at a lovable, boyish sheepish-
ness. "I was too hasty there, Vinnie. You were the
wise one. A man needs to be tided over the dangerous
age. But once he's over it, you've got him for life."

"But, Chambers," she protested with a sudden desperate, trapped feeling. "what about my article?"

"Your article? Why, everyone loved your article! Even people who ordinarily never read that kind of thing. Shelby Gage, for example, of Gage & Dunne, told me that he thought it . . . Now, let's see, how did he put it? Oh, yes, 'the most honest piece of prose ever written by an American woman.' And Clitus Tilney himself told me it was a minor classic. Oh, they're all for you, Vinnie. Florence Newbold compared you to Harriet Beecher Stowe . . ."

"I know," Lavinia said drily. "She wrote me."

"Then, why worry about the article?"

"I don't. I thought *you* might."

"Me? Why should I mind?"

"Because of the things I said about you!"

"Oh, those." Chambers seemed suddenly embarrassed, but it struck her oddly that his embarrassment was all for her. "Well, of course, I'm not much of a sentimentalist myself, but I understand that when you're writing for women's magazines, you have to go somewhat by their conventions. There may have been a sentence here and there that was a bit slushy for my tastes, but let's face it, Vinnie, no man's going to hold it against his wife that she loves him."

As Lavinia stared into the complacent eyes of the stranger who was having dinner with her, she wondered how even a person of his passionate egotism could have so misconstrued her. And then a stranger truth was borne in upon her. He hadn't read the article! Or if he had started it, with its romantic beginning, he hadn't finished it. He hadn't even been interested enough to finish! All he cared about was that she should have attracted the notice of Shelby Gage.

"You're a very tolerant man, Chambers," she said with a laugh that was half hysterical. "I wonder if I could ever deserve you!"

And as she laughed again and held out her champagne glass to be replenished, she knew that the purpose of writing her article had finally been accomplished and that the business of living which she had once thought almost over was now to be fully, perhaps even painfully, resumed. Miss Tilney had said that most people's problems were without practical solution, but Lavinia knew that her own had one. She would telephone to Mr. Cup in the morning and tell him to accept the terms of her husband's divorce offer.

THE AMBASSADOR
FROM WALL STREET

MISS JOHANNA SHEPARD, like so many of the older members of the summer community at Anchor Harbor, had become a legend in her own lifetime. The renewed public interest in survivals from the "gilded" age had given her her own small corner in American journalism and letters. Cholly Knickerbocker described her as "Maine's most formidable dowager, who rules the summer world of Anchor Harbor with the absolutism of a czarina." Cleveland Amory related in *Holiday* Magazine that "when she entertains at dinner in her rambling stone and shingle mansion on the exclusive Shore Path, the limousines of her guests line up ahead of time so that the first one can roll under the porte-cochere at exactly eight o'clock." And a more critical observer from abroad, in a letter to the London *Daily Mail*, observed:

> In America the term "dowager" signifies an embattled, elderly female who has triumphed over the fact of sex rather than one who has survived a member of the opposite. The virgin queen of Anchor Harbor, Johanna Shepard, has the long features and solemn mien of a Hapsburg archduchess and dresses with the same sumptuosity. Set in the irrelevant brilliance of her hat and scarfs, her face is like a stone sun dial in a rich flower garden. To watch her cross the lawn to her umbrella table at the swimming club on the stroke of noon is to watch a ceremony that seems to have been borrowed from the opening of parliament.

Nobody laughed at this kind of exaggeration more than Miss Shepard herself. "I'm just another old New York seal," she would protest, "who likes the Maine rocks in summer and the scream of gulls." Nobody, certainly, tried harder to keep abreast of the times.

She played bridge for high stakes and into the small hours of the morning; she was propelled each spring, by jet motors as far as Hong Kong or Singapore, and it was she who had inaugurated the bold move, as chairman of the admissions committee at the swimming club, to take in a select group of "natives," as the year-round residents of Anchor Harbor were known. "Their families are *much* older than yours or mine," she would retort to any objectant, crushing his opposition by the simple expedient of bracketing his own dim origins with those of a descendant of John Jay, Gouverneur Morris and Chancellor Shepard.

But in recent summers it had begun to seem to Miss Shepard that people were taking her denials of rank a bit too literally. Their interest in the social routine of the older group at Anchor Harbor was friendly and even at times enthusiastic, but it was essentially the interest of the drama school audience at the revival of a Jacobean masque. The idea that Miss Shepard, or even the admissions committee of the swimming club, could have any direct impact on, much less jurdisdiction over, their own lives seemed not to occur to them. Thus Miss Shepard found that although the younger people were always quoting with delight Amory's account of the limousines queuing up for her dinner parties, they rarely felt obliged to be on time themselves. Everywhere she looked she saw further evidence of the rise of this same egalitarian spirit: in the bank teller who was not in the least confused when he failed to recognize her, in the library clerk who fined her for overdue books, in the young doctor, giving her a midsummer checkup, who asked her if she had ever had a baby. There was no hostility in the attitude of any of these persons, but Miss Shepard was beginning to wonder if she did not regret the old class animosities of the depression years. With animosity, there was at least recognition. Was it hopelessly reactionary to want to stand out a *little* from the dull grey mass of everybody?

She was always hoping better things of each new summer colonist and always being disappointed, but when Mrs. Tyng bought the old Strong place next to her own, she decided, as usual, to be her first caller. It was rumored that Emmaline Tyng was a rich and attractive Washington widow, but Miss Shepard's little group, knowing how apt social climbers were to use a summer resort as a way of attacking the soft underbelly of the old guard in their home towns, always held aloof until their leader had scouted the field.

"But I was told that nobody in Anchor Harbor would come near me for years and *years!*" Mrs. Tyng crief with infectious gaiety. "And here the great Miss Shepard comes in person. I declare, if it isn't the sweetest thing!"

Mrs. Tyng was small and just a bit plump, with bright shining black eyes in a round pale face and black bangs like Mrs. Eisenhower's. There was a trace of Southern accent in her tone and much more than a trace of Southern effusiveness in her manner. She had painted the Strong living room white and filled it with Chinese things. Miss Shepard was unable to elicit any particulars about her, other than that she had lost a great many dear ones, but did not believe in being "morbid."

"Do you think we could be friends, Miss Shepard?" she asked disarmingly when her approving visitor rose to leave. "Or would you be bored to death by a poor little rattle like myself? That's what they call you in Virginia, you know, when you go on too much about yourself. But it's all your fault. You're so sympathetic, everything just tumbles right out."

Miss Shepard wondered just what it was that had tumbled out, but she was nonetheless touched. "I'd like to have you meet some of your neighbors," she replied. "Would you come to the swimming club tomorrow at noon and sit at my table?"

"Oh, Miss Shepard! Of course, I'll come, but I warn you, I'll be scared stiff!"

Mrs. Tyng presented herself the next morning, dressed discreetly in navy blue, but she did not seem very scared. She chatted volubly yet modestly with all of Miss Shepard's group, with old Colonel Townsend, the collector of doorknobs, with Mrs. Potts, the richest widow of the resort, with Tommy Landon, the golden-haired, epicene muralist who had been their "youth" for twenty years. They all agreed that she was charming—and impenetrable.

"I'll bet it's nothing but an act," Miss Shepard suggested, enjoying the independence of seeming to depreciate her own protégée. "If I wanted to crash 'us,' I'd try to seem mysterious. Here we are, all talking about her past when she probably doesn't even have one!"

All that summer Miss Shepard never gave a big party without asking Mrs. Tyng, and her delight in her new neighbor steadily increased. The latter seemed ready and able to exercise upon her aging group of pleasure seekers the rejuvenating influence of a Madame de Pompadour in the court of Louis XV. It was Emmaline Tyng who organized picnics by buckboard along the old carriage trail to Porpoise Rock where they could watch the sun plunge behind the White Mountains and the cold sapphire sea turn to a phosphorescent ebony. It was Emmaline who thought of renting the old tea house on top of Hamlin Hill and serving a champagne lunch before the panorama of pine forests and crags. It was Emmaline who organized the tombola lunches at the swimming club and who got Sunny Dixie from the North Shore to play at the Tennis Week ball.

"She's taken us over, Johanna," Mrs. Potts told Miss Shepard at the end of Emmaline's first season. "She's taken us over, and we're all the better for it. You were right, my dear. I had my doubts at first, but I should have known. You're always right."

Miss Shepard accepted the compliment as simply her due. She had already conceived the idea of her new friend as a successor to herself, as a person who would preserve and maintain in a chaotic future some of the standards of hospitality and graciousness of the old Anchor Harbor. Like a late Roman emperor, she now began to invest her adopted heir with the purple and to insist that equal honors be rendered. She and Emmaline were inseparable, a sort of Mutt and Jeff, as in her own brusque way she liked to put it. Heads turned at noon at the swimming club to watch them cross the

lawn to what was now *their* umbrella table: Miss
Shepard, so tall and broad shouldered and big chested,
so lanky and pale and long nosed, and yet at the
same time so frilly and flowery and gauzy, hobbling like
a rolling vessel with her cane, one hand on the shoulder
of Mrs. Tyng, so round and smiling, so bouncing and
vivacious, so simply and impeccably dressed, so giggling,
as much aware of all who were looking on as her
companion seemed aloof. They had even developed a
special way of talking to each other, an elaborate exchange of mannered truculences.

"Don't bring anything to my friend, Mrs. Tyng,"
Miss Shepard would say gruffly to the white-coated
waiter who hurried to take their order. "Unless it's a
glass of tomato juice. I'm afraid she overindulged last
night."

"It's true, Johanna. I found myself in some pretty
bad company."

"Is that so? I heard you were seen about with a
respectable old body, a most virtuous spinster. I trust
you did not expose the poor dear to the temptations of
your fleshpots."

"The poor dear, indeed! There's a smell of brim-
stone in the very daisies on her straw hat!"

The waiter would smile and bow and bring them
their martinis as usual.

If the friendship, however, in its early stages, might
have suggested the Well-Beloved and his Pompadour,
alas, it was not the sovereign who was the first to be
bored. Emmaline Tyng, having established her rule at
Miss Shepard's, began, as early as her third summer,
to sigh, like another conqueror, for more worlds. There
were a number of old summer families, older even than
the Shepards, particularly from Boston, who held aloof
from the social life of the swimming club, in dowdy
shingled isolation, without lawns or formal gardens,
who came to Maine only for the sea air and the pine
trees and whose wives and widows were to be observed
padding along the sides of roads in sweaters and sneak-
ers, even sometimes pushing bicycles. Of such were
the Motley Goodriches, regarded by Miss Shepard, and

by her parents before her, as the natural targets of summer levity. She really stared when Emmaline suggested that they be included in a charade party.

"My dear, they're the most terrible frumps. What on earth put that idea in your head?"

"They have that divine old turreted castle on Porpoise Point. Wouldn't it be fun to give a picnic there?"

Miss Shepard, to tell the truth, was becoming the least bit tired of picnics. Even with the efforts of her old chauffeur who toted a camp chair and wrapped her knees in a steamer blanket, her limbs tended to stiffen in the night air.

"My father used to say that Anchor Harbor had never recovered from two things: the road up Hamlin Hill and the Goodriches' August clambake."

But Emmaline simply smiled the formal smile of the child who knows that she has only to wait till teacher's back is turned, and a week later Miss Shepard had the mortification of learning that invitations had gone out to a charade party without finding one in her own mail.

"Of course I'd have asked you," Emmaline pointed out when she protested. "Only I was afraid you'd be bored to death. The Goodriches are coming. If you think you can stand them, come along!"

Miss Shepard came to her friend's party and was very gracious indeed to the Goodriches, but she did not delude herself about the extent of her concession. She could tell, from the more pebbly note in Emmaline's Southern chatter, that her heir no longer expected to await her demise before coming into possession of her rights. It was soon only too clear that Miss Shepard's younger cohort in the imperial purple intended to enroll the entire colony under her standard. It was not enough for her to assemble a chosen few around the best umbrella table at the swimming club and live with the satisfying knowledge that there was nobody on that long lawn by the swimming pool who would not have gladly exchanged his canvas chair for one at that charmed circle. No, such were the joys of mere society creatures. Emmaline's ambition was more imperial. She wanted to know the old families and the new, the smart and the dowdy. She wanted to give lawn parties that were like palace receptions, to control the clubs, to sponsor the debutantes and hand out the silver cups at Tennis Week. She wanted the admiral to call first at her house when the fleet came in. She wanted, in short, to be Mrs. Anchor Harbor.

But only of the summer colony. She had no interest in the "natives" or in the village fathers except to form committees to protest their real estate taxes. Emmaline subscribed to the prevailing opinion on the Shore Path that the Anchor Harborites existed only to "do" the summer people and went to Miami every winter to spend their ill-gotten gains. Miss Shepard, on the other hand, conceived of her relationship with the village people more as that of a landed aristocrat with the local peasantry. Old ties and obligations held them together with a bond that was stronger than any between herself and mere summer swallows from distant metropolises. Did not Mr. Durand, the druggist, remember her mother's heart flutter pills? Had not Mr. Wiley, who ran the Anchor Motor Company, started his business with a loan from her father?

It was not surprising, then, that the ultimate break between the two friends should have come over Miss Shepard's policy of sponsoring natives for membership in the swimming club.

"I think," Emmaline announced at a board meeting, with a little smile at the gentlemen on either side, which betrayed a preconcerted move, "that, with all due respect to Miss Shepard, the time has come for an 'agonizing reappraisal' of our admissions policy. We have at the moment not one, but *two* local candidates up for consideration."

Miss Shepard decided immediately that so open a mutiny called for the sternest measures. "The Durands and the Wileys," she said gravely, "have been in Anchor Harbor since the end of the eighteenth century. I suggest we consider their qualifications in the light of how long some of our more recent members have been here."

But Emmaline positively snatched at the gauntlet so thrown. "I never heard that membership went according to length of squatting," she exclaimed with a hard little laugh. "Why not take in the seals and the moose and have done with it? It seems to me that the clear duty of this board is to preserve a club that will continue to attract new and desirable families to Anchor Harbor. And you won't do that by filling it with a parcel of druggists and haberdashers!"

"At least," Miss Shepard retorted, "we know where *their* money comes from."

Emmaline flushed deeply and lost control of her temper. "You needn't take that tone, Johanna!" she cried shrilly. "Everyone knows that the Shepards only came here because they couldn't make the grade in Newport!"

Miss Shepard stared down at the green cloth on the table of the committee room without deigning to reply. She was not surprised when her candidates were blackballed. She was not even surprised, a few days later, when she had resigned from the board, to receive a purely formal letter of thanks for the two decades of her service on it. Mrs. Tyng had won, and words, of course, would never again be exchanged between them. The umbrella table on the other side of the bricks leading down to the lawn would henceforth be occupied by a rival group.

Yet it was not one of her satisfactory rows. Anchor Harbor was too small a place for a serious feud, particularly if one's enemy lived next door. Emmaline had taken to having music at her evening parties, and it was terrible for Miss Shepard to be kept awake by the sounds of a frivolity in which she was no longer included. Worse still was the modern pavilion for suppers and dancing which her neighbor proceeded to erect, at obviously great cost, on the rocks overlooking the sea directly abutting Miss Shepard's border. It was not simply that the pavilion obstructed Miss Shepard's own view that angered the latter; it was that it blocked the shore path, so the sailors and their girls, who had formerly done their necking at the end, just beyond Emmaline's house, now did it on the rocks in plain sight of Miss Shepard's porch. When she wrote to the Mayor's office to protest Mrs. Tyng's arbitrary action

in closing off a public easement, she received the mys-
tehious answer that the Village Board of Anchor Harbor had by "mesne conveyance" transferred the "public easement over the lands of Emmaline Tyng" to
Emmaline Tyng herself. After that there was nothing
for Miss Shepard to do but close her windows to the
making of music and her shades to the making of love
and await with a vibrant indignation the annual August
visit of Waldron P. Webb.

Miss Shepard's relationship with her lawyers had
been the most satisfactory of her life. She knew that
they flattered her, but it was nice that there were still
people who cared enough to do that. In fact, the partners and associates of Tower, Tilney & Webb, alone
of the reading public, seemed to take literally the legend
of the "formidable dowager" evoked by Messrs. Amory
and Knickerbocker. In their Wall Street offices she
could play to sympathetic countenances her favorite
and inconsistent roles: the shrewd old girl whose flare
for business was worth a library of book-learning and
the art-loving, beauty-loving, "fay" creature who had
no comprehension of the deeds and mortgages and
leases that made up her little brownstone empire. She
suspected that if admiring Johanna Shepard was a lawyers' game, it was a game, nonetheless, that they enjoyed playing, from the receptionist, with her emphatic
"And how are *you*, Miss Shepard?" to Mr. Webb's
secretary who came beaming to the reception hall to
greet her, to the nice young law clerks who smiled
so feelingly and seemed to have so much time to give
her. There was none of the casualness to be found
now in the oldest banks and even in the oldest Fifth
Avenue stores; a Shepard there was a gold coin that
still rang with its full value.

With Waldron Webb, who had triumphed over the
unspeakable woman who had sued her father's estate,
alleging the most terrible things, she had developed
something like a friendship. He was actually less congenial than Mr. Madison of the Tax Department or Mr.
Buck in real estate, but Miss Shepard was so anxious to
keep him close to her, in case that filthy hand from the

cesspool world should ever strike again, that she invited him and his wife for a long weekend every summer in Anchor Harbor. Actually, she rather enjoyed the importance of this "visit of counsel," with its implications to the community that her affairs in the distant simmering city were too important to go even three months without a conference. She would give a small dinner for the Webbs on their last night, and she had contrived to make invitations to this party seem like tokens of her especial favor. "Mr. Webb is tired and hates parties," she would murmur at the umbrella table, "but I think if we had just a congenial few, we might get him going on one of his cases."

Webb himself was a trying visitor, almost impossible to entertain. He was one of those lawyers who were frankly bored by everything but the practice of law. He was a big, stout choleric man, with a loud gravelly voice that was made for the cross-examination of hostile witnesses and not for gossip under the umbrellas. He indulged in no known sport, would not even swim, and expressed his contempt for the country in the uncompromising black of his baggy linen suit and the damp cigar that was always clenched between his yellow molars. He wandered about the house, pulling books out of the bookcases which he would then abandon with a snort, and asking for whiskey at unlikely hours. Mrs. Webb, the kind of forlorn creature that loud, oratorical men are apt to marry, contemplated him with nervous eyes, hoping, perhaps, that he would wait until they were alone before abusing her.

He brightened, however, on the visit when she told him of her troubles with Mrs. Tyng, his nostrils whiffing immediately the gamy scent of a law suit.

"I shouldn't dispute the Village of Anchor Harbor's right to release its easement to *all* the landowners on the Shore Path," he said, after clearing his throat emphatically, as if to discharge all idle summer accumulations. "But I certainly question its right to release it to *one*. That smacks of discrimination."

"How do you suppose she obtained it?"

"How?" Webb glared at her as if naïveté were a kind of impertinence. "Why, how else but in the time-honored fashion of crossing the palms of the Village fathers?"

"Oh, but we're in New England, Mr. Webb. Things are different here."

Webb's snort was positively joyous. He was the kind of litigator whose fixed belief in the corruption of man gave a buoyancy, almost a gaiety to the moments when he could demonstrate it. He was never satisfied, reading the newspaper, at finding only a single crime. A rapist had to have been led on, a murderer blackmailed, an embezzling politician the cover for a higher-up.

"Here in New England, as elsewhere, apes will be apes," he said with a chuckle. "But, of course, it will be uphill work to sue a Maine village in a Maine court. Let me explore first to see if there isn't an easier way."

"How?"

"Let me prowl around, Miss Shepard. Let an old wolfhound prowl around. I may drop in at the Register's office and have a glimpse at your title papers. I was trained by a great trial lawyer, John Carter Stokes. He used to tell me: 'Waldron, remember one thing. Always start at the beginning. If your enemy has a gun, find out if he's got a license.'"

Webb spent a large part of the next two days in the village, and at mealtimes he seemed preoccupied but content. He said very little and occasionally whistled under his breath. The third day he spent strolling about the place, consulting a crumpled paper that appeared to be a map. Miss Shepard, watching him from the veranda, where she sat with his wife, felt an odd combination of comfort and apprehension. There he was, her legal protector, so large and alien, a strange blob against the radiant blues and greens of the coast line, yet curiously dominating it, as if, an ambassador to a world of sea and pines from the greater world of asphalt and brownstone, he might suddenly assume vice-regal powers and say: "Waves, you are only waves, and trees, you are only trees, and I bring the word that relates you to men." He seemed to hurl an articulate challenge into the astonished face of eternity, shouting that the rights and prerogatives of Miss Johanna Shepard were more than the transiently enforceable squat-

ter's claim of a withered old maid to a bit of top soil on
the Atlantic Coast, that they were, on the contrary, fixed
and eternal and had their place—their important place
—with the mountains and the forests and the tossing
sea.

When he fixed his attention on Mrs. Tyng's property,
on the other hand, when he raised his arm and squinted
down it towards her new pavilion, as if he were aiming
a rifle, he seemed the very figure of Nemesis, a dark
devil from a sulphurous underworld who would destroy
the enemies of Johanna Shepard but only at a terrible
price to her. It was in this latter guise that he appeared
at cocktails one night on the veranda, puffing at that
damp cigar and obviously bursting with news that he
nonetheless was determined to repress and discipline
into more dramatic form.

"My old sage was right, Miss Shepard," he began
with a pleased sigh, after a long sip of whiskey. "Mrs.
Tyng's gun is not hers. Or at least not all of it. But who
cares how much? Who can shoot with part of a gun?"

"What on earth do you mean?"

"Simply that the barrel of her gun is yours."

Miss Shepard was always frightened when her heart
began to beat too hard, and she exclaimed almost
querulously: "Please, Mr. Webb, don't talk to me in
riddles."

"Very well then. That beautiful new pavilion of your
neighbor's. That very expensive summerhouse. It
stands half on your land. I suspected it the other day,
but I didn't believe it until I'd paced it out. Of course
a survey will have to prove it, but there's no doubt at
all of the fact."

Miss Shepard still gaped. "But how can that be?"

"You mean how could anyone be such a fool as to
erect a structure like that without first making a new
survey? But that is typical of such a woman as Mrs.
Tyng. Habitually living beyond her means, she will
always save in the wrong places. And will lose a pavilion to pick up a hundred bucks."

"Beyond her means? What makes you say that?"

"I had a little talk with the president of the local
bank. Mrs. Tyng is well known as bad pay among

the tradespeople. If she loses her pavilion I doubt that she can build another. And the beauty of it all is that she's been hoist by her own petard. Her only possible defense to an action in trespass would be entrapment: that you had knowingly watched the construction of the pavilion and bided your time. But by closing the shore path (which I find she accomplished by the simple expedient of giving a garden party for the Mayor's wife) she shut off your view of what was going on. It's too perfect!"

"You mean, I can simply tell her . . . to remove her pavilion?"

"Or remove it yourself. At least, the trespassing half. There is absolutely not a thing she can do about it."

The Webbs extended their visit until a survey had been duly made, and when they left Miss Shepard was in possession of a map that showed, with a terrifying precision, how the purple line of the Shepard-Tyng boundary neatly bisected the poor little oval that represented the expensive pavilion. Miss Shepard carried the survey about in her pocket and kept pulling it out and furtively examining it. Each time she had to reassure herself that this dizzy vision of inconceivable power was not the illusion of a premature senility. No, each time, there was that line slicing through the offending pleasure dome with the laminating edge of an executioner's sword. It was justice, the strong, dazzling justice that falls with the final curtain of a well-made melodrama.

Webb had pleaded with her to allow him to call upon Mrs. Tyng, survey in hand, and to present her with his demands, but she had insisted on time to think it over, and he had departed sulkily for the city, deprived of his well-earned scene. She sympathized with his disappointment, but she wanted to savor her triumph. She had reached an age where she knew that there was no greater joy than anticipation. At her umbrella table at the club, when she heard Emmaline Tyng's high, shrill laugh, the particularly high one that was designed to create at Miss Shepard's table the uneasy sense that its occupants were targets of the Tyng wit, she would smile grimly and reach a finger into her handbag to touch the folded paper that she always kept there. Similarly, at night, when the offensive strains of dance music were wafted across the lawn from the doomed pavilion to Miss Shepard's window, she had only to reach a hand to the table by her bed and sink into gentle slumber at the reassuring touch of the survey. She felt younger and gayer than she had for many a summer, and it was not long before her mood began to be felt at the Tyng table where it caused suspicious glances. What in the name of Hamlin Hill was the old girl up to?

She could not, however, live indefinitely on anticipation. Labor Day was approaching, and soon the summer swallows would be gone. Miss Shepard rose one afternoon from the wicker chair on her veranda, reached for her stick and strode slowly across her lawn. As she paused in the little path through the copse that separated her property from Mrs. Tyng's, she opened her bag to take one last quick look at the survey. It was safely there. Erect again, she proceeded up her enemy's lawn and around the house to the big porte-cochere. But as she passed under it and placed her foot on the first of the big stone steps, her heart began beating so rapidly that she stopped in terror. Was she going to die and miss her famous scene? Breathing hard, she sat down on the top of the steps and rested her chin in her hands.

After only a few moments, her heart resumed its normal beat, but her exhilaration seemed to have vanished with her panic. As she gazed back at her own house, viewed from the now unaccustomed angle of her enemy's fort, it appeared suddenly, like her spirits, a poor sad jumble of weatherbeaten things. The heat of the day, the stillness of the air, the buzz of bees in the clematis on Mrs. Tyng's driveway, were all oppressive and stifling. She herself was an old, weak, about-to-be-dead female, and the paper in her pocket was a fable for children.

Where was reality? What had happened to hers? It had fled the hot void of out-of-doors to find refuge somewhere behind the screened doorway in the wide, dark, shade-drawn interior of Mrs. Tyng's domain. In the sunlight, amid the buzzing bees, lingered the attenuated ghosts of fantasy, walked with faltering feet the old maid "queen" of Anchor Harbor, Amory's "formidable dowager" and the all-powerful client of Waldron Webb. Miss Shepard understood at last that she would destroy herself in destroying the pavilion, that Anchor Harbor would unite behind an injured Emmaline. For the rivalries of a summer colony had to be played by the gentle rules of parlor games. To bring a blunderbuss from the distant city of true conflicts and blast away would be to stand up suddenly, like Alice in Wonderland, and show that the community was only a pack of cards. But she could not wake up like Alice; she had to live with those cards, and how long could one live in a cardboard world as the legend of Waldron Webb?

"Who is that out there?" came a shrill, suspicious voice from behind the screen door. "Who is it sitting out there?" There was a pause, but Miss Shepard said nothing. "Is that you, Johanna Shepard? What do you want? Are you ill?" Now the screen door opened, and Miss Shepard heard the quick tap of high heels on the porch behind her. "Shall I call a doctor?"

. She rose slowly now, very slowly, and turned to gaze calmly into those bright, agitated black eyes. "I'm all right, Emmaline," she said quietly. "I think I must have had a touch of the sun. I came over to tell you that I couldn't endure our silly quarrel any longer. Will you forgive me and make up?"

There was another pause in which those black eyes seemed to penetrate every inch of Miss Shepard, even to the handbag with the folded paper.

"Well, of course," Emmaline said at last with a perfunctory little snort, "it's all too ridiculous, isn't it? Come in, my dear. Come in and let's talk it over."

As she held open the screen door, Miss Shepard moved painfully forward. One thing and one thing alone sustained her. Under the scrutiny of those suspicious eyes it had flashed upon her that there was still a way in which the last word might be hers, a way in which Emmaline could be made to learn, without embarrassment to her friend, of the latter's dread but unexercised power. When Johanna Shepard had gone to take her place in the Chancellor's mausoleum on top of a wooded hill by the Hudson River, it would be the duty of Waldron Webb to instruct Mrs. Tyng that his client's will contained a devise to her of a small strip of land in Anchor Harbor.

THE CROWNING OFFER

CLITUS TILNEY had had to work all his life to keep melancholia at bay. The attacks were never so severe as to require the help of a rest home or even of a prolonged vacation, but the disease made up in persistence for what it may have lacked in intensity. He had long recognized that it was his doom to live on the outskirts of a mild, damp hovering fog that tended to creep slowly towards him when he was not watching. As soon as he became aware of the first wispy tentacles stealing about his eyes and ears, he would shake himself and dispel them by enumerating all the things from which he was deriving any present satisfaction. The new bond issue was going well; the firm gross would be larger that year than last; the Columbia Law School had asked him to preside over a symposium on changes to the Federal Securities Law. On some occasions he could dispel the grey cloud simply by recalling that he was going to a good concert that night or that he and Ada were expecting amusing people for dinner. But then there were the days when the fog was naggingly persistent and when he had to turn on all the fans of his imagination to blow it back, days when the very whirring of these mental motors kept him from attending properly to business. Such a day was the day when he received the telephone call from the President of Barnes College.

He was working in his office with Jake Platt, studying exhibits for the government's second anti-trust suit against the investment banking firms, of which no less than three were his clients. It was one of those early spring days of unexpected heat, and his winter tweeds hung about him with a damp heaviness. Ahead lay months of what promised to be a very dull case—a case that could be won only by the production of mountains and mountains of correspondence—and his trip to Scandinavia with Ada had had to be put off. Two good friends had died in the preceding winter, each at precisely his age, fifty-eight, and he was beginning to think, as well as to feel that all the good things in life were past. It particularly bothered him that the firm's new offices, the magnificent new offices for which he had been responsible and of which he had been so proud, struck him already as rather showy and shabby. No, shabby, of course, was too strong; they were *not* shabby. They were simply like . . . well, like other people's offices.

"What a commentary on our society an anti-trust case is!" he exclaimed with a snort. He was standing at the window, his back to Jake, leaning forward as he stared out over the harbor. "What a grotesque parody of our ideals! If you put one on as a show in a Communist country, everyone would laugh their heads off. Can't you see Uncle Sam as a schoolmaster applying his ruler to the knuckles of pupils who won't compete? 'I smell a conspiracy! *Prove* to me there's none.' 'Oh, no, Uncle,' the defendant protests. 'I promise you I competed. I put a spoke in Johnny Jones' bicycle wheel so he sprained his ankle. And I spilled ink all over Billy Smith's notes and messed up Fred Doe's athletic clothes. So *I* was the pupil with the best attendance and the cleanest copy book and the neatest locker!' And Uncle Sam relents and quashes his anti-trust suit."

"Would you rather do things the Communist way?" Jake asked, without looking up. He was used to the master's moods. "Would you like to cut out competition?"

Tilney slapped the windowpane. "I'm sick and tired of this modern habit of impugning a man's patriotism every time he enunciates the smallest criticism of how things are done here. Will you deny, Jake, that there's something radically wrong with a system that requires a defendant to prove himself a son of a bitch to beat a criminal indictment?"

"It depends what you mean by a son of a bitch," Jake said, shrugging. "I suppose you're thinking of Shelby Gage's telling old Art Hunter that he was pulling out of the bond business when he was secretly trying to grab three of his best bond men. But that's part of the game. It's like poker."

"And a game, I can see, that you find precious little difficulty playing," Tilney retorted. "You belong to your times. That's all right, I'm not sneering."

"Not much."

"I'm not, believe me. I'm the one who's out of joint. Why don't you turn me over to the Un-American Affairs Committee? I feel in a mood for Un-American affairs."

"Perhaps you're tired," Jake suggested, looking up at last.

"I'm *not* tired."

"All right, all right."

Tilney remained at the window in the silence that followed, reflecting that Jake would be twice as good a lawyer with ten percent more imagination. But then, in all honesty, he had to speculate whether it would have been possible for Jake to *be* twice as good a lawyer. Jake was pretty good. But, damn it all, that was just it. Tilney was weary of lawyers who were simply good lawyers. Jake had no juice. He had brains and looks and even charm, in his stubborn American way, but he had no juice. Tilney sighed, wondering, if he and Ada had had a son, whether he would have been a Jake. Probably. The telephone rang.

"No, I'll get it, you're working, I'm doing nothing," he muttered irritably as he turned to pick up the instrument for which Jake was reaching. As soon as he heard the high, faintly-quavering, far away tone of Albert Berringer, he felt an easing of the pressure about his heart, as if his veins had been injected with a fast operating drug, and he ached again with his old nostalgia for the oblong green campus of Barnes and its quaint, rusty-red, somber Romanesque buildings, dignified in the quiet, melancholy way of upstate New York in the 'seventies.

"Clitus, my boy, it's Albert. Are you alone?"

"Except for my faithful Jake," Tilney replied with a little grimace at his most junior partner. "You remember Jake Platt, who did the amendments to the charter? My right hand?"

"I remember him well, and gratefully, and please give him my best," the high voice continued. "But do crave his indulgence for an old man and tell him that I wish to speak with you on a matter of the greatest confidence."

"How mysterious you are today, Albert. But all right." Here he winked at Jake and pointed to the door. "Now we are quite alone," he continued when Jake had left, "unless Miss Hanley at the switchboard is listening in. Are you, Miss Hanley?"

"Clitus, I am going to ask you to do something crazy. Something against what most people would consider your best interests. But before you say no, before you turn me down flat, hear me out. I know what a brilliant and successful man you are. Nobody knows better. You've pulled your old Alma Mater out of the hole more than once. As a leader of the bar you could look to a judgeship, even the Supreme Court, if our Republican friends ever get back in. And, of course, I know you make oodles of money, even if you do have to give most of it to the government."

"What is this? A Valentine?"

"Clitus, listen to me. You know I have to retire. You know the difficulties we've had finding a new president."

"Hell's bells, man, aren't I chairman of your board? Haven't I been beating the bushes for you these last six months?"

"That's what I mean. You know what a job it is."

"Albert," Tilney said with a groan, "will you come to the *point?*" But when he swallowed, he bit his lips until he was sure he had drawn blood.

"Clitus, listen to me. I woke up the other night with a brainstorm. I thought: What about Clitus? Oh, sure he's too big a man for the job—everybody would say he'd be mad to take it. But I began thinking he grew up here, and he loves the old school, and maybe now that he's made his pile and is no longer in his first youth, he might like the academic life for a change. Maybe he'd appreciate the chance to make something big of Barnes, something that an old fuddy like myself could never dream of. Maybe he'd get a kick out of turning his Alma Mater into the leading intellectual small college of the Eastern Seaboard. Maybe—"

"My God, Albert!"

"I don't want an answer right away. I'm afraid I know what that answer would be. I've sounded out your fellow trustees, and they all say I'm crazy to think you'd even consider it."

"What makes them so damn sure?"

"Don't try to answer me now, Clitus. Think it over, my friend. And try to dwell on the pleasanter aspects of it. You could teach courses yourself, you know. In government or economics. Presidents do in small colleges. I know you'd like that kind of contact with young men. And maybe you could even start a law school. We need a law school up here."

"Look, Al, I—"

"No answer now, Clitus. Please."

"Al, will you listen!"

"No. As a matter of fact, I'm going to hang up right now. I won't even talk to you if you call back!" And the old man hung up.

For the first time that he could remember Tilney closed his door and locked it. He telephoned to Miss Clinger and told her to take his calls.

"Is something wrong Mr. Tilney? You sound so tense."

"Just do as I say," he snapped and did not bother afterwards to regret the sharpness of his tone. Miss Clinger was used to him. He was her job. Would she like to go to Barnes? Of course not. Nobody but Clitus Tilney wanted to go to Barnes.

It had been his dream from boyhood. He still saw himself, after a lecture, descending from the rostrum and walking out to the fountain in the middle of the campus, followed by the brightest of the class, to continue the discussion informally with cigarettes. He saw the young men everywhere, on his doorstep, in his study, beside Ada as she poured tea, the young men who would take no easy answer, who would wrestle with every dogma, who would squeeze out of him every thought they could. He heard his own voice and laugh; he saw himself admired, even a bit revered. Oh, it was a harmless fantasy—or at least it *had* been. Unless it now became a fact? He sat at his desk and pounded his temples with his fists as though physically to drive away the objections that swarmed, the objections that were gathering like locusts, the host of them that would soon darken his sky and beat at his eyes.

"Why can't I be happy?" he moaned aloud. "Is it too much to ask to be happy in the few good years that may remain?"

Barnes had everything. It was small enough to be exempt from the vulgarity of athletic excesses, small enough to be totally directed by one man. As senior trustee he knew all about the graduates, the board, the finances. There was nothing he could not accomplish at Barnes! And then to be free of the little meannesses, the cloying demands of clients, to be able to espouse a higher ideal than the particular case one was handed, to serve the muses and them alone, to love truth, with long summers in which to travel, perhaps to write— well, after all, why not? At fifty-eight?

When he unlocked his door, he went straight to Chambers Todd's office. Todd was also a Barnes graduate, which was why, as a young man, he had come to Tilney for a job. He was not yet a trustee, but as chairman of the alumni fund he was active in college affairs, and would probably have heard of Berringer's proposition. Berringer was a great talker. Tilney pushed his head in the doorway and found him dictating.

"Come to lunch."

"Sorry, Clitus, I'm tied up."

"Untie yourself, then."

Todd looked up quickly to see if he was serious and saw that he was. It was rare for Tilney to be dictatorial, but all his partners knew and respected such moods. Todd gave his secretary instructions about breaking his engagement, took up his hat and walked after Tilney down the corridor. Neither spoke until ten minutes later, when they were seated at a table at the Down Town Association. Tilney, who rarely drank at noon, ordered a martini.

"Berringer just called. I suppose you know what he wanted."

Todd shrugged. "I told him to save his breath. That there wasn't a chance."

"Oh, you did, did you? Why did you assume that?"

"I thought you were the indispensable man around here."

"Oh, come off it, Chambers. You know what I am. Nobody better. You know everything I do, every client I see. You know that you could do it all yourself. Just as well. As a matter of fact, if I *did* take the Barnes job, you'd damn well have to take over mine. You're aware of that, I suppose?"

"Somebody'd have to step into the breach," Todd replied, looking at his senior with steady, expressionless eyes. "And I guess I'm about the only one who could do it. Administrators are hard to come by. But I certainly don't relish the prospect. I know how lucky we've been to have you taking care of the office headaches while the rest of us practiced law."

"Does that mean I have to do it forever?"

"That's up to you."

Tilney was exasperated by the other's impassivity. "How is it up to me," he grumbled, "if everyone thinks it's my duty to stay on here?"

"Your duty?" Todd frowned and shook his head. "When did anyone say anything about duty? Your duty is to yourself, man. What do you *want* to do?"

Tilney stared. "I never imagined you were such an epicurean, Chambers. I thought you believed it was a man's duty to get ahead and stay ahead."

"I believe in getting ahead for myself because that happens to be what I want. But if I wanted to be a beachcomber, I'd damn well be a beachcomber!"

"Is that what you equate with the presidency of Barnes?"

"Don't be so prickly," Todd retorted. "I respect Barnes as much as you do. All I'm trying to say is that if Barnes wanted me and I wanted Barnes, I wouldn't let anything in Wall Street stand in my way."

Tilney rubbed his chin as he thought. "Suppose you'd taken on a case? A big case? One that you felt committed to?"

"Like your anti-trust matter? I'd turn it over to Waldron. You may be a genius, Clitus, but it's not going to take a genius to win *that* case."

Tilney's cocktail now arrived, and he drank half of it at a swallow. His sudden joy was pricking painfully against his ribs. "Do you know what, Chambers? I've done you a great injustice. There have been moments when I've thought your eye was just a bit too glued on the main chance. It shows that we should never oversimplify. Why, man, you're a great natural philosopher!"

He felt as if his joy could not help but elicit some show of enthusiasm from Todd, but the latter was very sparing with enthusiasm. "I think a man does less damage to others in the long run if he sticks pretty close to his own interests," he said gruffly, eyeing the lowered level of Tilney's drink. "At least, he has a rough idea of what they are. But when it comes to other people's, he's all over the place. The only person who knows what's best for Clitus Tilney is Clitus Tilney himself. And if he doesn't know—" Here Todd shrugged. "Well, if he doesn't know, he's probably going to make a mistake whatever he does. So he may as well try to be happy."

Euphoria ended with his talk that night to Ada. On evenings when they were alone they always sat before dinner in his study in the rear of their old brownstone, surrounded by his sets of reporters and framed court certificates. Over the white marble Victorian mantelpiece was a portrait of Tilney in tweeds, a pipe in mouth, against a background of more reporters, giving to the picture some of the effect of a mirror. As he now gave a slow and careful account of Berringer's proposal he watched Ada as cautiously as if she had been a jury. But she never once blinked or smiled. Her only sign of reaction was a tiny crease down the middle of her high, pale forehead, a seeming extension of the straight part which divided her straight brown hair. When he had finished and paused, she still said nothing.

"You don't seem very dazzled by the prospect," he said with a touch of sourness. "Obviously, it has not been *your* dream to be first lady of Barnes."

She looked faintly surprised, and he realized that she had not even considered the proposal in the light of how it would affect herself. How typical! And yet for once he could have wished for the smallest portion of a Chambers Todd in her make-up. "Isn't it a rather curious climax to a brilliant legal career?" she asked. "Isn't it even a bit of an anticlimax?"

"You think I'm too big for the job. Of course. Everyone does. Obviously, I'm a giant."

"Now, don't be testy, dear. It's too important for that. I *don't* think you're too big for the job. Barnes Barnes should have the best. I was simply wondering if you're the right man for it. And if it's the right job for you. Have you worked all these years in one profession to give it up for another? Now that you've reached the top?"

"After thirty-one years of marriage I discover that my wife has worldly ambitions!"

"I've always been ambitious for you."

"Can't I be the judge of what's best for my own ambition?"

"Certainly." She shrugged. "Only I thought you wanted my opinion."

"Oh, don't be so damn reasonable!" Tilney got up and strode to the back window to stare out at their little bit of garden. "Can't you see I want you to agree with me?"

"If I only could!" Ada's voice trembled with sincerity. "It hurts me terribly to oppose you. But there are times when I simply must. Do you remember when you wanted to take that year off to raise money for missions? It would have cost you your place in the firm."

"And maybe I'd be a happier man today!" he retorted. "The firm isn't everything. Neither is the law. There's such a thing as doing one's duty to the community."

"Exactly. And I think you'd do more for the community staying where you are, looking after your employees and clients and charities, than jumping into a brand new career at almost sixty."

"But don't you *see*, Ada? That's just the challenge!"

"Of course that's the way you *would* see it," she said with another shrug. "If it's a challenge, it's quite all right to give everything up for it."

Tilney now lost his temper. "I suppose you mind about the money."

It was so unfair that Ada smiled for the first time that evening. They both knew that she spent no more on her clothes than when he had been a law clerk. In fact, their few quarrels had been over her parsimony. "You must want the job very much to say that. Darling, you *know* that if I thought it was the right thing for you, I'd follow you to the North Pole and live in an igloo. But what can I do about my conscience? You should sympathize with that. You have one too."

"Forgive me, Ada," he muttered, flushing. "I didn't mean that you'd want the money for yourself, but for the girls. Anyway, they have their own trusts now. And the loss of my legal income would make surprisingly little difference with taxes what they are."

"I don't care about the money!" she cried indignantly. "*Or* about the taxes. That's not the point!"

"I know, I know," he said with renewed bitterness, turning from the window as the maid came in to announce dinner. "You only care about me. Please don't say it again. Let's agree to drop the subject for now. Only I do have to add one thing. I'd never have believed my ears this morning if somebody had told me that before the day was out I'd be offered the presidency of Barnes and that Chambers Todd would be for it and my own wife against!"

But Ada, taking him at his word in the irritating way of a woman, passed before him into the dining room without replying.

Tilney was surprised and exasperated to discover in the morning that the news of the Barnes offer had already spread over the office. Miss Gibbon, the file clerk, stopped him in the corridor to congratulate him, and in his own room he found Miss Clinger in tears. No sooner had he reassured her that no decision had been made when Jake Platt, with a stricken look, came in to beg him to deny it. He called Todd, when he had sent Jake away, and asked him angrily why he couldn't hold his tongue. Todd, however, insisted that he had said nothing.

"You know Al Berringer, Clitus. He's the greatest old gabber in the world. He's been talking to everybody he can think of for a week. He wants them all to work on you."

"Well, he's been going about it in the wrong way," Tilney muttered.

It was all very annoying, but worse was to come. In the middle of the afternoon, he received a visit from Shelby Gage of Gage & Dunne, investment bankers and principal defendants in Tilney's anti-trust suit. Gage was a recent trustee of Barnes, having consented to go on the board at Tilney's urging and despite the fact that he was not an alumnus of that or any college. It was clear from the moment that Gage seated himself that his visit would be concerned with the offer.

"Have you decided?"

He had all the looks of an aristocrat; it was hard to believe that he had started his business life as an elevator boy in Wall Street. At fifty-five, Gage had kept his trim figure and his thick brown hair, and he played with the platinum cigar cutter at the end of his watch chain with the tapering, indolent fingers of a duke's son. He took it magnificently for granted that the man who could predict the rise and fall of the market was the man to rule other men. Lawyers, accountants, inventors, engineers—they had all their uses, and no one appreciated such uses more than he—but in the last analysis what were they but the handmaidens of the financier?

"I haven't decided a thing."

"Then it's actually still possible you may accept?"

"Why not?"

"Don't give me question for question, Clitus," Gage enjoined him, in a cool, firm tone. "I'm here 'in double trust,' as Macbeth said of Duncan. First as your client and then as your fellow trustee. I think I'm entitled to a definite answer."

"I can't give you one."

"But you're *thinking* of taking the job?"

Tilney's eyes narrowed as his anger mounted. "I'm thinking of it, of course," he said defiantly.

"In that case, my dear fellow, I'm afraid I have a

bitter pill for you to swallow." Gage sat up straighter in his chair and put his thumbs in his waistcoat pockets. He was evidently accustomed to the dispensation of pills. "I consulted last night with the other defendants in Uncle Sam *versus* Gage *et al.* I'm sorry to relate that we are of the unanimous opinion that you are bound to complete the case before undertaking other responsibilities."

"Bound?" Tilney queried softly. "Bound, did you say?"

"Morally bound, of course. We don't propose to go to court about it."

"You mean you would ask me to give up a position I've wanted all my life to finish a case that one of my partners could do as well?" Tilney's voice had risen at the end to a note of near shrillness.

"Now try not to get excited, Clitus. It happens that we don't consider that one of your partners *could* do as well."

"What about Chambers Todd? What about Waldron Webb?"

"Both excellent men, no doubt, but not Clitus Tilneys." Gage shook his head imperturbably. "You have only yourself to blame, my friend, for making us believe in you. Rightly or wrongly, we're all of the opinion that you're the man to win our case. We know you won't let us down."

"Of course, if you put it that way, I can't," Tilney said suddenly. "But I hope you won't mind my saying that I think it's most unfair. I've been one of the principal architects of this firm. I've always tried to build it into an entity that was greater than the sum of its individual partners. When Tower, Tilney & Webb takes on a job, Tower, Tilney & Webb finishes it. But that shouldn't mean that the particular partner who starts has to finish!"

"In your case, it's precisely what it does mean. We paid our money for Clitus Tilney, and I hope I'm not being vulgar in reminding you that we paid a pretty sum. Perhaps we could induce Al Berringer to stay at Barnes another year, until the case is over."

"No, no, no," Tilney said impatiently. "You know

yourself that's impossible, Shelby. Al's had one bad heart attack and has got to take it easy. No, we must have a man by autumn, and that's that."

"I'm sorry, Clitus. I really am, old man. You don't believe that, but it's true." Gage rose now, put his cigar cutter back in his waistcoat pocket, buttoned his jacket and gave the front a little tap. "This interview has been extremely painful to both of us. I suggest that it's wise to conclude it at the earliest possible moment."

Tilney had been staring in deep discouragement at the blotter on his desk. Without looking up he called after Gage's retreating figure. "Just a minute, Shelby. There's one thing I don't understand. Why didn't you, as a trustee, tell Berringer, when he proposed my name, that you wouldn't release me? Wouldn't it have been kinder to spare me this disappointment?"

Gage paused, but he did not turn. "I didn't think I had the right," he replied. "I hadn't had a chance to discuss the matter with the other defendants. They might have felt that Todd or Webb would do."

"I see," Tilney said slowly, weighing the plausibility of this. "Well, I suppose that's that." He rose and walked to the door to open it for his visitor. "There's one member of my family who will thank you for this. Ada couldn't bear the idea of my leaving the firm."

Gage turned quickly and placed a hand on his arm. "Ada thinks only of you, Clitus. She'd go to the North Pole for you."

Tilney stared for a tense moment at his friend's inscrutable face. "I'm sure she would, Shelby," he said grimly. "I'm sure she'd live in an igloo there. Isn't that what she told you?"

He left the office early that afternoon, took a subway to Columbus Circle and walked home through the park. The bitterness that had overcome him at the end of his interview with Gage was not something that he could afford to have seen. It was only in the park that he could properly let himself go, the park of New York's dirty spring, the long, green, oblong escape valve for the city's frustrations, the ambling and sitting space for the bereaved, the abandoned, the idle, the lonely, who exhale to cloudy and sunlit skies alike the endless highs of their self-pity. Tilney thought of himself as one who despised self-pity, but that afternoon he wanted to wallow in it. For he saw it all now, the whole shabby plot. Ada had gone to Shelby Gage, or telephoned to him, and begged him to prevent her husband from accepting the Barnes' offer, and Gage had obliged her with his customary smooth efficiency. Yet even in his anger Tilney did not again accuse his wife of worldly motives. She was simply afraid that they were too old for change and challenge. Unconsciously, of course, she had been influenced by her desire to remain close to the girls and to have ready cash to meet their every need. For who did not have a hand in Clitus Tilney's pocket or a rope around his neck?

"Suppose I were dead?" he demanded irately of himself. "Suppose I dropped dead tomorrow? Then what would they all do?"

But that was just it. If he were dead, they would all adjust to it, and in two days' time. They would not eat carrion; they had to tear with their beaks the flesh off a living thing. While Clitus Tilney lived, he must supply his daughters with Frigidaires, his clients with consolation, his partners with sanity, his associates with hope, his trusts with capital increases and his charities with new contributors. There was to be no end of it. If he asked, for his later years, after most men had retired, for a little while to himself—and not really that, either, for it was only another chance to serve—what did he get in answer but a shrill, angry clamor of negatives?

Something familiar about the seated female figure a hundred yards ahead and the old Airedale at last impressed itself upon his vacantly staring eyes, and with a snort of irate satisfaction he recognized his wife. Ada had the gift of never seeming surprised. She rose, as he hurried forward, as if she had been waiting for him.

"I hope I haven't surprised you on your way to a rendezvous," she said. "Argos and I keep looking for a new walk. Perhaps it's indiscreet."

"Shall we head home?" he asked briefly, and for a few moments they proceeded together in silence. "Ada," he said at last, in a voice that trembled. "I think you might have appealed to me before Shelby Gage. If you felt that strongly about the Barnes job, you had only to tell me. I wouldn't have taken it."

"Oh, *why* did Shelby have to tell you?" Her voice was taut with sudden anguish, and she pulled up short and took a deep breath. Then she walked straight to the nearest bench. Seated, she threw her head back, her eyes closed, as if she were fighting off a spasm. Tilney stood before her in dismay.

"He didn't tell me. I guessed."

"Why was he so stupid as to let you?" Her eyes were open again and vivid with indignation. "I thought he was supposed to be so much of a diplomat. And now, of course, you've been thinking all sorts of horrible things about me. You've been thinking I wanted to keep you in harness, like an old horse, for the girls' sake. Oh, dear God, what a bungler I've been!"

Tilney was startled to discover now, in his instant relief, that the worst part of his day had been distrusting Ada. "Don't be unhappy about it, Ada. It's not worth being unhappy about."

"Haven't *you* been unhappy about it?" She looked at him and shook her head sadly. "Of course you have. You and I are much too close to be able to fool ourselves about these things. And now I must tell you all. I had *prayed* that I'd never have to. I had so longed for you to believe that Barnes wanted you for yourself!"

Tilney found that he could actually laugh. "What *did* they want me for?"

"They wanted a fund raiser!" she exclaimed scornfully. "They wanted you to raise ten million dollars. They figured that by the time you'd done that, you'd be ready to retire and then they could get a *real* president. A pedant or a general or maybe even an exgovernor!"

Tilney's laughter increased with her ire. "Wait a second! How do you know all this?"

"Shelby Gage came to see me. Oh, weeks ago. Don't ever think *he's* not your friend. He told me that Chambers Todd had started a campaign to persuade the

Barnes trustees that you were secretly longing to be president."

"The son of a gun!" Tilney whistled. "How did he *know?*"

"Because he wants to be senior partner," Ada said grimly. "He wants it so badly he can see right through you. That was always clear to me. But where I made my mistake was in not letting Shelby head the whole thing off. I wanted you to have the satisfaction of being *offered* the presidency. I thought if you had that, it might be enough. I thought you might really hate to leave the law and might grab at the excuse Shelby would hand you. Oh, I was greedy for you, Clitus! I wanted you to have your cake and eat it, too. And now I'm paying for it the way greedy persons should pay."

"Ada, you're a wonder!" he cried happily. "Do you think having such a wife isn't worth a thousand college presidencies? The only thing that appalls me is to think that if I hadn't been lucky enough to sniff that something was up between you and Shelby, I'd never have known what a magnificent wife I had or what a magnificent friend!"

But Ada was still gloomy. "And you wouldn't have had to resent Chambers. And Albert Berringer. And Barnes itself."

"No, Ada, that's quite all right, I accept my universe." He took her hands and helped her up. "Of course the trustees want a fund raiser. It's their job to find one. By hook or by crook!" He waved an arm expansively as they sauntered slowly on. "And why shouldn't Chambers want my job? Why shouldn't he angle for it? Hasn't he always been that way? Haven't I always known it? Hell, am I so different? How did I get where I've gotten? No, Ada, I tell you, all is for the best in the best of all possible worlds!" He threw back his head and emitted a hard, loud laugh. Still, it was a laugh.

"The best for Barnes, anyway," Ada said sourly. "I wouldn't be surprised if Shelby made a major gift to Barnes in the near future."

"You see? It all works out. Barnes will get its money and a *real* president. And I will have served my college. Oh, yes, I will have served it far better than if I made a fool of myself playing at being President Tilney. Dear old darling President Tilney, so whimsical and philosophical, entrancing his disciples with his wit and wisdom under the crab-apple trees! I belong where I am, Ada. Bless you for seeing it!"

"But do you know something?" she demanded. "Something you've never guessed? I, too, had a yen to go to Barnes. I, too, had that fantasy."

"Well, you see, you belong here as well as me," he said consolingly and squeezed her arm and smiled benignly but a bit vaguely, for his mind was already returning to *United States v. Gage et. al.,* and he was weighing the chances of winning a directed verdict when the government had completed its case.

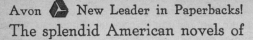